A Battle for Fire

by Jake Stehman

© Copyright 2024 Jake Stehman

ISBN 979-8-88824-289-6

All rights reserved. No part of this publication may be reproduced, stored in a retrieval system, or transmitted in any form or by any means—electronic, mechanical, photocopy, recording, or any other—except for brief quotations in printed reviews, without the prior written permission of the author.

This is a work of fiction. The characters are both actual and fictitious. With the exception of verified historical events and persons, all incidents, descriptions, dialogue and opinions expressed are the products of the author's imagination and are not to be construed as real.

Published by

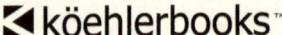

3705 Shore Drive
Virginia Beach, VA 23455
800-435-4811
www.koehlerbooks.com

A BATTLE FOR FIRE

Jake Stehman

VIRGINIA BEACH
CAPE CHARLES

This book is dedicated to my mother, Karen, and mother-in-law, Sharon. Your selflessness and support of family and friends is something I hope to instill in my own children.

CHAPTER 1

Twenty Years Ago

The harsh Antarctic air just beyond this realm was nonexistent as he limped into the main chamber of the temple. Instead, a warm breeze whipped around the cracked but enduring original pillars soaring to the marble ceiling above.

While the serene backdrop was breathtaking, the vast darkness told the real story of this long-forgotten place. Cobwebs and vines, rare sights in the region, dangled from the damp crevices of stone arches. The old paintings that worshippers—human and lumi—had created long ago were faded, the previously vibrant colors no longer visible. One dark pew remained toward the front.

It had been hundreds of years since anyone last set foot on these floors. The moldy tile lay in shambles, and moss flourished in the Essence's humid environment. Each drag of his wounded leg up the steps brought flashes of his last encounter here. He could still feel the grainy parchment of the treaty he had signed, and an echo of the hallowed prayers for the lives lost in that long and useless war remained, as if uttered from the vacant pulpits below.

Something seemed to call to him from a table in the shadowed distance: an icicle almost as long as his forearm that had once produced a piercing blue light but now only glowed dimly. Through the haze of exhaustion and pain clouding his mind, he staggered toward the object, which was soon joined by another that no longer existed in this realm. The aura of the two great relics became clearer, shining as brightly as the Christmas Day light show at Rockefeller Center. While he knew the mirage was not real, the fact that it was Christmas Day in the human realm prompted a laugh.

He pulled a chipped plastic pocket watch from his pocket as he steadied himself beside the icicle. The watch's warmth was comforting, though it conjured a rush of remembrances he usually blocked out.

The image of a red flame bursting from a golden cup danced through his head. The gems and pearls that encrusted the cup represented everything right and wrong with the humans he had been forged to protect. Its flames licked the air in his mind's eye, the pull of its power forcing him nearer to where it once rested as he rolled the watch around in his palm.

A rusting set of armor crashed to the floor to his right, jolting him upright and out of his trance. A curse preceded the sharp return of the watch to its hiding place as he opened both hands. "Stupid." The aura of this majestic sanctuary had swept him up again, blurring his focus long enough for the creatures he had been battling to gain position on him.

The deep, painful gash on his thigh was problematic, the blackish liquid oozing from the wound a clear sign that his assailant's poisonous fangs had done the intended damage. His next step, toward the sound, was hobbled. A grimace and long exhale were the best he could do to stabilize himself.

Not that long ago, the wound would have meant nothing. The poison would have been a brief nuisance as his powers worked to drain the black toxins from his simmering blood. Tonight, however, things were different. His former powers had dwindled, and the decision he had made years before was coming back to haunt him in the very place he had been created.

Another crash brought a creature into view on a balcony, silhouetted against the moonlight streaming through the windows above.

The ferlup's matted mane held signs of moisture from the recent precipitation. Its two muscular back legs flexed before it took a prone position, allowing him to size this one as at least seven feet tall. Extremely fast, these wolflike creatures Chaoic liked to use in battle were fierce and skilled in close combat, aided by poisonous fangs and four-inch claws that he had only been marginally successful at dodging on the journey to the temple.

Their careful, predatory approach was familiar to him. Blood pounded in his ears, signifying his body's instinctual rise in temperature as he prepared for another encounter with these vile creatures.

An ear-piercing howl was his only warning before a third ferlup lunged from behind the pew. This one had caught him by surprise, and he stumbled back before locking his feet to the floor.

"Clever." He smiled slyly and stopped his attacker dead in place with one hand. The beast's yellow eyes grew wider as he tightened his grip on its furry neck, ignoring its struggles to escape. Giving the creature one final moment to contemplate all it had done, he thrust with his opposite palm and spiraled the assailant into the air to erupt in flames upon impact with the far wall.

Unsurprisingly, the ferlup that had knocked over the armor took this chance to advance, its claws clamping into his shoulders as it strove to drive its fangs into his throat. One swipe of his arm threw off the creature's weight, but the damage from its claws added to his agony.

"Bastard!" His shout was followed by a swift kick to the beast's ashy midsection, launching it spitting and shrieking in the opposite direction. "Shit!" He had inadvertently sent the creature toward the icicle at the top of the landing. Its attempted scramble to the relic sent him shambling forward with a gasp. "No!"

The ensuing thrust of his hands propelled a fireball so fast that the ferlup had no chance to react. As a gray cloud smelling of burnt, wet hair plumed to the ceiling, he couldn't help wondering if they thought or felt anything.

Above him on the landing, the third creature rocked back on its hind legs to jump over the railing, its empty yellow eyes unwavering during its descent; it squealed when his powerful fingers snatched its throat. His muscles coiled and released as he smashed the monster into the marble floor. With a deep inhale, he summoned the powers his master, the Essence, had granted him thousands of years ago.

"My turn!" The thought of the many innocent humans this thing had killed energized him as he plunged his hand through the ruffled fur and muscular chest. "You won't be the last one!"

Adrenaline kicked in, a burning sensation that coursed through his veins as fire erupted from his fingers and torched the creature from the inside out. All that remained as it vanished into the musty air was a black, beating heart—an ironic outcome that perhaps only he found funny.

"I see you still enjoy killing my friends." The familiar voice was like nails on a chalkboard, causing him to cringe even as he crushed the heart to powder in his palm. "But I also see that your powers are quickly leaving you." An arrogant, humanlike laugh reverberated around the cavernous room. "I thought you had given up on them. I thought you had—"

His twist was instinctual, and his arms locked in anticipation of the last battle he would ever fight. "You know nothing about me!"

His response drew another laugh from the shadows.

"Tell me something, Ignati." He tensed at hearing the baritone voice speak his name. "Do you think she can protect you tonight? Do you think that, after all of your failures, she would want to?"

It was a question Ignati had contemplated many times; he wished he could answer.

He tried to eliminate the lingering doubt. "I'm not here for the Essence's protection!"

"Then you are here to stop me from taking that?" A long, scaly finger jutted out of the shadows and pointed to the flickering icicle in its iron base. "That is not your job. That is the job of Iclyn, who has long forgotten about you, just like her people have forgotten about this temple and that relic!"

The last word brought an eerie silence. Then the thing he had battled so many times before stepped forward to be revealed in the splintered rays of the moon.

No matter how many times the Ignati ran into Chaoic, no matter how many hundreds of years he put between them, the sight always gave him pause. This horrified hesitation came not just from the fact that this man—or creature—was the soul of darkness and was responsible for the extinction of so many of the Essence's creations. The most terrible aspect was that no matter how hard he looked at this thing, with its pointed nails, fangs, and leathery skin, he could not help but see its resemblance to himself.

It was taller than most humans, towering ten feet high and slightly hunched over when not engaged in battle. However, its mop of black hair and its bulging stomach neatly summed up the worst aspects of the Ignati and the people he was born to protect.

"I know you brought it as well. You have tried to hide it for this long, but I know you, Ignati!" The smile on the demon's pursed, drooling lips widened. "Are you looking to make a deal?" The question caused the Ignati to stiffen; the thoughts and images he was trying to block out fought harder to push through. "Do you think if you do, I will spare your young boy's life?"

He could not stop the flick of his wrist. A fireball sailed across the room, but Chaoic's indifferent swipe deflected it to the torches above before the Ignati recovered from the effort. The light from the extra flames only made the failed offensive more embarrassing as more creatures came into view.

"Still so passionate, Ignati!"

A new count showed that at least ten more ferlup and two dozen minima had joined the fight.

"I see you brought more friends."

The soul-snatching soldiers hissed at him. Though they had no faces, their white eyes gleamed in the shadows of their black hoods.

"You have failed, Ignati. All these years, you have cast yourself away. And all these years in the darkness have made me too strong! You will die tonight, and when you do, I will have my relics and my army!"

The Ignati's scoff was rife with sarcasm, a characteristic of human communication he employed whenever possible.

"You want this?" He grabbed the watch and set it ablaze in his hand. Both sets of creatures backpedaled from the flames, but Chaoic held his ground. "Why don't you come and get it?"

"So stupid not to try to bargain." A bony finger extended toward him. "But if you wish to die this way, so be it!"

There was no hesitation as the howls and hisses closed in on him from every corner. Closing his eyes, he thought back to a place he had once cherished.

"I'm sorry I failed you." His whisper invoked the image of a beautiful woman. The temple disappeared, and he stood in a home that no longer existed.

The fairest skin he had ever beheld made a perfect complement to the woman's straight black hair, now dampened by the line of tears streaming down her face. The yellow-and-red tint of her cheeks and the softness in her eyes were impossible to forget as they settled on the small child resting in her arms.

"He's perfect." Her sniffle drew him closer. He leaned over the boy, who had the same complexion as his mother. "He looks just like you."

The baby's crooked smile mirrored his own. The roaring flames within subsided instantly—something he had never felt before—as he placed a kiss on the boy's forehead.

"Just like his father."

The scene dissipated as snapping jaws and shrieks drew closer. His wounds finally overtook his weakened legs, and they buckled with his last grab at a show of strength. He locked onto the memory of that baby's face, the smile of his son—the reason he had come to this godforsaken place tonight.

"Be strong, Chris."

The heat rising inside him was coming to a boil, his body preparing to unleash it, when an icy blast whipped through the temple.

"Perfect," he chuckled as he blocked the frigid gust.

The sculpted figure that appeared on the balcony above unleashed a blizzard of ice on the approaching creatures before they could retreat.

She had impatiently bided her time, watching the man she had spent millennia loathing suffer at the hands of creatures he had tried for so long to ignore. She knew she could not show her hand until the timing was right, until the logical moment for her to join the battle—her last—had presented itself.

The burst of ice glistened as she rolled her shoulders, every fiber of her body coiling as she reached for a strength she had thought she no longer possessed. A ferlup straggler had suffered the most damage from her entrance. Its labored retreat could not save it as she thrust everything from her veins toward the scattering group that, just seconds earlier, had set their sights on a fresh kill.

An icy wall snapped into place no more than twenty yards away, encasing the demon wolf before it had time to bark.

His voice scarcely a murmur, the Ignati said, "You came." The two words were the first she had heard from her warrior kin in many years.

"You thought I would not?" Her snarky response surprised even her, but her amusement lasted only a moment before he slumped down on a step. "You're wounded?"

This was not what she was expecting to see, his forged muscularity diminished by multiple bleeding wounds that she feared would soon fester.

"The poison . . ." She stopped, the glimmer in his eyes manifesting in a tear that ran down his tanned cheek. "You are weak." Again, she trailed off.

"And so are you." His grip on her hand sent a shock wave through the temple as he peeked at her empty neck. "That ice won't hold them much longer." The clawing and grinding at the wall meant nothing to her. The expression now directed her way was far from what she remembered of the many times they had fought and argued. "But I'm still glad I wasn't at the end of that avalanche this time." He tried to laugh, and more black blood spewed out as the poison spread faster.

The sight of this once spectacular warrior was so upsetting that the Iclyn turned away, toward the table where the lonely icicle flashed, drawing her toward it.

The smell of the burned ferlup still hung in the air, its body smoking where the potent fireball had struck it directly in the chest. She rested her hand on the table where they had both signed the piece of parchment that laid the groundwork for separating their two species. The pain from that decision, along with the others that followed, mounted, her shoulders sagging.

"You did not have to protect this." She plucked the icicle from its base and spun to face him.

The absolute power he radiated was stunning, even as he struggled to his feet and pulled the tattered remains of his human clothing around him. The outline of his chest and the toned definition of his midsection resembled the musculature of a lumi warrior. She had never seen his stance waver like this, though. The mighty legs had always held him firm, like the redwood trees one might find in the forests outside the frost. Tonight, however, she rushed to his aid.

"It was time I finally kept up my end of the deal." He gave a crooked smirk, the incessant clawing growing louder with each passing second.

"No," she chuckled softly. "I mean, you really did not have to protect this toy."

As the fake icicle crumbled, he tilted his head, a smile she had not seen in years budding as he shrugged.

"Seems like you did learn something from the humans after all."

He dropped the watch, and the sound of plastic hitting the ground confirmed that it was not the original she had given him.

"I guess we are not as different as we once thought," he murmured.

The two embraced. The wobble of his body worsened until she was forced to gently set him down on the rotten pew.

"Maybe," she exhaled, peering over at the wall as their attackers gradually pierced through, "maybe we should have figured that out long ago."

His soft laugh became a pained cough. He shook his head and rubbed his trimmed, charcoal-black sideburns.

"And miss all of this?" His outstretched arms quieted them both. "But I must know: who is he?"

She had forgotten his audacity, which unexpectedly made this easier to cope with.

"Really?" she demanded playfully.

"I'm sure he was the least arrogant of them all."

His shrug was so human that she snorted. "You just could not resist!" A sly smirk appeared again. "And you?"

"Lee." He did not hesitate. "Her name was Lee."

The delicate, quick way he said her name carried the full force of his feelings.

"She sounds beautiful."

Another twinkle, followed by a tear, was the end of that subject as he clambered painfully to his feet. The squeals and howls grew clearer.

"I should have been there for you." It was all she could think to say as they straightened to face their impending attackers. "All those years behind my wall . . ."

"I know now why you could not."

The pause following his interruption signified silent acknowledgment. His smile was full of a warmth he had never shown her before.

"The name you picked?" He seemed to genuinely want an answer.

Images of her daughter flooded her mind. "Eira."

Remembering the tender, pale softness of baby cheeks brought a tranquility that cascaded over her.

"She's perfect." Her husband cupped the back of her head and placed a gentle peck on her cheek as she cradled their daughter in her arms. "She looks just like you."

The phrase repeated in her head as she held tight to the vision of her baby girl's joyous blue eyes—until a shriek from the army of creatures that had waited hundreds of years to feast on her broke her from the trance.

"Yours?" It was worth knowing the name of the child who had so changed this man—someone special enough to bring the self-exiled warrior back to fight for a people he had sworn to leave forever.

"Christopher." The response was again soft and filled with so much love and pain that her heart swelled.

"We will see them again." It was her job to stay composed, the rising anticipation of battle chilling her body and sending a mist rolling down her back. "And when we do—"

He grabbed her hand, generating a force that rocked the temple anew. The creatures hesitated.

"I never understood my existence, Iclyn. Never understood what I was really created to do." His strength returned as his body began to smolder. "But as soon as I saw that boy, I knew."

She nodded; she could not have put it better herself.

"No one leaves here!" he shouted. "Tonight, we meet our destiny to allow our children to fulfill theirs!"

It was the last thing she would hear him say. The next pulse of heat was a decisive indication that it was time to face the monster now visible on the other side of the wall.

"You two think I won't find them!" The scaly finger from her nightmares pointed at the two false relics on the ground. "If this is how you wish to die, with your dwindling powers and toys, so be it!"

The gigantic monster's scream was echoed by a cacophony of screeches, snarls, and barks.

"I will never forget you, Ignati." She bent down and placed her hand on her neck. The necklace that had been there now awaited the beautiful baby who had inspired her actions tonight. "And if you don't mind"—her insides turned to a heavy, icy rush as her fingernails froze over—"as your people are so fond of saying"—a final, brief snapshot of that smiling little girl appeared, her pureness bringing the last ounce of Iclyn's strength to the surface—"ladies first!"

CHAPTER 2

Today

A fire burning in the darkened gallery gave way to shadows creeping from the paintings on the wall. The emptiness of this room provided a stark contrast to the others in the castle, which were generally filled with eccentric decorations or linens. In this lonely castle above the sprawling city below, the gallery was an unwanted reminder of the past, shunted aside to rot and disappear from memory.

"We should not be in here." The tremor in the young woman's voice brought a slight grin to her friend's lips. The absolute truth of that statement was the main reason for wandering away from their mundane studies on the first floor. An immense door covered in thick vines stood open behind them.

"You worry too much, Ivy. And we have already finished our training for this morning."

Her smile did little to ease her best friend's tension.

"Eira." Ivy's impeccable cheekbones, which Eira had always admired, clenched even tighter. "We really should be getting back so we can prepare for your party." Her intense blue eyes, a trait she shared with every lumi, were particularly vivid as they darted in all directions. "I would hate to anger your father." She wrapped her strong yet delicate hands around her shoulder-length blond hair in a familiar gesture of worry, strands sparkling elegantly in the light of the crackling fire.

"My party." Eira scoffed as she stomped to the far end of the room, stopping beside a picture that hung there. "I do not have any interest in pleasing my father with this party. It is bad enough he is two days late."

"And you should still respect his wishes," announced a stern, raspy voice.

Eira grinned, imagining how scared stiff Ivy must be in this moment.

"Class let out early, Bernard?" The question was for show as she faced the burly trainer, who just an hour ago had told her not to leave.

"It would have helped if two of my best students had stayed for the full session."

Ivy was practically a statue as she stared straight ahead.

"Ivy dear, can you please leave Eira and me to speak?" This question did not need an answer. Scarcely a moment had passed before she scampered from their sight with a hurried wave.

The silence held until the plant-covered door was closed. The warrior's exhale as it creaked shut was one of slight amusement, which he let linger briefly before continuing. "You enjoy getting that poor girl in trouble, don't you, Eira?"

She already had other things on her mind.

"Was she really this beautiful?"

Though the nearest painting was difficult to see in what little morning light strained through the lone, partially covered window, the green tint the artist had chosen made the Essence's skin glow powerfully. Her brown hair, which flowed to the ground, was a perfect match in color to the dirt farmed in the outside villages.

"The stories say she was." Bernard placed his arm around her shoulders, the strength of his touch locking her to the marble floor.

"However, I doubt any mortal artist could capture the true visage of the creator."

She struggled to wrest her gaze from the eyes of the painted figure. The vivid blue matched her own, and they clung and held her still. She leaned forward, noticing for the first time the red fingernails peeking gracefully from the green light of the Essence's hand. "Did she project fire?"

"Legend says that she did not have the power to project, only the power to create." She had heard the story many times, yet she felt she needed to hear it again today.

"But *he* did?" She had been trying to avoid the picture to her right, the black canvas giving way to a broad-shouldered man who better fit the description of a grizzled lumi warrior than a human.

"Yes." Bernard's answer was precise as he steered them over to it. "The Ignati was gifted with the power to project fire, the element that saved humans from the Darkness during the extinction." The use of the D-word sent a shiver through her. Thoughts of what could be powerful enough to destroy the Essence's creations crept into her mind. "It is said he was forged from the fires of our world, tasked by the Essence to protect the humans from Chaoic and his forces."

She was not about to peek toward the covered portrait of the dark being in question. The stories she had heard about Chaoic were plenty, given this room's empty, haunted feeling.

"He looks strong and powerful, similar to . . ." She trailed off, studying the Ignati's satin robe. Scattered with red jewels, it reinforced the tales she had heard about his wealth and hubris.

"Your mother was just as powerful." The man's reply veered her over to the adjacent canvas, where he released his grip on her and analyzed the painting, rubbing his bearded chin in silence.

"She was perfect." Eira could not imagine what other words would do her mother the justice she deserved.

The painting rendered the Iclyn with icy white hair cut right below the shoulders and a soft, caring gaze in her blue eyes. But while her faultless facial features held a smile, the hands settled on the lap of her modest silver dress told a different story, one that could not be hidden by a healthy set of polished, light-blue nails and one that sent a dire warning to potential threats.

The image spoke of the true power her mother had possessed—a power Eira seemed to be missing.

"There is no denying you look just like her." Bernard broke the quiet. "In fact, you have a lot more in common than just your hair color."

She spun away. "I am nothing like her." The lie made her feel better after the last few days, and she stalked to the other end of the gallery to gather herself.

The next painting depicted not one figure but many: an elaborate battlefield that shifted from sandy beaches to huddled forests and even into the snow said to bless the area right outside their own realm. This fascinating picture captured all the regions of the human world, most of which she had only read about in books. The sheer barbarity of its content, however, made it difficult to truly admire. The red blood of the soldiers, both human and lumi, splattered every section of the parchment. Cries seemed to erupt through brush-kissed lips. The scene always mesmerized her with its sheer volume, but the dark shadow slithering in from the bottom of the image sent a familiar shiver up her spine.

"How many died during the Great War?"

Bernard's loud steps echoed off the marble floor as he joined her and settled his arm around her shoulders once more.

"Many, and no matter what anyone else says, the losses on both sides were heavy." His tone had changed; it was as if Bernard were himself living out the events, the squeeze of his eyelids tightening his grasp on her shoulders. "Until your mother and the Ignati ended it with the treaty." He tilted his head and chuckled, "If you believe the stories, that is."

He released his hold and made his way toward the door, but his vagueness drew her ire.

"Why does everyone refuse to speak of my mother's sacrifice? The books wax on about this Great War, but no one mentions her bravery in the Battle of the Frost. They are cowards for it!" The high-pitched shout stopped him cold and was not remotely becoming of her status. It felt like someone else had taken over and spoken for her.

She sheepishly peered at the floor.

"Eira." The whisper brought her gaze back up. "Sometimes those who care about you do things to protect you." This recurring lecture felt hollow today. "However, you are correct that there are many cowards among us. Cowards who seek to bury our history, or at least run from it. And your father must face them every day."

The painting she'd so far avoided felt like an anchor pulling her down, the creature underneath the cover demanding acknowledgment.

"I'm sorry," she muttered honestly as the hairs on her neck stood up. She quickly put space between her and the covered canvas whispering in her head. "I just—"

"I know you want answers, my dear." Her trainer pushed her out and closed up the gallery. "And in time, I promise you will have them."

He nudged her shoulder in the opposite direction, toward her chamber.

"No one ever mentions what happened to the Ignati," she suddenly commented. Bernard glanced at her inquisitively. "You and my father have told me about my mother, about our people, and about how we settled behind the frost after the treaty. But no one ever talks about what happened to him."

The drawn-out silence almost compelled her to storm back inside the gallery and ask the man's portrait, but Bernard finally replied,

"Most believe that he gave up on the humans, gave up on all of us after he saw what we were capable of. You must remember, Eira, that the Ignati was forged *for* humans. He was powerful but also headstrong in his own right."

"So, he was a conceited fool?" she asked bluntly.

"As I said, my dear—"

A sudden banging below signaled that her father had returned. Trumpets blared in the distance, a pompous noise that meshed well with what she could only assume was his self-satisfied enjoyment of every citizen's wave.

"In time, I promise you will have answers."

"Chris, goddamnit!"

He knew who was shouting for him, but having just seen the delivery guy exit, he was not eager to respond.

"Where is that son of a . . ."

The seething twenty-something manager stomped through the opening by the coffee bar, which was still decorated in Christmas colors. The small crowd of customers gathered for their early-morning lattes appeared unbothered by the impending confrontation.

Chris had always been amazed that his boss found the time to slather all that wavy hair in place. The sheer amount of gel needed to do so likely contained enough chemicals to take down a full-grown elephant.

"My dad told you to order straws, not these flimsy pieces of shit!" A paper straw headed his way, the slight dip in its flight allowing him to avoid it.

Chris had been waiting for this shipment to come all week. In fact, he had been tracking it for days, imagining the reaction he would get from the former high school linebacker who now awaited a response.

Chris barely reached the man's eye level on tiptoe. While the height difference was obviously a factor in why the muscular man so easily dismissed him, Chris was sure his lanky, garden-variety body type was the real reason. The man was a bully through and through.

"Well?"

"Your dad posted something about us being more environmentally friendly, so I decided to take the—"

The man's arrogant laugh made Chris's stomach boil with heat, a reaction that had recently become quite prevalent and that no amount of acid reflux medicine pacified.

"What were you going to say, Cho? Initiative?"

Answering would surely get him reprimanded or worse. However, as the pompous man laughed louder, Chris could not help but mutter, "Not like your steroid-taking ass would know anything about initiative."

He knew it was over the second he let the words slip out, but consequences rarely meant anything to him when he was caught up in the moment.

The coffee shop was just another front for this dickhead's father, a feeder program for the stripper-and-drug fund he blew on the weekends. Even the post about going green, which was only made in response to bougie college kids' daily complaints, was designed to keep the money rolling in. The store had no intention of taking real action, and the green-and-red recycled cups during the holiday season were for show.

"What did you say to me?" The hulked-out day manager's searing glare bore into Chris, and the eyes in the café finally shifted their way.

"It's not a secret, Stevie." It was the wrong tone, but he decided to take a swing at the sarcasm. "Steroids have a side effect, and based on the whispers from the ladies in the back, you know all about it."

Chris tugged off his apron and deliberately placed it on the side table.

"Are you serious, Cho? You do know who you're talking to, right?!"

That question preceded another arrogant snicker that brought the customers in line sidling closer to gawk at the drama.

"Look, Stevie—" The rush of air past his cheek was his only warning. "Whoa!" He chuckled as he ducked away, backpedaling from his red-faced, soon-to-be-former boss.

"Come here, you piece of shit!" Stevie's next punch was wild and uncoordinated. "Stand still!"

A few more flailing swipes had Chris dancing like a boxer in the early rounds of a fight as he maneuvered toward the exit.

"You know"—one more useless swing sent him leaping all the way to the door with a swiftness that drew a few tilted heads from his now former coworkers—"maybe I should just take the rest of the day off?"

At this point, his huffing assailant was out of gas. All the amino acids in the illegal substances comprising his fake muscles seemed to be breaking down at the same time.

"You're fired, Cho! Don't even think of showing your face in this coffee house again! Go work at the Chinese restaurant down the street and stick with your own kind!"

The shop's activities ground to a sudden halt. Chris's amusement evaporated as the warmth from his stomach crept to his chest. Curling his hands into fists, he felt his body coil up. A new, pulsating thump from his neck mixed with the heat of his insides and made it hard to breathe as he stood motionless in his old Nike Jordans.

No more jokes ran through his head, no more witty retorts or sneering remarks. At this point, the only thing revolving in his mind was the last sentence the man had spat out, the anger with which he had said it, and the clear meaning behind it.

Chris had never been one to get physical; it wasn't his forte. However, the last few days had been difficult, and his calm demeanor was in a losing battle with urges from another part of his brain.

"He's Korean, dickhead!"

The voice was like a splash of cool water. His former boss retreated a step or two at the appearance of Chris's best friend. "And don't worry. He doesn't want to work for garbage like you anyway!"

A pull on Chris's arm was the final dousing of the fire, leaving an ashy taste on his tongue and the scent of charcoal in his nostrils.

"You good?"

Under the guidance of his friend, they finally exited onto the sidewalk. The door to the café swung shut, and his own golden irises were the last image he saw reflected in it before he turned away.

"Chris?"

The ashy taste disappeared, replaced by the city's polluted air.

"Me?" Chris chuckled and ran a hand through his black hair. "Psh, you know I could have taken him."

This quip kept the two laughing through a crosswalk, a car horn mere background noise as they reached the sidewalk on the other side of the road.

"That little stunt cost me my morning coffee!" CJ's ebony skin glistened as he let out a genuine laugh and patted Chris's shoulder. "I finally get a day off to just relax in a coffee shop, and *bam*! Chris Cho strikes again."

The lighthearted conversation and the bustle of their surroundings returned the calm to Chris's scrambled mind. His muscles started to relax as they approached a familiar area.

"I guess." A strange inner tug, which seemed to come from the heat that sometimes overtook Chris's body, begged for a change of plans. He peered up at Independence Hall, the building reflecting the early sunlight. He had a crazy idea that he knew would not go over well. "Since neither of us are working now, I can get my stuff from Amber's."

It struck him that he might just be looking for more punishment. A meeting with his ex-girlfriend was not really the best follow-up to being fired and assaulted.

CJ seemed to have the same thought, even as they headed toward the apartment complex. "You can give it time, man. It's only been a few months."

"Does it look like I need time?" He tried to make up for the snappy, emotional response with a half smile. "It was mutual, remember. She's happy and . . . I'm happy." Chris had meant that to come out much more forcefully. The squeak at the end exposed one of his rare breaks from form.

CJ sighed and nodded uneasily. "Okay, man. If you want to ruin your Saturday even more, well, I'm right by your side."

A chime echoed from the church tower down the street. The faint smell of charcoal was already wafting back to Chris's nostrils as they turned down another crowded Philadelphia street.

CHAPTER 3

A swirling, circus-like atmosphere greeted Eira through the double doors. The party halted as she eased onto the shiny wooden floor, and the round of applause that followed her curtsy cooled her cheeks with an icy blush.

"That dress!" Ivy was the first to approach; most of these military and business leaders were here to see her father and had already resumed conversing with each other. "You look stunning!" The compliment was welcome after the crazy afternoon. A fragrant glass of fruity wine helped calm her mind.

The constant commotion of staff entering to drop off dresses, along with her inability to choose one, had done nothing to relieve the residual tension from her conversation with Bernard. She had settled on this blue-tinted, floor-length ball gown out of exhaustion. The sparkling droplets at the bottom were a bit much, and the shiny baubles accentuated a daringly snug fit that made her hesitate before leaving her room.

Her preferred outfit was the training uniform she donned each day, which was designed for battle rather than politics. Her strong legs always nestled nicely into the dark-blue leggings, the fabric of which could withstand a thrust from some of the more robust projections thrown her way. A thin, armored top allowed for optimal movement. The sleeves, made of the same fabric as the pants, flowed down to her hands, which were always left uncovered for maximum efficiency and speed.

A few steps in heels flexed her sore calf muscles, and she longed for her boots. Yet as she sipped from the clear, ice-sculpted glass, she could not help but fondle the smooth, cool material that wrapped her up tight. The eyes of a few male visitors reinforced the appeal of her selection.

"You picked an amazing dress yourself, Ivy." The compliment brought the two face-to-face as they both took another sip of wine. "I am sure Andri will find it quite pleasing."

On that teasing tone, they ventured further into the party. The overhanging icicles and snowflakes glowed blue as the setting sun danced across the walls.

"It's not like he would even notice. He'll probably be busy talking about his fun by the frost." While "fun" was not a suitable descriptor for what Andri and the others had been sent out to do, Eira understood her friend's annoyance.

One of the reasons they had become so close so quickly was that Ivy was rarely afraid to hold her ground when it came to their peers, though she balanced this fearlessness with a reluctance to admonish her elders or superiors. She was also endlessly curious and thirsty for knowledge, which was sometimes frowned upon due to her status as a warrior but often came in handy, especially when Eira looked to counter whatever foolish idea the council was trying to force on her father.

All of this made it surprising that Andri had been chosen as her suitor. A mighty warrior in his own right, he and Ivy had sparred on many occasions, with her best friend coming out on top most of the time. But Andri gave every appearance of lacking Ivy's scholarly side. His unwillingness to pick up a book suggested an utter disregard for any hobby or dream his future wife might have. And while Ivy looked stunning tonight, her crystal gown a perfect complement to her blond locks, Eira was sure Andri would not bother acknowledging her until he was fattened with food and drunk on wine.

"As radiant as the moon in a nighttime sky!"

A grab of Eira's hand and a spin of her body brought a grizzled warrior into focus. His graying hair was perfectly trimmed on the sides tonight, and a small scar flashed on his cheek.

"You always know how to get the attention of an entire room, my dear."

She plunged toward the firm chest of the man who had supported her family throughout her life, taking care not to slosh her wine on him.

"General Aquilo!" Her childlike shriek signified a love she could not hide. "I'm so happy you made it!" A tear ran down her face, but a quick swipe flicked the frozen droplet to the ground.

"I would not miss it for the world! Even if we are a few days late."

She giggled. He was the only one who could have turned this into a joke, and her sharp, frosty anger dissipated as she playfully shook her head. "I'm just glad you're home safe."

She couldn't hide her interest, though, and he met her eyes knowingly.

"Eira, you know I cannot tell you what happened, even if we returned home two short, while the enemy minima lost triple that." The thin strap of her dress grew tighter around her neck as her shoulders filled with tension. "The kin have already been notified—one of the reasons why we were so late returning from our travels."

She sighed, trying to alleviate the breathlessness the words had given her.

"All of the kin?" The question was only to confirm what she had heard; composure returned as she replayed the information a few times.

"All." Another voice cut through the party's chatter, and any chance at openness evaporated.

"Father." She followed the curt word with a fake smile, and it took her full willpower to face the king, who awaited her attention.

"General Aquilo. Why don't you give my daughter and I—"

"No need!" Her interruption was as icy as her breath, prompted by a sharp bite in her stomach. "I was actually just heading to get another drink."

With a pivot and flick of her heel, she escaped to the back of the room. If she were younger, he undoubtedly would have grabbed her for a stern tongue-lashing. But given the setting and the eyes on them, she had little fear he would pursue her.

By now, the council had arrived and would be looking to get her father alone to discuss what he and the Legion had discovered on their trip to the village by the frost. Her hope—and based on past experiences, she was likely correct—was that their little show would soon be over, and her father would be distracted by the usual political rhetoric that had become his strong suit over the years.

The sharpness was already dulling in her stomach as she sat and considered the general's words. The loss of two great lumi soldiers was undoubtedly another coup for the council, which sought her father's grace to go to war with the humans.

"You should not be so hard on him." The warm touch on her neck sent a quiver through her body, and she squeezed her wineglass. "It was not a vacation he has returned from."

Relief mixed with an avalanche of other jumbled feelings as she laid her eyes on the future leader of the Legion.

"Cole," she whispered as he sat by her side. "You . . ." He placed his strong hand on her thigh, and the next tremor was more robust, clinking the glass of her heel against the wood. "You're alive."

His grin took her breath away. The perfect jawline he'd boasted since his youth was steady, and the broad shoulders she was sure had brought down at least one minima nicely filled out his crisp uniform.

"Sure am," he said, grabbing her hand and placing it on his powerful chest.

"I'm glad." She trailed off as he slid closer.

A slight hint of fruity wine wafted as he leaned over. The whisper by her ear did not help with the nervous tapping of her feet. "It has been a long day, and my chamber is open. You look like you could use some rest."

The wine smell and his grasp on her leg suggested that his desires had nothing to do with rest.

A peek over at her father showed the beginning of an intense conversation with the council, including Cole's father. She placed her palm on Cole's cheek and brushed a blond lock aside to fully reveal his blue eyes. "That sounds amazing."

His lurch to his feet showed that he had been desperately hoping for that response.

Most at the party would hardly notice their hasty exit; they were present primarily for political appearances. However, Eira felt one gaze on her. She let it linger just a bit as she paused in the doorframe, slowing her eager fiancé.

"Some party, Father." The glare she received showed that he had heard her over the hubbub. "Thanks for everything," she laughed as she let herself be dragged down the hallway.

Each beep of the elevator made Chris regret his decision a little more as he attempted to tune out his best friend's lecture. The issue for Chris was not so much what was being said but what it meant.

Being fired was nothing new to him, and scouring online job ads seemed merely an inconvenience. However, CJ might have been right that this undertaking was an emotional response to what had just unfolded, coupled with the fact that he had spent another birthday alone just two days before.

"A freaking paper straw, dude?" CJ had spent the hours of procrastination and their lunch break letting it sink in. "Like, of all the hills you want to die on: that?"

Chris shrugged it off with a crooked smile and stepped through the doors as they finally opened. "The world is dying, CJ. Just last year, the average temperature of the earth increased by—"

An elbow to his chest stopped him. "Please, don't!"

Chris's smile grew wider as they turned a corner.

He had forgotten the musty odor. The building's subpar maintenance work and likely below-code plumbing were probably the main culprits. After all these years, he was still astonished at how shabby the buildings in this city could be, especially with the high costs that handcuffed the tenants, most of whom were struggling to put food on the table to begin with. The constant construction around the area suggested that the city was preparing to open some grand landmark, not repairing a leaking sewage system that was past its expiration date.

"You really sure you want to do this?" CJ broke him from his dreary thoughts, and he realized he had stopped in front of an old, familiar door.

"Absolutely." He grabbed the doorknob on reflex, but the rusting brass refused to turn. "Locked."

He was shocked at how surprised he sounded, knowing full well that he had been kicked out two months ago by the woman he once thought he would marry.

"Well then." CJ knocked before he could stop him, the sound echoing.

Chris took a deep breath at the sound of shuffling on the other side of the door. The soft jiggle of the latch forced a final hard swallow as he prepared to face the consequences of his decision to come here.

"Chris?" The young brunette woman looked uneasy. A slight brush of her ponytail hardly made it sway as she blocked the entrance. "What . . . what are you doing here?"

He had hoped Amber would be more excited to see him. Their last text exchange a few weeks ago—at one in the morning after a night out—had produced a small rekindling of old feelings that he had almost acted upon.

"I, um . . ." She stood firm as he edged closer. The inside-out T-shirt she was wearing clung tight to her chest. "I figured I would come get my stuff today."

Finally, she swung the door open. "It's in the back," she said flatly. "I left it all for you." Without a hello to CJ, and before Chris could respond, she disappeared into the kitchen.

The one-bedroom apartment was much cleaner than when he had moved out. The addition of a few more paintings was the only other difference he could see.

"I thought you had work today?"

He was not about to answer. He crept through the living room, heading for a door that stood ajar. As he poked his head into the bedroom, the generous window to his right admitted enough of the early-afternoon sun to illuminate the bed where he had once held Amber close.

This room by no means screamed luxury; the nightstand by the bed was a yard sale item they had recovered when they first signed the lease, and the bedspread was as plain as they came—a clearance purchase from a local retail chain. However, despite its simplicity, the room carried more memories than he could begin to process at the moment.

The two years they'd spent together were outwardly summed up by a box marked with his name just outside the room, and the barely legible scribble brought back more memories he had been trying to block out. The box's sparse contents included a few old shirts he would not miss and three pictures of him playing sports. A final object drew him deeper into the box: the gleaming gold pocket watch.

Growing up, he had been told it was a gift from his father, someone he never met before his death but quite frankly had no interest in getting to know after being abandoned so young. Nevertheless, something about this watch made him keep it, even if the white, icicle-looking hands never budged from twelve. The small engraving on the inside was, he assumed, from the maker. A few numbers and the city name, Boston, were even less visible in the wintry, partly overcast afternoon.

"You got fired, again!" The scream shot him upright, an all-too-familiar glare meeting him.

"Amber—"

"Don't, Chris!" She thrust her hand into the air, the T-shirt riding up as she tugged up the university sweatpants hanging from her waist. She rubbed her forehead, and her huff gave him a few seconds to prepare for her words. "This isn't my problem anymore." Her smile was more a baring of teeth, the jutting of her hips expressive as she pressed her hands on them. "I have an offer to paint overseas this summer, and when I do, I'm going to be leaving this city, Chris. I can't keep dragging myself down trying to save you!"

A pained gulp kept him from saying anything in retort.

"You just have no idea how hard this has been on me—to support you all this time while I go to art school and try to build a career!" She seemed to be explaining it more for herself than for him. "I am trying to make something of my life, Chris. I want to be something, and if you can't . . . You just have no drive to make anything of yourself!"

With this final shout, she pointed him to the exit. CJ's eyes were so wide that Chris thought they might pop out.

The muscles in Chris's neck relaxed, the finality of her statement making it all the more real as he started back toward the front door. He took one last look around the place he had lived for so long, the memories of how happy they had once been pouring more salt on the wound that had torn open in his chest.

It had hardly been perfect, but it had been home—something he had never had before. He struggled to let go.

"Amber . . . I'm really sorry." A last glance at the wall caught a picture she had painted for him three years prior, when they met—a view of a castle overlooking an immaculate city.

"Chris." Her voice trailed off as he reached the door. "Your stuff?" She seemed determined to erase all memory of him as she motioned down the hallway to the old box.

"Throw it out." He needed no remembrance of her, either.

He slammed the door, a childish attempt to make a point as a rising tide of something he could not explain threatened to explode from his chest. The quiet elevator ride gave him space to somewhat calm the roiling inside. He cleared his throat around the returning ashy taste before they stepped into the lobby.

The sun cast a glow over the putrid, spirited city as the two friends exited through the double doors. The smog-filled air that coated Chris's airways with each inhale strengthened his desire to run away from his hometown.

"Hey." CJ grabbed his arm as they joined a group of Philadelphians at a crosswalk. "Why don't we go get a drink?" This was a delicate question that could have sent Chris either way. "Come on, Chris." The tug on his shoulder took them down a side street. "I owe you this."

As his senses settled, he nodded and forced a smile. "You fucking do!" He tried to sound as cheery as possible and bear-hugged CJ. "You're two days late on my birthday drink!"

A fake but vitally needed shared laugh echoed as they continued on to their favorite bar. The tightness in Chris's chest, a worrisome recent symptom, finally released as they left the apartment building behind.

CHAPTER 4

The bustle of the bar escalated with each passing hour. All the regulars gradually filtered out, replaced by newly minted twenty-one-year-olds home for winter break. A pop song being played religiously on the radio continued to blare, its bass taking over the makeshift dance floor that had formed in the rear.

Spending his nights out was not a regular occurrence for Chris. CJ had been working longer hours at the university he attended, and most of their other friends went to school elsewhere, in the suburbs or out of state. Since his split with Amber had sent him back to his best friend's apartment, Chris's nights consisted mainly of video games or the occasional sporting event on television.

"The Birds suck this year." CJ's slur had grown more pronounced over the past hour. He firmly clasped the shot glass he had just emptied as he shook his fist at the TV. "They got no heart! No goddamn heart!"

His shout drew a nod from an old man standing nearby. The man, who was cashing out his tab, quickly pointed to his worn football jersey, which looked to have not been washed in years.

Chris didn't necessarily hate sports; during his high school days, he had been quite an athlete when he engaged himself. The problem—not limited to his athletic career—was that he could never find the commitment needed to finish a season.

"You're drunk!" CJ again stumbled over his words as he grabbed at his beer. "I should probably cut you off!"

His laugh was euphoric, and Chris grinned widely as CJ slapped the table.

"I think you're the one that's had too many." With a sip of his own beer, he turned his attention back to the TV, which was playing a commercial for a hybrid vehicle. He added, "And you don't have to pick up the entire tab."

It had to be at least a hundred dollars at this point. The several hours they had spent on these stools, drinking shots and overpriced, watered-down beer, had probably racked up one of their highest-ever bar tabs.

"Shit no!" CJ lurched forward and slapped the table again. "I missed your birthday, man! I mean, I missed your birthday and Christmas, which, well, now that I think about it, falls on the same day!" Another belly laugh caught the attention of a couple of women, and Chris stiffened at their judgmental glares.

"Well, man," he said, his eyes following the two girls, who started conversing with a group of Rolex-wearing fellows, "I know how busy you've been with school lately, and I know your professor has been trying to get you—"

"I'm taking the study-abroad opportunity in Cairo."

The interruption jerked Chris's attention back to his friend, who suddenly seemed more sober and in control.

The two had been close friends from a young age, and their shared progression through a series of group homes strengthened that bond. Once they'd turned eighteen and the system had all but forgotten about them, the two rented a small apartment with whatever money they could string together while CJ attended his first year of college.

Living with Amber had been a difficult decision at first, but the longer Chris was gone, the more CJ seemed to enjoy his independence and life at the university.

"I'm sorry, man." CJ's grin was apologetic as he fiddled uncomfortably with the top button of his polo shirt.

Chris tried to play it off and ignore the obvious elephant in the room. "You deserve it. You worked really hard to get there, and I know your ass will have a ball playing in the sand all day."

It was no secret that CJ's professors had been pushing for him to take the opportunity when it was offered in the fall. CJ was at the top of his class, and, unlike Chris, he had never had a problem sinking his whole life into anthropology. At first, it had seemed like an odd choice; orphaned kids from the south side of Philly rarely ended up studying prehistory and digging up artifacts of the ancient past. However, one conversation with the young man would make anyone realize that CJ's intelligence would take him far.

"I'm just worried you might get yourself killed out in that barren wasteland."

CJ scoffed playfully at the notion.

"I might not be as big as that steroid fuck that tried to kick your ass today, but don't forget how much I benched during off-season workouts back in high school!" The sarcastic flex brought another chuckle from them both. "But you can stay in the apartment, man. I wouldn't do that to you. We can figure out rent arrangements once you get a new job, and I'll make sure to wire—"

"CJ." Chris could tell that many hours had gone into thinking about this. "I'll be good. Always have been, always will be."

CJ's nod was only a little doubtful. Another overplayed pop song began to blare.

"Maybe you can find something you actually want to do in your next job?" The question came after a slight pause and sounded more cynical than CJ likely intended.

Unable to help himself, Chris responded with a downright nasty tone. "I get it. Because you found your passion, it's probably time I do as well?"

"No, man. I'm sorry. It's just—"

"What do you want me to do, CJ?" His stomach simmered as the day's events played out in his head. "You want me to go to college? Want me to take out a few student loans that will charge ridiculous amounts of interest to some poor, orphaned kid like me just so the banks can get richer?"

At this point, he could not have cared less who heard him.

"Or how about I do what every other poor kid does and join the military? Try and get my college paid by getting sent over to some country where I don't belong. All for a bunch of old shitheads down in Washington, DC, counting money they got from deals they made off my blood!"

CJ kept his head down as Chris pushed away from the bar.

"And in the end, does it really matter? The planet is burning, we are running out of food, and the people who could do something about it would rather play us against each other so they can put more money in their pockets!"

Their part of the bar had gone quiet, though the game was still playing on the TV.

"Jesus, man, I'm sorry. I just thought, well, I don't know."

He had overreacted again. The nearby said as much, but after all the foster homes that never wanted him and the girl of his dreams cutting him out, losing CJ felt like the final straw.

"I gotta take a piss," he said abruptly, jumping off the stool.

It was hard to focus. He practically sprinted away, his eyes vibrating with tears as he burst through a giggling crowd of girls huddled in line for the bathroom. A forceful shove sent the swinging door to the side.

His breathing nowhere near calm, he rubbed his face and unzipped the fly of his jeans.

"Fucking Cairo!"

His fist on the fake tile wall did not hurt, but it brought him back to himself in what he now realized was an empty bathroom. Another, deeper sigh shrank the ball rising toward his chest, the heat subsiding as he let the beer and tequila flow out into the urinal.

He had never thought of himself as having anger problems. Living on the streets in Philadelphia could humble anyone, and despite his big mouth, it was wise to avoid fights whenever possible. Lately, however, he'd found himself in this sort of situation more often. A swirling heat of something he could not explain was trying with all its might to break free.

Whatever it was that brought on the ashy taste and charcoal smell had never actually made it to the surface. Maybe it was simply a result of his terrible diet, which was his only diagnosis when he was lucky enough to have a doctor's appointment a few months back.

"*Christopher.*"

The sound—if it could be called that—of his name shocked him into an upright position, the final droplets of pee splashing his jeans.

"What?"

As he quickly zipped up, he noticed that the lights seemed much dimmer than when he had entered.

"*Christopher.*" The hiss sent a scorching shiver up his spine.

"Who?" The question had barely even squeaked out when a shadow started to emerge from the furthest stall. The voice, still repeating his name, tugged on that dark part of his brain he always tried to ignore, and every hair on Chris's body stood straight up.

"Dude!" CJ's unexpected yell had Chris grabbing the side of the urinal. "Are you okay?"

Chris's neck refused to twist back to the stall where he had seen the advancing shadow. "I . . ." When he finally built up the courage to face it, the figure had disappeared, and the lighting had brightened. "I, um . . ."

CJ looked concerned as Chris went to the sink and fumbled with the automatic tap.

"We both had a lot to drink. I didn't mean to bring up Cairo tonight. I'm sorry."

Now the city name put him at ease, returning the atmosphere to normalcy as he tried to puzzle through possible explanations for what he had just seen and heard.

"No, I overreacted," he said, wiping his hands on a towel. "I shouldn't have yelled. I got defensive in the heat of things, like always." Another peek at the far end of the bathroom was a vital confirmation that the figure had not lingered. "I just, well, you know me."

A tiny flash in the corner of the last stall made him pause, and an almost overwhelming urge to confront the thing arose until a patron's loud laugh just outside eliminated that foolish thought.

"Come on." CJ tapped his chest as they supported each other. "We are way too drunk for this. Let's go home."

Their next steps took them out into the crowd, but Chris's eyes remained on the dark corner stall until the bathroom door swung shut.

A quiet, peaceful night awaited Eira as she threw open the blinds, the midnight moon rising high over the city of Noella. It was such a calming view. Though the harsh, rigid mountains to the north offered their own sort of beauty, they were never as pretty or serene as the architecture sprawled out before her to the south.

She was sure the partygoers had left by now, their stomachs full of wine and food. They would head to bed and whisper an ironic prayer to the Essence as they slid under the fine furs of their beds, but the words were lip service, as they took in far more than they needed to survive at each event.

A brush against the long satin curtain sent a twinge of cynicism through her body, and the dress she had worn—now spread out on the bed—added to it. Her much-preferred nightgown, which she clasped tightly to her body, was made of cotton from the mills at the Eastern Tier. The loose-fitting material allowed her to breathe easy after the stressful night.

Sure, it had been fun to go back to Cole's chamber and skip the party. It was not like she had been missed, and the new scar on her fiancé's shoulder needed her gentle touch. They typically spent only a few hours together, with the strong avalanche of ecstasy rarely leading to conversation afterward. He was never one to talk about his work, and her prying was useless against Cole's word to her father. This night, however, he had been more open about where they had been, though that meant spending an extra hour with him under the sheets—not an unpleasant price.

Cole had made himself a viable suitor from a young age. Their connection was not based solely on his fierce ability on the training grounds or his charisma. It was also based on shared experience, with his mother passing in the Battle of the Frost twenty years earlier, just as hers had.

To say she was not attracted to him would be a lie. Every girl she'd grown up with would have given anything to be paired with this man, with his well-sculpted exterior and deep-blue eyes that could melt one in place. The wavy hair he was constantly flipping about with his sturdy fingers was probably the feature she enjoyed the most, though. The dampness from exertion during their time in bed always made it darker, which she had just recently begun to prefer.

"Eira." The voice yanked her from her thoughts, a slight creak of the door jolting her upright. "I see you are back."

As her father entered, a glance at the dress on the bed showed that he knew where she had been.

"I know you enjoy embarrassing me in front of the council." His inhale was a disapproving, fatherly one. "But please, if you can, try not to be so blatant about it in front of Lord Colden."

The corner of her mouth twitched in wry amusement. Her goal had been accomplished.

"I'm surprised Colden even realized Cole was home." She closed the curtains and drifted toward the fireplace. "I thought he would have been standing on tables and yelling about exterminating the humans."

Her father rolled his tired blue eyes.

"Well," he said as he sat on her bed, the grand goose-feather mattress sinking under his weight. "You would not be wrong that he tried to get my ear. And when it comes to the humans—"

"Why do you give that fool the time of day?!" Her sudden shout was probably loud enough to wake the castle staff. "He cares nothing about the villages outside these walls and merely comes to try and convince you—"

"Eira." He sounded so weary that she had to face him. "Lord Colden is all for his politics, which is one of the many reasons I am happy Cole is nothing like him and will be leading the Legion after General Aquilo retires."

It was the first thing the two had agreed about in months. Cole was nothing like his father, who sought only political success. The lord's rise to the top of the council had been met with concern, mostly from military leaders who feared that his boundless hatred for humans, whom he blamed for his wife's death, would lead to unnecessary conflict.

His son, on the other hand, had never shown much interest in the politics that came with his power. However, that could change in a few months' time, as his marriage to Eira would bring them both to the head of the bargaining table.

"You're mad at me," her father said softly. "You're mad at me for missing your birthday."

Every frigid knot inside her began to unravel. A few quick steps took her to his side, and she finally noticed a new box on her wooden nightstand.

"I know why you were late." She lowered her head, the overwhelming urge to humiliate him from earlier gone, and she began to wish she could take it all back.

"Eira." Again, he sounded so defeated. "This time of year. Your birthday and all that comes with it . . ."

A chill cut through her body; the direction of the conversation was not remotely to her liking. "You know how I feel about lying to all of them." Her stern, low declaration contained a warning she hoped he would heed.

"Eira." He seemed to be unable to do anything but repeat her name tonight.

"Don't, Father!" She was up again, pacing the carpeted floor, her bare feet freezing with each step. "To bring her up now, after her sacrifice and what she did that night!" She struggled to get the words out, her mind twisting like a blizzard.

"You think I want to lie to them?" The shout stopped her cold, the volume something she had not heard from her father in quite some time. "You think I do not want to tell them what she did that night? About how she faced down Chaoic's army and battled those creatures, just for us?"

He was the one pacing now. A jab of his hand through his white hair left it untamed.

"Do you think I do not hear the whispers of my own people? The blame they place on me for what I have done?" Eira had no response in the face of her father's pain. "She was our savior, created for us, and

I have to hear the murmurs blaming me for choosing her as my wife!"

The weary man dropped back onto her bed, sending her to him at a run. His apparent exhaustion inspired her to hold him tight, and they collected themselves in the break that followed.

"Father." Scarcely a murmur escaped past the frost building in her throat. "It was I who took her powers. It was I who—"

He grasped her hands, locking gazes with her as a tear ran down his face.

"Don't ever say that, Eira." The whisper was more a plea than a demand. "Your mother and I, we made our mistakes. But you were never one of them."

It had been years since they had spoken like this, years since she had seen her father shed a tear; the longer they held each other, the more she understood why.

It was no secret that most of the citizens still blamed him for the Iclyn's death. The legends said that she had lived since the beginning of time and had never once taken a suitor from the lumi she had always protected. Her father's rise to power and his choice of bride could easily be taken for hubris—something she knew was a lie.

"I know you loved her, Father," she muttered, the truth of it soothing them both. "And if it is your will that the people still believe that she sacrificed herself in the frost to strengthen it, to keep Chaoic's creatures away, well—"

"I only wish to give them hope, Eira," he interrupted as she squeezed tight again. "To let them know that she is still with them and still protecting them."

Knowing the words were not meant to hurt her, she stared down at her palms, which lay helplessly open.

His lean away was an acknowledgement of the error he had made. "I did not mean . . ." The pause once more allowed them to collect themselves. His next drawn-out sigh ended abruptly as he went to the nightstand, where he grabbed the box. "Please." A tilt of the lid produced a sparkle so bright that she had to squint. "Take this. It's from your mother. She made me promise to give this to you after your twenty-first birthday."

The necklace was flawless, an immaculate blue sapphire shining in the low light of the dying fire. Shaped like a teardrop, it was so perfectly carved that it seemed to have come into being in that very shape. A silver chain kept the astonishing gemstone in place. Her father's delicate movements as he unraveled the chain and placed it around her neck made it feel like much more than an ordinary birthday gift.

"Is this . . ." A tear froze as she sniffled and tried to compose herself. "Is this the relic she created?"

"No, my beautiful girl. It is so much more," her father said, pulling a note from his pocket. The metal chain's warmth made it feel like it had melted into her skin as he handed her the parchment. "But when you are alone, please, please read the note." He kissed her forehead and started for the door. "You are destined for amazing things, Eira. Believe in yourself, trust who you are, and I promise you will discover them."

His last words floated behind him as he disappeared into the hallway, and her trembling hand wiped away another tear before it froze on her cheek.

CHAPTER 5

The morning sun flooding in through the kitchen window magnified the drumming of his headache. Each step toward the sink sloshed the cheap beer and shots still in his stomach.

"I'm never drinking again." He had uttered this phrase many times before.

Getting home from the bar had been a blur. The city nightlife, a spectacle they normally refused to be sucked into, had swallowed them up and spit them out before they somehow found an Uber to carry their tired bodies back to the apartment. A half-eaten slice of pizza on the small table in the living room was the final remnant of their mini after-party, which left one of them still passed out cold on the couch with the blanket pulled up as the clock approached nine in the morning.

"CJ! Get up!" The spiritless shout was mostly to himself as he rummaged through the cabinet. His frantic search for medicine made his head throb more vigorously.

When he had first lived with CJ, they'd always kept the Advil above the kitchen sink. After a few more pathetic blind swipes, he realized that things were not how he had left them when he moved away. The apartment's stale aroma had not changed; nor had the typical, cramped city feel or the dingy appliances. But CJ's new job at the university had enabled the addition of a recliner beside the old couch. A Samsung flat-screen also stood out, the attached sound bar reeking of unnecessary expense, given how little time they spent watching television.

"CJ!" His scream carried more desperation this time as he slammed the old cabinet door shut. "Where the hell is the Advil?"

He rubbed his forehead, hoping to stymie the thumping. His best friend's loud moan indicated he was not too far behind Chris in needing the pills.

"Top drawer of the bathroom." With another groan, CJ sat upright. "And why are you yelling?"

He got up to rifle through the refrigerator as Chris headed to the bathroom. "I'm seriously never drinking again!" CJ rambled on about his own headache and how they had to find a new place for coffee after yesterday, but it was all just a mumble to Chris as he swallowed the pills and locked his hands on the counter in the pitch-black bathroom. The darkness grew heavier as the faucet ran. He peered into the space where the mirror hung and tried to focus on anything that would eliminate the pounding in his temples.

"Stick with your own kind!" The memory made his skin crawl. He'd heard similar statements many times growing up. Another shout churned in his thoughts: *"You just have no drive to make anything of yourself!"*

He preferred the headache to these echoes.

"Christopher."

This voice was different: a screechy, soulless shriek that made him shiver with heat as sweat poured down his face. He heard it again and again, the shadow from the night before creeping closer in his mind's eye as he stared directly at the mirror he couldn't see in the dark.

The blood in his veins started to cook as he held his breath. The headache was now the least of his worries.

"*Christo*—"

"Chris!" CJ's yell from the other room broke the spell, and he pulled away from the sink with a loud gasp. "You have a delivery!"

Chris slapped his hand to the light switch. The sudden illumination of the bathroom showed no other guest, but something else unexpected sent him backpedaling as CJ yelled again. The sides of the sink were charred black and smoking from what looked like an intense encounter with a hot flame.

"Yo, man, is something burn—" He burst through the bathroom door before CJ could enter and forced a smile in a desperate attempt to hide his unease. "Um, are you okay?"

The question reminded Chris that he was dripping with sweat. The smell of sulfur wafted from the bathroom, and Chris tried his best to fan it away with his hidden hand.

"I'm sure I smell—"

"A package? On a Sunday? For me?"

As CJ grimaced over his shoulder toward the smelly bathroom, Chris steered them into the kitchen, where a square box covered in stamps sat on the island.

His best friend peeked from behind him. "The guy didn't look like the regular delivery guy. He actually looked real shady and had this crazy-messy red hair. I would have thought he was homeless if not for his nice suit."

They studied the package, which besides the stamps was oddly bare.

"Where the hell was this sent from?"

An instinct Chris could not fight off had him already slashing at the tape.

"Should you really be—"

It was too late to second-guess; Chris pulled apart the cardboard.

"What the . . . ?" Every concern fled his mind as he removed a piece of paper. He unfolded the old parchment and turned, hardly noticing when CJ tugged a heavy duffel bag from the box.

Christopher—Answers to the past will not soothe your mind, but when the time is right, your future you will find.

—*Love, Dad*

"Is this some type of birthday present?"

He vaguely heard a zipper.

"Um, Chris?"

The word at the end of the note kept Chris frozen as he tried to process what he was staring at.

"Chris?"

He read the words yet again, his hands shaking.

"Chris!" Chris whirled to face a flabbergasted CJ. "What the hell are you into, man?"

This strange inquiry brought Chris hurrying around the island to see what his best friend was holding. "I don't . . ." His hasty grab of the large bag crinkled the cash inside, the twenties and hundreds shifting with the movement of his hands. Both men struggled to speak. A small slip of paper with a phone number and New York City address became visible between the bills.

"Chris, do you want to tell me something?"

Chris pondered this question as he handed the original note to CJ, who accepted it hesitantly.

"This paper is so old, man. Who would send . . ."

Chris kept silent, waiting for his friend's verification of what was written there.

"Dude." The next question was entirely expected: "Who was your dad?"

Warmth rushed through Eira's body as she fiddled with the metal chain, the blue gemstone sparkling in the morning rays that pushed through the training room's broad bay window. She had not slept the night before: the encounter with her father, the gift, and the note filled her mind as she lay in bed.

Eira—Perfection on the outside can leave one blind, but when you find the strength on the inside, your future you will find.
—Love, Mother

The simple yet inexplicable message now had her staring blankly out into a blue sky as yet unmarred by a single cloud.

She had repeated the sentence at least a thousand times since reading it, scrutinizing each word and trying to discern what it could mean. However, after a few hours of mumbling to herself, her attention stuck fast to the last two words. A swirling inner storm seemed to strangle her lungs.

"Love, Mother." Her whisper brought her hand to the cool glass of the window, which offered little relief from what had become alarmingly cold blood.

A gust drew her eyes down to the quad. The training ground started to fill with her peers, who were honing their skills in the art of battle.

"Control yourself, Ivy!" she heard General Aquilo call. The general was easy to work with; his ability to get the best out of any student was a calling card that had lifted him to the highest rank in her father's military. "That's it!"

Her best friend found her center of gravity in the pitch below. A swivel onto her back leg brought her hands up as she prepared to unleash the power growing inside her.

"Poor Andri." Eira could not help but smile as Ivy's concentration produced a whirling wind. Her friend's grip on the long, circulating energy staff that suddenly appeared set the stage for her impending spar with the man assigned to wed her.

Eira had always wondered how it felt to hold a spiratus, which was produced from its wielder's energy. Having been gifted with her mother's powers, she did not have the ability to produce such a weapon when training. Instead, the cloudy stick was always used against her. The force of it in the hands of a trained and powerful lumi could break the neck of whatever stood in their way during battle.

The ability to wield the two-inch-thick cane offensively was the first thing young trainees sought to learn when working on the grounds, thanks to the stories they had heard of great warriors. Powerful gusts frequently circulated the castle whenever the windows were left open as they showcased their skills. But the spiratus's defensive qualities were what most often led to victory in these sparring matches. A spiratus could block almost anything thrown at it; this included, according to legend, the powerful weapons developed by humans and even the claws of Chaoic's infamous ferlup.

"You are too aggressive, Andri!" General Aquilo's shout drew Eira's attention back to the match. Ivy's blond hair danced in a gritty wind as she sidestepped a blast from her fiancé's staff and effortlessly pirouetted to maintain her guard.

To say that Ivy had improved over the last few years did not do her justice. The many nights she had spent researching the techniques of the great lumi warriors and the extra hours the two women had spent perfecting every step and maneuver were on full display as Ivy gracefully jumped from a log on which she had been perfectly balanced.

There was an art to how they were taught to fight: a foolproof design directing one's thought and movement when engaged with a target that sought to do harm. In these scenarios where both combatants had been trained equally, it came down to mental strength. The ability to control what churned inside them was paramount to gaining the upper hand.

"Now!" The general's command sent Ivy's hands twirling. The spiratus spun faster as she rocked on her legs and exploded toward Andri, who was still gasping from his whiffs earlier in the match.

The resulting wind whipped Eira's curtains into a frenzy. As high as she was above them, the power Ivy produced was obvious, and a hush fell over the area below as the dust settled.

General Aquilo beamed. "Great job, Ivy!" Her staff disappeared as the burly Andri climbed to his feet. "You are finding your true strength, and I must say, it is quite incredible!"

A chuckle reached Eira's open window, and the person who produced it appeared by Ivy's side. Eira's muscular fiancé did not hide his glance up at her as he announced, "I would not mind having her train with the Legion today!" Cole directed Ivy toward the soldiers in the corner. "That type of power can be useful in the field; let's see what else you can do."

Ivy's slight eyebrow raise was another acknowledgment that everyone knew who was watching. Cole's wink brought a cold blush to Eira's cheeks before she ducked away.

"She has lots of potential," said Bernard from behind her, causing her to jump. "I see a bright future for her."

She instinctively grasped the gemstone hanging against her chest. "Ivy's been practicing a lot," she managed to say. She consciously exhaled, releasing the stranglehold on her new gift.

"A birthday present?" Bernard stared at it intently. "Is that—"

"Just my mother's necklace." She had been asked that question four or five times so far today, unfortunately leading her to snap at Cole when he met her for breakfast in the grand hall. "You know the stories." Yet again, she forced out the lie her father had promised her to keep. "The ice relic no longer exists. It was used to strengthen the frost many years ago."

The next part was something she had not spoken out loud yet, but she needed someone else to hear it. "Besides, she would have never trusted me with such a powerful . . ."

The sigh evinced more defeat than she intended. She clenched her hands at her sides as frost clung to her fingernails.

"You put too much pressure on yourself, Eira."

"I am twenty-one!" Her petulant stomp was prompted by an accrual of tension from the night before. "I should be able to fully harness my powers by now! Every one of them down there can, and yet I sit in this room and struggle each day!"

"You are different, Eira." Bernard's statement was blunt. "You are not like any of them down there, and you should not be comparing yourself to them." His response, which seemed to encourage arrogance, made her cringe and slouch. "A lumi's power is concentrated in our spiratus, an object created solely to project all our energy into one place. It is the only way to reach our full potential and master our art."

This was a lesson children learned, yet he seemed fixated on getting it across.

"You, Eira," he continued, grabbing her hands and chilling them even more, "you project something stronger. You project the very element that saved our people so many years before. You do not focus squarely on one object but on multiples, and you possess a strength that no one, not even I, could comprehend." She had never heard this tone from him, and her cheeks froze as she tried to focus on Bernard's vivid blue eyes.

"I don't"—a wave of emotion took over as she started to shake—"I just don't know if I can do this!" She flung herself away and returned to the window. The training group had intensified their sparring, and their roars echoed up the castle walls. "The attacks are getting worse. People—my people—are dying! People I am supposed to protect, and yet . . ." She struggled to finish, the previous night returning to her as she squeezed her eyelids tight. "My father says that he believes in me, says that I am destined for special things, but everything I have been told says otherwise: my selection; his actions to keep me in this castle."

She shook her head. Her grip on the window produced an icy outline of her hands as she gazed toward the city wall that had held her captive for so many years. Her breathing grew labored, as it always did when she attempted to discuss this subject.

"You need to control yourself, my dear." His gentle rub on her shoulder refocused her as she stabilized her temperature. "And be careful what you seek outside these walls. Your fiancé and the Legion have performed quite well against the creatures, and the council believes—"

"The council wants nothing but more power and a war with the humans!" she shouted, darting to the other side of the room as she clasped the sparkling necklace between her fingers. "Bernard." She sized up a question she had long wanted to broach with this grizzled warrior. "Do you believe that Chaoic controls the humans? Do you believe the council's verdict that they are sacrificing their souls to increase his power?"

Bernard moved toward the fire burning at the far end of the room, but he didn't seem to be ignoring her. He was likely searching for the right words—and those words would no doubt break a promise he had made to her father.

Politics were to be off limits during her training. Nevertheless, her ability to extract information from General Aquilo kept her updated on the latest events. After she transitioned to Bernard for more advanced training, she'd quickly learned his trigger points, even if it sometimes took a few extra sessions to get him to talk.

"You spent years with them as a liaison to our traders when they used the leaps to travel into their realm," she continued. "You have spent time around the humans and were one of the last to come back from their world before we closed trading during the Battle of the Frost. My father trusts your information on them."

Bernard turned to her with a smirk. "History, stories; they have a way of changing one's opinion of something one struggles to understand." The hook in his words reeled her in.

"But are they barbaric as the stories say? They are weaker, right? They do not possess the power to project."

"The inability to project does not make them weaker. Only our arrogance supports that view." He started to pace, his hands folded in front of him. "That arrogance, the very fact that we learned nothing from our war with them, is the reason that Chaoic stands at our front door now."

"Then how have they fought him off for so long? If he has been stuck in their world, has the Ignati . . . has he come back? Has he started to fight?"

"The humans possess something we can never truly understand, something we have struggled to comprehend since we started to trade with them." Eira drew close to him as he dropped his voice to a whisper. "Free will."

She frowned. "So, the Ignati gave them this free will to—"

"The Ignati did not give them this power, Eira. They are born with it. It's why they have survived and why the Ignati left his post as their protector after the Great War."

She straightened at attention, waiting for more.

"By imposing the treaty, the Ignati stripped them of their free will, the very thing that had allowed them to prosper. Lumi arrogance that we could show the humans a better life led to that war, and the Ignati's relic removed their memory of our existence in an effort to stop the death and destruction."

This was another lesson she had already heard but had spent little time studying or contemplating when she was younger.

"The relic your mother created strengthened the frost to serve as a barrier between the humans and our own realm so that we can both live in peace. Together, the two relics sealed the leaps, preventing unnecessary interactions."

Bernard's tone dropped lower.

"A small amount of trade was all I was to supervise, and I approved vendors who knew nothing of our actual identity."

The speech ended abruptly, which felt odd given his buildup.

Her curiosity filled the silence to bursting. "Then if the humans are still fighting, Ignati must still have some power to help us repel Chaoic. We can have my father open one of the leaps in the city, or if he refuses, we can go to the Temple of the Essence and find the master leap that the books speak of! We can use it to find the Ignati and—"

"Eira!" His shush and stern frown cut her off. "Do not speak of such things! If your father knew that you would even consider going to the Temple of the Essence, what you might find or see . . ." His eyes widened, an obvious sign that he had said too much.

"What do you mean by what I might find?" She narrowed the distance between them, but Bernard pivoted quickly and started for the door.

"But Bernard! My training!" she cried to keep him in the room; she wanted to get to the core of what he meant.

"We are done for today!"

Before she could retort, he was around the corner and gone, a meager sliver of sunlight illuminating the spot where he had been standing.

Her mind raced. The lesson she had expected that day had transformed into something completely different—something that had her questioning everything she had been taught.

"I am sick of this."

A new idea sprang into her head. Though it would undoubtedly get her in trouble, it sent her sprinting for the door.

CHAPTER 6

Dirt crunched beneath Eira's feet as she ran down the walkway and emerged into the welcoming, brisk winter air. Snow-covered trees rustled on either side, and the path's slope allowed her to hit top speed in no time. She whipped past an outside caretaker shoveling fresh flurries from the night before. The ominous mountainscape in the distance provided a stark backdrop to the serene foreground shimmering beneath its white blanket.

"Eira!" Ivy huffed, struggling to keep up after being yanked away from a long training session with little time to recover. "We should not be doing this! Your father will be furious if he finds out we went into the city."

A cool breeze whipped through Eira's hair, the icy white strands splashing against her face.

Another caretaker smiled over at them and received a hurried wave from Eira. The dirt finally gave way to a cobblestone sidewalk leading out through the open gates. Another chilly gust picked up at their backs, accompanying them out of the compound and down to the city of Noella.

Eira had been contemplating this visit for a while now. Semiregular trips into town were considered necessary for her people's morale, especially in light of the current political situation, but recently her father had only allowed her to visit if accompanied by Cole or a few Royal Guards. Bernard's cryptic last statement about the Temple of the Essence was her main reason to expedite such an adventure without notice today, and she didn't want a bodyguard stifling necessary conversation.

She felt out of place in this setting. Even today, with the cobblestone streets more barren than usual, the eyes of the few citizens outside the castle were fixed on her as she moved past a store selling pastries and bread. The aroma of the baked delicacies helped to shut out some of the awkwardness, bringing Eira back to her younger years, when she did not have to deal with the unnerving judgment around her.

"Slow down!" Ivy gasped as she grabbed Eira's arm. "Why are we in such a hurry, and why did you not want to tell your father?"

Eira's presence was already drawing a crowd. A beefy milkman in a wagon creaked to a stop not far from them and lowered his head, bowing—an appropriate response to her appearance yet one she wished he had forgone.

She dipped her head in acknowledgment, but he had disappeared around the corner and out of sight as if she had the plague.

"Eira, come on. Why are we here?" Ivy's impatient question matched an urgency within Eira that grew stronger as they continued down the city street. Even the ordinarily bustling vendor stands with their mounds of fruit and vegetables were eerily desolate.

"I need to talk to Whittaker." Eira kept her voice down as they approached the end of the stone road, her boots skidding to a stop when a young girl ran up to them.

"Eira!" The delighted scream made her smile more genuine. "I have not seen you in the city in so long! I have been practicing so much!"

Their embrace was full of warmth, and Eira's icy shell retreated in the heat of the hug.

"I missed you, Aspen, and cannot wait to see all you have learned." Her heart swelled as she patted the little girl's blond head. "Are you ready for your selection?"

She tried with all her might to shake off the stares around them.

"Yes! I just know I am going to be a warrior like you." The little girl puffed out her cheeks. "Are you here to help me some more?"

"Actually, I am here to see your father. Is he in the shop today?" Two older women passed nearby, where a few torchlights stood, their stiff faces locked on her until they entered a clothing store to the right. Eira barely hid her annoyance as she focused back on the little girl. "I have some business I would like to speak with him about."

"He is!" The pure excitement in Aspen's shriek prompted another hug. "Follow me!"

All the lingering eyes, the judgments, both good and bad, faded to the background as the trio continued toward the flawlessly constructed brick building Eira knew so well.

"Daddy, we have visitors!" Little Aspen's shiny hair bobbed as she hopped through the entrance and disappeared behind an interior door.

"I love this place." Ivy stationed herself by one of the bookshelves decorating the walls, her fingers running along beaten leather spines.

The faint smell of herbal tea scented the shop, wafting from the white flowers beside the small table of boiling water. Quite some time had passed since Eira last entered this place. Growing up, she had vastly preferred its cozy quietness to the castle's massive library with all its pupils constantly roaming about. With the worsening breakthroughs near the outer villages, her last few trips to the area had been brief, mainly to mingle with business owners Cole wanted to see and leaving little time to visit old friends.

"Eira!" A bearded man emerged, his broad shoulders swallowing her as she returned his embrace. His vibrant personality radiated through his glowing skin and graying hair, which sparkled in the sun. "What are you doing here, my dear? And where are your guards?"

The question irritated her. She had never needed an escort to visit the man who had run the castle library when her mother was alive. Since Whittaker's retirement to Noella, he spent most of his days teaching the children not selected for warrior training, and while Eira enjoyed most aspects of her combat instruction, she envied those students.

The pupils inside the library walls spoke reverently of his knowledge, but even they did not understand the full extent of what his mind had stored up over many years of work.

"I have my guard."

Ivy smiled self-consciously as Eira gestured in her direction.

"I see." He had always been too discerning for her games, and his narrowing in on her neck showed that he already suspected something was up. "Radiant." He delicately fiddled with the gemstone, her face freezing as he shifted to a warm smile. "You look just like her with that necklace on."

A hard swallow gave her time to collect her thoughts. "I want to know more about the Temple of the Essence." The grin dropped from his face, and his shoulders stiffened. "I want to know what my father is not telling me about that night."

An uneasiness settled as Aspen peeked from behind a door.

"Eira—"

"I know you swore to my father not to say anything." She was desperate, an internal itch compelling her to persist. "But I need to know. I need to know why she would go out there."

It was the only question that meant anything to her.

"Eira, your mother . . ."

She strangled the necklace harder as she watched him struggle, a deep pain growing in his cobalt eyes.

"Was it to protect the ice relic? Was Chaoic's army coming to steal it and destroy the frost? Is that why?"

Whittaker played with the frosty tips of his sideburns, looking pained.

"I know I took her powers. I know it was me who drained her, and for her to just leave us, to face those creatures by herself like that, it would have had to be—"

"Don't ever blame yourself for any of this," he burst out. "Your mother made a choice that night. But that choice, it was not to protect the ice relic or the frost!"

Her legs weakened under the weight of this new piece of information.

"Whittaker!" The familiar bellow brought her around as Cole stomped into the shop. "You are breaking the king's orders!" Eira shivered, and the tips of her fingers glistened as Cole barked, "Her father has specifically stated—"

"How dare you act like I do not exist!"

All eyes in the room turned toward her.

"Eira?" Cole asked, taken aback.

"How dare you berate this man, to whom I came on my own to find answers my father refuses to provide!" Ice percolated through her veins, her vision focused on Cole as he retreated a few steps. "And why is it that you had to come down here to grab me? Are you afraid that if you do not follow my father's wishes, you will lose your spot by the throne? Your spot at the head of the council?" This unbecoming outburst was nowhere close to reflecting the control expected of a warrior of her degree.

"Eira, you know that means nothing to me! Your father sent me after Bernard left."

"He left?" She leaned toward him, her body rigid with astonishment. "What do you mean?"

Cole tugged at his fur coat and seemed to regain his composure. "I was told that he left after your training session today. King Rori sent me down to get you when he heard of your trip because he was worried—"

"Worried?" That word triggered a blizzard within her. "My father cares only about controlling me."

"Eira, please—"

"Let's go, Ivy." She was done with all of this: the shouting, the questions, and the wall her father had built around her. "And if you even mention this to my father . . ." The incomplete threat was as blunt as it could be. She smashed through the door and exploded into the street.

"Eira!"

"I mean it, Cole!" Her scream reverberated as her palms opened, the swirling frost forming into one of her rare emotional projections. His eyes went wide. "Not one word!" Her final shriek echoed behind her as she took off down the cobblestone sidewalk with Ivy in tow, a line of disapproving stares following them as they left.

A pungent bouquet of body odor and dried urine filled Chris's nostrils as he replayed the last few hours in his head. The shaking of the subway car did little to distract from the scent.

The original shock of the package, along with the note from his father, had left Chris and CJ in stunned silence as they counted the cash in full. The staggering total of ten thousand dollars had left them in a daze until Chris finally decided they needed to act.

"This is stupid." CJ fidgeted with the string of the duffel bag in his lap as another bump of the subway car pushed their shoulders together. "Opening the package was one thing. Hell, I can even understand making the phone call to see what it was all about, but going to New York City? This is how people die, Chris."

"I know this doesn't feel right—"

"Feel right?!" CJ paused and lowered his voice. "Chris, I'm holding a bag with more cash than either of us have made in months, from a package sent from God knows where, presumably by someone who knew your father, a man who you were told died when you were an infant!"

To punctuate his point, CJ slapped the pole in front of them, drawing glances from fellow passengers.

"Chill out, man." Chris was normally the one acting irrationally, but he felt a strange sense of calm as he scanned the car. "I said you didn't have to come, but you of all people should know that I have to do this."

It was a low blow, and the way his best friend straightened showed that he had felt it.

"Don't do that." CJ shook his head. "Don't drop that orphan shit on me right now. That's not fair, and you know it."

The two rarely brought up why they had each been placed in group homes. Only after a night of cheap beer and their first blunt had they truly opened up to each other.

"I'm sorry, man. But I need to do this. I know nothing about my parents other than that my mom died giving birth, and my dad passed a year later." His gaze fell to the rubber floor as it jerked. "I always asked myself why. Why would he just drop me off? Did he blame me for—"

"I get it," CJ interrupted, saving him from finishing the painful thought. "I at least have answers, even if that terrible answer is that my pops went to jail after my mom passed from cancer." The two fell silent once more, signifying a truce.

After a few more stops, Chris studied the map near the window. The red lines and black dots indicated a few more blocks to go before they reached their destination.

"So, the bank really had your name ready to go when you called?"

"Yeah, it's weird because I don't know many banks open on a

Sunday. But it was like they were waiting for me to call."

CJ's scoff was expressive, and he shook his head harder. "Yeah, *that's* the weird part."

Another stop brought a homeless man onto the train. A couple of patrons showed their displeasure by rolling their eyes as he took an isolated seat in the corner. The December air had done a number on the man's face. The red of his cheeks peeled as he blew into a pair of tattered gloves that matched his patchwork long-sleeve shirt and jeans.

This was nothing Chris and CJ hadn't seen in Philadelphia, where every corner had a story: a man or woman, or sometimes an entire family, begging for a dollar or two to survive. Chris always cringed when he passed the cardboard boxes they spent the nights in. His life and all of its issues did not seem so bad then.

"What are you doing, man?"

Chris had not even realized he was removing his coat, his feet drawn like a magnet to the man.

"Here." The nylon windbreaker would probably do little to help, but it was all he had grabbed in his rush to leave earlier.

"For me?" The perplexed inquiry curled the man's chapped lips. He struggled to raise his arms to accept the gift. "But why—"

"It fits you better than me."

The man pulled it in tight, the gratitude crystal clear in his watery eyes.

"Just enjoy, sir." Chris's body seemed to act independently as he removed a few of the hundred-dollar bills he had placed in his pocket. "And take this for whatever you need. I hope . . . I hope it helps." The man's eyes now showed a tiny spark that had been missing when he entered the car.

Chris didn't give him the chance to say anything else as he darted back to his seat and dropped next to CJ.

"Always trying to save the world." His best friend sounded more lighthearted and relaxed.

A lurch of the subway was followed by the doors opening and a muffled announcement over the speakers. The homeless man paused by the exit, as if he expected Chris to regret his decision, to ask for the jacket and money back before the man reached the platform and left for good. A subtle nod from Chris sent him on his way, and the battered fellow returned the gesture before disappearing.

"He has very little time left in this world."

The stern, raspy voice jerked Chris around as the doors closed. "Excuse me?"

He couldn't tell who had spoken. CJ grabbed his shoulder, and together they edged closer to where the voice had come from.

"That thing will not last much longer. To give your coat and money to it, why?"

A hulking, muscular figure sat, arms crossed, two seats down.

"That 'thing'?" Chris took extreme exception to that word. The critical eyes of the well-nourished man in his fine fur coat widened at Chris's aggressive tone. "That 'thing' is a human being. He deserves decency, just like anyone else."

A slight shrug from the burly shoulders showed only the faintest understanding, but given his flawlessly designed leather boots, Chris had little reason to hope for more.

"Not like you would understand, though."

The subway train rocked to a stop at their destination, which was for the best; he and CJ did not need to get caught up in another physical confrontation.

"Why is that? Because of the way I dress? Or because I merely asked you a question?" The man followed them onto the platform. "Your response is very human of you."

The crowd in the subway station was moving too slowly for Chris's liking, making it impossible to shake their unwanted companion.

"Look, man." CJ pushed through the turnstile and spun around. "We don't want any problems."

"I guess it should not surprise me, though," the man continued as if CJ had not spoken. "You probably got it from your father."

The statement stopped the pair in their tracks. A wave of heat washed over Chris's face as he straightened. "What—"

"From the stories I've heard, he was always quite cynical—one of the many human traits that unfortunately rubbed off on him."

The crowd gradually dispersed around them, but the man held firm and looked to be waiting for them to speak first. Chris could get nothing out as he studied the towering stranger, who loomed over them with a mane of white-streaked blond hair that accentuated striking blue eyes.

"I know you have business in this city, and I do not wish to disrupt that." Chris and CJ had to lean in to hear him. "I only wish for you to listen to what I have to say. When I am done, you can decide if you want me to leave."

The friends shared a momentary, confused glance. Chris tried to fight off the impulse building inside him as sunlight crept down the steps leading to the city above. CJ grabbed him in warning, but the desire to hear more about his father was too great for Chris to deny.

"What do you want to tell us?"

CJ sighed.

"I wish," the man said with a wave of his firm, calloused hand, "to tell you a story."

CHAPTER 7

"I knew this was a bad idea," CJ whispered as they stopped in front of the bank. A few car horns blared in the street, and the afternoon sun sparkled off Brooklyn's buildings.

In the last twenty minutes, which had felt like an hour, the enormous individual had drawn nary a stare in this city that had seen it all. Chris had lost patience. The strange folklore the man was trying to sell them seemed to have nothing to do with his father, and his arms were frozen in the long-sleeve shirt that was his only protection against the bitter winter breeze.

"Look, um, Bernard, was it?"

The man nodded as he settled his hands behind his back.

"I know you might have overheard some things in the train. Maybe you thought you could use that to have us join your church, but I promise you, we have no money to give."

"Church?" Bernard's confusion seemed sincere.

CJ snorted. "My man, I wouldn't go spouting off in this city about God being some green woman who can paint." Bernard raised a perfectly groomed eyebrow. "I would make it more believable if you want any traction. People with wind sticks who fight humans in some great war? Come on. We have better movies out right now."

Bernard's coat rocked up and down as he laughed unexpectedly. "You humans!" Chris immediately took offense. "If you want me to show you—"

"Dude." It was time for this to end; the bank behind them called to Chris. "We're not interested. Take your stories about warriors from Antarctica somewhere else. We have places to go, so please just leave us alone." His twist away was emphatic. He and CJ stomped up the steps, sharing annoyed glances.

"I never got to the part about your father! But I guess if you think hard about it, you might be able to figure that out!"

Chris halted, trying to ignore the pull in his brain that always reared its ugly head when he was alone with his thoughts.

CJ grabbed his arm. "Chris, he's just trying to bait you."

That was probably true, but Chris could not help but linger as the slight taste of ash returned to his tongue. With a final nod to the gigantic man, he went inside. The urge to look back through the glass lost out to his fear of giving in to the part of his mind that desperately wanted more answers and would put him in absurd situations to find them.

The internal struggle ended quickly as the aroma of mint greeted their entrance to the pristine interior of the bank. But while the smell was welcoming, the sight of empty teller booths and a barren receptionist desk put Chris on edge.

"Mr. Cho!" The shout echoed against the high ceilings. "I am glad you made it; any problems coming in?"

The russet color of the man's face highlighted a few scars that grew more pronounced as he drew closer in a form-fitting suit. He was not nearly as tall as the storyteller who had chased them for ten blocks, but his short haircut and rigid walk screamed military.

"No sir, not at all."

"Very good, and I see you brought a friend." The suit wasted no time steering them through the open lobby, their isolated footsteps emphasizing that they were alone.

"Are you the only one here today?" CJ asked incredulously.

"There are others," the man said with a dismissive wave as he opened a steel door and gestured them in. "We are heading to the back. We have the vault waiting for you, Mr. Cho."

"Vault?" Chris squeaked, hesitating by the door.

"Please, Mr. Cho," the man said pointedly as he motioned again down the white hallway. "If you will?"

It did not seem to be a request, but Chris's curiosity outweighed his irritation, so they made for a partially open steel door at the far end.

"Jesus," CJ muttered when they entered the room. Steel bars encircled the vault. The rest of the room slowly took shape as they drew closer to the center, congealing into an unmoving darkness that did not alleviate Chris's growing concern.

The lockboxes, arranged on one wall of the enclosed area, were fronted by a small metal desk that held an open laptop.

"The keys are on the desk for you. The paper by the computer will give you the information you need for the account number, and the card under it can be used anywhere in the world." Chris's eyes widened as he listened to the man tick off instructions, none of which made sense. "The lights are all on motion sensors, and when you are done, I can get you a car to escort you home."

Without another word, he vanished into the void of the room and was gone.

The two friends stared at each other in disbelief as CJ stuttered, "What the fuck, man?" He'd said the only thing that could sum up this moment.

The place held the air of being long forgotten. Cobwebs glinted in the corners, reflecting the gloomy light that kicked on with their guide's exit. The dusty floor seemed to invite them to create footsteps, and the tug Chris had been fighting was finally too insistent to ignore.

"Chris!"

It was too late; again, Chris had no control of his body as he eased past the bars and under the spotlights. The vault had a strong, musty smell that became more prevalent as he neared the pixelating computer screen.

"This is not a good idea." CJ stated the obvious, but it had little merit now, as they were both standing inside a makeshift jail cell in an empty bank.

The keys beside the laptop glowed in the light. Chris did not hesitate to reach for them and scamper toward the lockboxes in the back.

"Chris, don't!"

The plea meant nothing to him, and a yank of the heavy alloy exposed a long tray, the contents of which sent him stumbling in the opposite direction.

"Holy shit!" CJ's loud whisper confirmed that he had seen them too: rows of diamonds and rubies sparkling in the light. "Chris."

The intrigue finally got the best of his friend, and CJ grabbed the key from Chris, shoving it into another lock and removing an even bigger tray.

"Dude!" An old painting rolled out, the picture like nothing Chris had ever seen before. "This . . . this looks like Monet." The parchment shimmered as a natural landscape took shape. "I've never seen anything like this!"

After pulling out an iron bust of a bearded man from another slot, CJ rambled on about ancient history, but Chris shifted his focus to the laptop. He took a seat in the lone chair in front of it. A small, ripped slip of paper lay to the right of the computer, and he studied the two long lines of numbers scribbled on it.

Chris had cashed enough checks to recognize banking numbers, the screen's display of two blank lines confirming that notion as he punched them in.

With a thud, CJ dropped another duffel bag on the metal desk, this one much larger than the first. The cash spilling from the zippered opening grabbed Chris's attention; the twenties and hundreds amounted to at least what had been delivered that morning.

However, the numbers that appeared on the screen called him back and sucked all the wind from his lungs. An unfathomable account balance with his name on it shot him to his feet even as his best friend remained focused on the bag. "There must be thousands of dollars in this bag! I mean, this is nothing—"

Chris shoved his best friend in front of the computer screen to shut him up, offering only one word: "Dude."

"That's . . . that's impossible!"

"This was a bad idea." Ivy's whisper did nothing to stop Eira's ascent up the hill. The farming village they had passed now lay in the distance, and swirling, frigid gales bore down on them from the cloudy frost barrier to their left.

Eira had never been this far from the city. In fact, she had only ever been to two other villages on the Southern Tier, and that was when she was a little girl, traveling with General Aquilo and the Royal Guard. The remnants of the Battle of the Frost, along with her mother's death, had driven her father to isolate her for her safety—a choice presently driving this very trip.

"I said you did not have to come." The swipe of a birch tree branch brought snow down on her, her thin, armor-plated top providing little protection from the moisture.

The cold had never bothered her. The mix of ice and lumi blood she had inherited from her parents meant that she was comfortable in almost any environment. However, since the confrontation with Cole at the shop earlier, her roiling emotions froze any liquid that touched her body.

"Like I had a choice! But you know we are not to venture into the Western Tier. I can understand taking the horses to check out the southern farmlands, but this is the sacred land of the Essence!" The toll of a full training day and the treacherous footing appeared to be catching up with Ivy, who panted as they walked.

Another few steps took them down a slope, snowy pockets from the night before providing little hindrance as they crunched through a group of woody dwarf shrubs that parted at their touch. Though the midafternoon sun broke through the gaps of the trees, the forest was an intimidating backdrop. The constant, biting wind from the barrier Eira's mother had died to preserve enhanced the eerie feeling, and her stomach churned with each blast.

"What about all the breaches by the frost? My father wrote to me that the Legion lost two soldiers just the other day not five miles down on the Southern Tier border. And now you think it's safe to go to some temple that has not been visited—" Ivy cut herself off and looked away. "I'm sorry, Eira. I know this temple means something to you."

Eira rested a hand on her best friend's shoulder. "Please, I need to do this. Bernard let it slip during my training that I might find something here, something my father has been keeping from me."

Clasping her necklace gave Eira a chance to take a deep breath. They paused only briefly before a quick nod between friends signaled the continuation of their trek through the wooded area.

"I need to know, Ivy. I need to know why she would come out here with her powers so diminished that night. I need to know why she would just leave."

Seconds turned to minutes as they slogged through another snowy patch of broken trees. Finally, an opening appeared, and the slit of sunlight pulled them into a field.

"Is that it?" Ivy seemed unable to contain her fascination as they approached this legendary place long forbidden to them by their elders.

A bright glow emanated from the mossy stone of the three-story cathedral. The old bell tower still stood, holding strong after a millennium of aging. The craftsmanship was not all that different from the shops in Noella or the homes in the outside villages, and its windows, which reflected the setting sun, seemed to undulate with each breeze from the frosty barrier in the distance.

"It is," Eira whispered, already tiptoeing into a meadow of flowers—a sight usually only available in the well-tended castle courtyard during a temperate summer.

This place seemed untouched; despite extreme storms and weather changes, the structure and its surroundings were undamaged. The chilly air that had accompanied them on their trip began to warm as they climbed the stone steps. Eira hesitated by the door, feeling moved to study the plant-covered handle.

"Be careful."

Eira tried to heed the warning as she wrapped her hand around the green and yellow vines.

"It's just a plant," she said softly. A tickle overwhelmed her senses and sent a chill up her back. An icy glaze moved over the vines, her palms freezing over as she effortlessly pushed the door open and stepped forth into the inviting scent of honeysuckle and magnolia.

Past the short entrance hallway, they paused to admire their surroundings. Eira had never seen the types of flowers spreading along these walls. None grew in the courtyard, but she had been told that some of the older traders who had once been allowed into the human realm still grew them.

A slow pace took Eira to a larger set of wooden doors. The pulpit that greeted her when she pushed them open was accompanied by a new smell—one that had her grabbing her nose and stumbling back a step.

"Oh my!" Ivy gagged as the odor reached her. The hazy lighting did not reveal the source of the rotten stench.

"The blinds." Eira rushed down the aisle, her hand running over the flower-covered window to open the blinds. Her fingertips were encased in ice when she pulled them back. She marveled that the mere touch of these plants compelled a projection she did not have to consciously emit.

As the rays poured through the open window, Ivy shouted from the pulpit, "Eira, look at this!" The light had illuminated a story of the past, the darkness no longer able to hide what was locked in this temple.

An icy wall stretched from floor to ceiling and from one wall to another. The middle had burst wide open, and Eira's measured approach gave way to hurried steps on her approach to the impressive structure.

"Is that . . . ?" Ivy did not need to finish; the menacing creature stuck inside the ice was unmistakable.

"A ferlup!" It was the first time Eira had seen one outside a book. The beast's matted fur was still spiked, and a rib had broken through the side of its chest.

"More!"

At Ivy's call, Eira shook off her paralysis and joined her companion farther along the wall, where Ivy was gaping at a robed figure likewise encased in the ice.

"That's . . . that's a minimal!" Ivy backpedaled to the middle of the room, where a few more ferlup lay crumpled. It did not take a master physician to diagnose the cause of death for these unfortunate wolf demons. The blunt force of a hard, chilled object was the culprit in each and every case.

The light crept farther back, reflecting off a table with high pillars that reached to the ceiling. Eira gazed around in awe. "It's all true, then."

The stories of her mother's sacrifice, the fight she had endured in this very temple against Chaoic's soldiers to protect the ice relic, were true. She advanced toward the table, her eyes adjusting enough to glimpse a stand seemingly designed to hold something important. "I should never have doubted my father." Her glance at the old paintings above was brief, the putrid smell of decay forcing her to cover her nose again.

The next ferlup corpse she found was curled up and just as dead as the others. This one, though, appeared to have met its fate in a different way: a gaping hole had split its chest, and the burned hair seemed to explain the scent coating her nostrils. The Essence's power must have preserved the creature at the instant of its demise.

"Eira!" Ivy had bent down near a dead minima by the other pulpit. The seared black hood barely covered a charred, blank face that was still steaming. "This was not done by your mother."

A marking on the main floor caught Eira's attention before she could respond. The light outside, which continued to drift with the setting sun, had made the middle of the floor easier to see. Eira tilted her head to examine the outline further.

"What could—"

Eira raised her hand, halting Ivy's question as she analyzed the soot and the long, thick silhouette headed away from it. The outline grew more defined nearer the ice wall. A closer inspection revealed the scaly shadow of an arm at the far side, which led to another circle directly in the center of the crater in the ice.

She inhaled sharply and followed one more outline headed back toward the pew area; this icy shadow led to a circle the same size as the others. "This is impossible."

Her mind jumped to all kinds of conclusions as she paced between the outlines of char and frost.

"Eira, you don't think—"

A loud bang from a dark corner interrupted Ivy. The creature that emerged, frothing at the mouth, was one of nightmares.

"Ivy!" The ferlup drew closer, its fangs dripping, as Eira braced her arm across her friend's chest. A deep breath brought a rush of ice through her veins. "Get behind me."

CHAPTER 8

The creatures were as hideous as she'd been told. Knots of dark-brown fur quivered like quills as the massive creature rocked onto its back legs, exposing powerful muscles. Her studies warned of the long, poisonous claws, but the six-inch fangs were what captured her attention.

Ivy shuddered. "I knew this was a bad idea."

"Just remember your training." Eira took stock of the huge room as the ferlup stalked closer. "They prefer close-quarters combat. Keep your distance, and use your spiratus wisely. Defense will be your best offense." It was as if General Aquilo were in the room with them, Eira ticking his lessons off one by one as she sized up their attacker.

"Eira!" Ivy gestured toward another ferlup, this one possibly seven feet tall on its hind legs, advancing from the double doors through which they had entered.

"Stay focused." That was meant for Ivy, but Eira also needed the reminder. "Don't make the first move." Another lesson from the great general, it repeated on a loop in her mind as she rubbed her fingers together.

The ice seeped to the surface as she locked her shoulders in place. Her temperature dropping at an extreme rate, she narrowed her eyes at their attackers. Every new breath produced a more substantial puff of vapor, which rose above the soon-to-be combatants as they inched closer.

She had never been in a battle. All those sparring matches with Cole, all those times battling Royal Guard members and other trainees, seemed little more than child's play compared to combat with the vile creatures seeking to kill her now.

The fading sun outside began to settle, and the shadows of the two gigantic monsters grew.

"Focus yourself," Eira said. "Get ready."

A rush of wind, no doubt due to the arrival of Ivy's spiratus, drew snarls from both ferlup.

"Here they come." The clink of the creatures' bony claws on the marble floor sent her into a fighting stance, her left foot slightly out as she shifted her weight to her right. Eira held her ground, still rubbing her frozen fingertips, and the frostiness began to morph into jagged ice. The flurries dancing around her circulated up to the ceiling as her body temperature lowered to a point no lumi would have been able to survive.

"I know you're with me," she whispered to herself, the chain of the necklace burning her skin with each successive breath. "Guide me." This was a message meant for someone who had once graced these grounds, and one she had repeated during every training session. "Guide me!" It was not so much a shout as a release of everything building up inside her.

The swirling of her stomach, the icebergs cascading through her veins, coiled with one roll of her shoulders. Each fingertip became a glittery spectacle as her palms opened wide. She was initially unsure whether only she felt the ensuing blast of wind, but the retreat of the two ferlup gave the answer; their heads tilted as the gust tore around them.

A profound inhale brought a blizzard of snow and ice into her hand. The appearance of this type of projection sent the would-be attackers back another step.

"Are we going to do this?" she challenged. The frigid rush of adrenaline swiftly overcame her lingering fear.

"Eira!" Ivy's scream jerked her head to the right. A third ferlup, the biggest of all, leaped toward her with its claws outstretched. An instinctual thrust prompted by a mix of born warrior blood and years of training sent the balled-up projection directly into the furry attacker. Its pained, ear-piercing howl lasted briefly, and the crash of its body against the wooden pew echoed between the shrieks of the other two.

"Ivy, get the high ground!" Eira pointed behind them to the winding stairs leading to a balcony overlooking the arena.

A slide to the left returned Eira's hands to a fighting position, and another jab with her palm unleashed a powerful blast of ice and snow at the ferlup in the middle of the pulpit. The thrust flipped it back to the ice wall, the impact breaking off more of the frozen barrier and making the temple shudder.

"Ivy!" Eira had no time to assess whether she had killed either of the others. The smallest one was trying to prevent her friend from reaching the second floor. A gust sent the ferlup stumbling, its nails digging into the floor as it prepared to return with a slash of its fully extended claws. The creature's advance was halted by a strike to the head. Ivy's thrown staff stunned the beast before spinning back into her grasp. Another whizz of the weapon just missed Eira to thud into the largest attacker, which had launched forward at a fantastic speed.

"Thanks," Eira managed to gasp as the spiratus found its mark again. "We need cover up top!"

Ivy took off up the stairs before either concussed creature could regain their feet.

A slight shuffle to Eira's side drew her focus now. The ferlup she'd tossed into the ice wall was preparing for its second advance. It shook its fur like a dog in the rain. A flex of its enormous muscles was accompanied by gravelly barks. The other two returned the sound, seemingly organizing a response. A final stretch produced its claws and a warrior pose of its own before it pushed off and sprinted at her with ferocity.

"Enough!" Eira clenched her body inward as the creature barreled toward her, its fierce yellow eyes showing that it thought it had a kill. With another howl and flash of its claws, it prepared to strike. However, a roll and flip of Eira's wrist flung an icy lasso at the beast, and a jerk of her quivering arms snapped the creature's neck with a whimper.

This would have given any thinking creature pause, but the sound of scurrying claws told her that Ivy's spiratus strike had scattered the other ferlup's mind. "Stupid." Eira opened her palm, her body temperature well below freezing as a long, sharp icicle flowed into her grasp.

The ensuing thrust was graceful but carried surprising force. The ferlup's tilted head jerked a bit, straining toward her with snapping jaws for only a second before it slumped over the ice in its chest, its black blood running down the icicle to the floor.

"Eira!" Ivy's shriek broke her from the gory scene, and a blast of air shook the flowers and vines coating the temple as she locked on Ivy's position. A fourth attacker was in pursuit of her best friend, who scrambled frantically down the stairs. The new uninvited guest prepared to pounce on the throat of the woman Eira had dragged here against her will.

"No!" In a first for Eira, a jab of her index finger sent a blade of solid ice directly at the ferlup, which was already midair, looking to finish what it had started.

There was no thought to this attack, no preparation; Eira acted on instinct and perhaps something else she had no time to ponder. Unlike during all those hours on the training ground, unlike every time she had tried to find the target with Bernard in the advanced weapons area, this was a direct hit—a clean, straight-through connection that not only cut the creature's throat but also nearly took its head off.

The final ferlup caught her by surprise, and a panicked thrust of both hands produced a messy and unsteady projection. The makeshift shield of ice had hardly solidified before her attacker lurched at her, preparing to clamp down with its fangs.

"Eira!" a familiar male voice shouted. "Stay down!"

A powerful whirlwind gave her no time to focus on the latest arrival as it whipped the ferlup off her. The creature contorted in an effort to recover and face this new threat.

A spiratus smashed into its face, flipping it backward. Its claws, once heading for Eira's throat, gripped the marble for a moment before another blast of the weapon ended the fight with a crack to the skull.

Eira let out a soft groan, and silence took over. Her temperature returned to normal as she tried to process what had happened. The scene that greeted her refocusing eyes was a war zone. Four freshly dead ferlup had joined the rest of their brethren, who had been laid low long before the women arrived.

"Eira!" Ivy ran over, frowning with panic and concern. "Are you okay?"

Eira's father entered her field of vision. His appearance eased her mind and froze her heart at the same time. As he bent down and pushed the bloody icicle away, the locked stare between father and daughter reduced the sounds around them to a murmur.

She finally managed to say, "I . . . I think we need to talk."

"Stop, Chris!" CJ chased him through the empty lobby. "Come on!"

The last two hours in the vault had produced more mysteries than

Chris's brain could handle. The art, gems, cash, and even weapons CJ had found compounded the sheer insanity of what they had discovered on the laptop.

"Where are you going?"

With a slap, Chris pushed past the glass door, his lungs in dire need of whatever passed for freshness in the city.

"Chris, come on, man. Just stop!" A yank on his arm twirled Chris around. Sweat dripped down his cheek, even as the wind whipped down the street. The moisture in his hair was increasing, and a swipe of his fingers made it worse.

He felt like he was overheating.

"I can't breathe."

He nearly choked on a cough as an ashy puff of breath shot up into the dwindling sunlight. As he unstuck his shirt collar from his sweaty neck, he was glad he had given away his windbreaker.

"You don't look good." This understatement was interrupted by shouts from the soldier in the suit, who was sprinting to catch them.

"Shit. Come on!" Chris was not sure why, but he needed to get away from this place and everything inside it.

"Mr. Cho, I should get you and your friend a ride home!" The shout followed them as they scampered down the steps and attempted to blend into a group of unimpressed New Yorkers. "Mr. Cho!" The man seemed tethered to the bank, and his face finally disappeared as they rounded a corner and came to a bus stop.

CJ was gasping, his hands on his chest as he leaned against the shelter's plastic window. "What the hell is going on?"

Chris had been considering this question himself but believed the answer was far from simple.

"I mean, the package is one thing; that shit is ridiculous to begin with. But the crazy guy on the train? The creepy, empty bank with just one guy working? And to top it all off—"

"I fucking get it!" Chris's sharp retort drew a few glances from the people around them.

His best friend took a breath and steered them away from the crowd. A walk to the subway station eight blocks away was their next move. "You do realize you're a billionaire now?"

It had to be a dream. He was sure that in a few minutes, he would wake up in his bed, and this crazy nightmare would be over.

Their walk in the cool afternoon shadows helped to ease the residual burning. His stomach returned to a simmer, and they strolled quietly for a few blocks. The ever-present anxiety slowly dissipated as they turned down an alley to avoid construction.

"Look." CJ's tone was soft and concerned, preventing Chris from firing back anything sarcastic. "This shit is crazy, man."

Chris could only muster a sigh of agreement as he fiddled with the plastic card in his pocket. The blush heating his cheeks remained.

"I can't imagine how you feel right now," CJ continued.

Chris's sudden appreciation for the fact that he wasn't delving into this gobsmacking mystery alone brought a relieved smirk to his face. They both shook their heads in disbelief, then embraced, clapping each other on the back.

"Shit." Chris's laugh was all he could offer in the face of the fundamental insanity of the situation. "I don't know what I would do without you."

A crash at the end of the alley sent them bolting apart. All slivers of sunshine vanished as darkness crept in around them. The unnatural stillness seemed to only exist where they stood. The noise of the city dropped to a low drone as an overturned trashcan rocked from side to side.

"Hello?" CJ's shout almost knocked Chris over, and he stumbled into a small stream of water at his feet. He shook his head in response to his best friend's shrug. The water wet his sneakers and was soon joined by a glass bottle rolling out from a nearby drain.

"Christopher."

The familiar shriek resounded in his head, but a terrified peek at CJ showed he had not heard it.

"Christopher."

He inched closer to the voice, which had hooked him like a fish on a line. Then a shadow emerged from behind the trashcan. The ghastly figure's appearance was so unexpected that it sent Chris crashing into his friend.

"What the—!" CJ's high-pitched squeal nicely summed up what anyone would feel at witnessing the image before them. The ripped black robe gliding across the pavement was accompanied by two bony hands extended directly toward them. One white, razor-sharp nail stretched out as it drew closer, and a drop of dark liquid rolled down it, hitting the ground in front of the figure, whose blank face sported only milky-white eyes.

"CJ" was the only thing Chris could get out as he spotted what was behind the creature. His windbreaker lay in pieces, and the man he had gifted it to was slumped against a building lining the alley.

A loud hiss interrupted anything CJ might say. The creature continued to advance, unrolling a full hand of sharp nails.

Any normal human being would be struggling to comprehend this situation. A character resembling the Grim Reaper with razor blades on its hands was floating toward them with clearly malicious intent. However, for some strange reason, Chris felt no fear, the initial shock already wearing off as he scanned for an exit. "When I say so, run back to where we just came from and head directly for the construction site."

A deep, hollow growl suddenly came from behind them.

"What is that?" CJ gasped.

This was something completely different—a wolfish being that looked as tall as an elephant as it stood on its hind legs.

"Holy shit!"

Chris concurred.

The monster's feet scraped the concrete as it extended horrifyingly long claws. A slow, predatory stalk allowed Chris to peek at the advancing Grim Reaper.

"CJ, whatever happens, whatever the hell this is . . ." A rising tide of some strange force was choking him, and clearing his throat hardly helped with the smell of decay and death that accompanied the two creatures drawing ever nearer. "I just want you to know I love you. You were always my brother, and I couldn't have asked for a better one."

The wolf monster rocked back, and Chris prepared to feel the bite of its fangs and claws.

Suddenly, a swirling, forceful wind cut down the alley. The whistling sound was soon accompanied by a sharp scream from the demon wolf, which went flying in the opposite direction.

"Huh?" Chris had no time to form a coherent sentence. An object whizzed by his head and caught the robed creature, tumbling it backward to crash into the trashcan from which it had emerged.

The object boomeranged back to its wielder. The massive storyteller from the train marched with clear purpose toward the hissing, blank-faced figure as it tried to use its bony hands to steady itself.

"Time for you to return to your master!" The fur coat dropped to the ground, and the man's muscles bulged as he twirled a staff-like weapon between his palms. "And tell him you will not be the last." A thrust sent the object back at the creature. Its shadowy skull shattered into a plume of black smoke.

The weapon returned, and the storyteller rotated to face the monster that was scrambling to its feet and grabbing at a fire escape.

"Now," said the man, baring his teeth, "you can join him!" The creature barked with fangs protruding and attempted another lunge, but the cane was already snapping forward. A squeal from the subsequent impact rang out in the dark as the monster dropped, sending another cloud of black smoke to swirl in the strange wind.

"So." With blatant sarcasm, the man pumped his fists together and turned to say, "Are you two ready for me to finish my story?"

Neither spoke as a few rays of sunshine seeped back into the alley. The body of the pitiable homeless man remained motionless, and the returning light exposed a dark pool of liquid around him.

CHAPTER 9

"I told you he had little time left in this world."

Chris tried to look away from the homeless man.

"The minima must have smelled your fragrance on him. They have been tracking you for a while—one of the many reasons I was able to locate you so quickly."

Chris didn't respond, instead replaying the attack in his head.

"You were following us?" CJ had not moved an inch since the robed figure first appeared.

"I can explain on the way. If those creatures vanished upon their death, Chaoic's forces are lurking not far away." Without further explanation, the gargantuan Good Samaritan threw on his coat and was off, heading for the alley opening.

A brief exchange between the two friends ensued, but the dead body and the thought of other lurking creatures sent them rushing after him.

They walked briskly, and CJ was out of breath as he stuttered, "So, like, everything you told us, that's all real?"

The man pivoted, bringing the group to an abrupt stop, and his smile grew as he sized them both up. "I promise you will have some of your answers very shortly."

Then he spun about and continued onward.

"Where are we going? And why were those things after us? You said Chaoic. Wasn't that the Darkness guy you spoke of? The one who killed off the dinosaurs?" CJ's rapid-fire questions did nothing to slow their pace. The three took a hard turn in hurried lockstep as horns and revving engines faded to background noise.

Their rescuer finally brought them to a halt in front of an old building displaying a real estate logo. His eyes darted about before he opened the door and ushered them inside.

"Quickly, in case they still have your scent."

"Scent?" Chris's yelp did not deter Bernard, who brought them to an elevator that looked nowhere close to code. They had no choice but to follow him in.

"Christopher." His name sounded harsh in the cramped space. "I know you have lots of questions."

"Are you some magical being?" CJ interjected. "I mean, I saw you throwing that stick around, man, and you just . . ." He shook his head, momentarily wordless.

"My friends, I promise—"

"And, like, the humans. Us. We fought your people in some war? A war ended by two great warriors who signed some treaty that separated our peoples and wiped our memories of it?"

CJ's bulldozing of the conversation was helpful for Chris. A general overview of what he had been trying to ignore on the way to the bank gave him more time to process all that had transpired.

"Yes." The elevator ticked past the floors. "The two great warriors were gifted with the powers of fire and ice: the two elements that saved our kinds during the extinction." An ashy film coated Chris's mouth as he tried to avoid the man's gaze. The fellow seemed much more interested in him than in CJ. "The powers they were given by our creator, the Essence, allowed them to fight Chaoic, the entity that seeks to kill you today."

CJ appeared to be on the verge of a breakdown. His hands were shaking, and a gentle nudge from Chris did little to help as he began to rock.

The metal doors opened on an abandoned office space filled with only a few toppled swivel chairs, painter's tape, and plastic tarps. Two large windows covered by black sheets left the group to be guided by ceiling-mounted floodlights.

"I know this a lot for you to comprehend." Bernard's tone grew softer as he directed them across the cracked cement floor. "But we must make our way to safety before more of Chaoic's creatures find us."

"There are more?" CJ grabbed the wall for support. "My boss, the university . . . Shit! If they knew about this, they would . . ."

The dim hallway they entered next brought on a flashback from the alley, and Chris half expected to see another gliding robe or wolf demon.

They stopped by a janitor's closet, the markings on the door worn down and barely visible. "I promise, if you follow me, you will find some of your answers." Like a shifting hologram, a turn of the knob unveiled a web of vines that spread from the top of the door to the floor. CJ's gasp perfectly reflected what Chris felt.

"This is a leap. A long time ago, the Essence created leaps all over the world so our people could trade with yours. They also allowed the Ignati and Iclyn to move about quickly when battling Chaoic's armies." The tang of ash made Chris sniff, his eyes watering as the char smell intensified. "After the Great War, only a few leaps remained open to provide minor trade passages for essentials—and in case Chaoic ever returned."

It could have all been fake. A door in an abandoned building overrun by plants was not all that uncommon, probably. However, the green of the intertwined plants was so vibrant that Chris thought he detected slight movements in them, as if they were conscious and inviting the group to walk through.

"I was a liaison for our merchants, a member of the Royal Guard sent to protect them in case problems occurred."

"Problems?" CJ leaned against the wall, his arms pressed across his stomach as if he might vomit.

"Humans and lumi have a checkered past. Moreover, some of my people believe that Chaoic himself runs this realm and will unleash the humans upon us when the time is right." Bernard chuckled at Chris's disbelieving expression as he settled his hands on their shoulders. "This was one reason we closed most leaps after the Battle of the Frost."

The two friends again exchanged a look, and the large man's grip tightened as he pushed them toward the door.

"What the hell is the Battle of the Frost?"

"You want to learn about who you are, Christopher." Chris snapped his mouth shut. "It is why you came to this city, why you followed me here." This was a good point, but one that he was second-guessing as the vines separated to reveal a small gap. "Our worlds are both in trouble. My people and your people are on the verge of something much worse than what happened twenty years ago."

"Twenty years ago?"

The man nodded. "The fire inside you is telling you to do it. It is your destiny, passed on to you by your father before he died. You can no longer ignore it."

"My father." It was not just the boiling in his stomach that pushed him closer to the door but also the part of his brain he had always pushed back. Never before had he let it decide for him. Never before had he even let it speak to him, but now it sounded clearer than the man whispering by his ear. *"Christopher, answers to the past will not soothe your mind, but when the time is right, your future you will find."*

The voice was not his own, but it was strangely familiar. The stern yet calming words grew louder as they repeated over and over.

"Chris?" CJ grabbed his arm, the touch sending them into a locked stare.

"When the time is right." He shrugged at his best friend, the voice in his head winning out as he stepped into the vines.

"Take the horses." King Rori had already dismounted from his, and the stable attendants scrambled as she gently lowered herself to the ground.

A few peeks from the staff shamed her into dropping her head as she ventured into the courtyard. After the silent ride back from the temple, the crunch of Ivy's footsteps beside her in the fresh snow was her only comfort.

She turned in response to a gentle hand on her shoulder and lifted her gaze to General Aquilo's blue eyes, which had been on her the entire ride home. Their empathy sent her diving in for an embrace.

"General."

Her father's firm voice quickly separated the two as they stood at attention.

"Please work with the Legion to secure the wall of the city. Make sure every village—"

"Eira!" The shout came from a figure sprinting down the twenty or so steps that separated them. "You're okay!"

Her fiancé's muscled arms wrapped her up tight.

"I was so worried." She pushed against Cole's firm chest, sending him backward. "Eira?" Her fiancé's fading words did not have their usual boisterousness as she veered to the nearby open door, which held a handful of Royal Guards. She stomped up the steps, struggling to prevent the power swirling inside from breaking through her palms.

The looks she received from the guards told her she was behaving poorly, and two cowering staff members confirmed the point. She tried to ignore the reactions.

It was obvious where this situation was going to end. The long foyer of the castle, which led to the doors of the dinner hall, was cleared in preparation for a stern scolding. While some may have assumed the area had been prepped for a meeting with the council, she knew better. Her father's fears for the southern and eastern villages had been overshadowed by his daughter's disobedience.

Her mind grew troubled at the thought of how Colden and the council could use this new attack to bolster their bid to invade the human realm.

"Cole." Hearing the name in her father's mouth spun her around as the rest of the group entered from the stairs.

"I have sent the Legion out to every village, my king. The council was contacted and will be here—"

"You did not go yourself?" asked General Aquilo.

"I . . . I wanted to be here for Eira when she came home. I intend to head back to the wall—"

"I will do it myself."

The stinging words made even Eira straighten.

"Cole." Her father did not seem interested in this back-and-forth. He waved his hand imperiously and removed his coat. "Please take Ivy to her training quarters. I have something I need to take care of before meeting with the council."

The group nodded in unison and followed his orders without hesitation.

"Eira." Cole drew near, and Ivy was not far behind as they approached one of the two spiral staircases leading to the second floor.

"You heard my father." His shoulders slouched at her sharp retort.

"You would not want to disobey an order he gave."

It was no mystery who had given away her location, and while the betrayal very well could have saved her life, she was not about to give him satisfaction. Cole did not say another word, only shaking his head as he trudged up the stairs with Ivy in tow. The rest of the staff eagerly dispersed in all directions as they returned to work.

Her father proceeded across the foyer in silence, the only sound the echo of his boots, which tracked in mud from the courtyard.

She had always hated the way the marble floor magnified all sounds. Her many childhood attempts to sneak out into the courtyard after dark always seemed to end with her getting caught because of that quality. Back then, trips to this hall had unfolded in a similar fashion, her father's deliberate pace making the journey last an eternity.

But tonight, with everything going on and her reasons for acting, this trip felt short. The punishment she expected to receive was nowhere close to the first thing on her mind. She wanted answers.

As she squeezed in past the tall wooden door, she found the hall ready for the council's arrival. The array of snowflakes glimmering in the moonlight hardly drew her attention as she clomped into the shadowy room. The only light came from the fire burning at the far end, the torches standing unlit in each corner. A grand table was already piled high with food, most of which would go to waste by the night's end. And while she would have loved to address that topic and the hypocrisy of these leaders, there were more pressing matters.

"Are you hurt?" The compassionate question did not match her father's expression.

"No." Her answer was brief but true. The flimsy defensive wall she'd erected at the end had stymied the attack of the ferlup, and though she suffered a few cuts from the fall, they were already at the end of the healing process, thanks to her mother's power.

"Good. Then I ask that you return to your chamber. I need time with the council to discuss what has happened, and when I am done—"

"Father." She needed more than this. The outlines on the temple floor begged for an immediate explanation.

"You should eat something."

"Father!" Her voice was loud, harsh, and full of everything she had held back. "I had to go." She had ventured this far and refused to apologize or cower. "I had to figure out what you were not telling me."

"What I was not telling you?" He spun toward her, his eyes wide and furious. "Do you think that I have lied to you after all these years?"

"He was *there*, Father!" His body stiffened, and the piercing blue of his glare stayed directly on her. "I saw what was left in that temple. Chaoic was there that night!"

That name would normally have caused an even bigger fight, but for some reason it seemed to come as a relief to him.

"Eira—"

"I could understand your lying to the people, to give them hope and conceal how close Chaoic was. But me? To not tell me that Chaoic had entered our realm and that Mother—"

"Your mother sacrificed herself that night to save us all. Is that not what I told you in the first place?" Her father's political answers kept them running in circles. "I told you everything you needed to know. She did sacrifice herself that night. And whether she faced Chaoic's army or the Darkness himself, it does not take away from the fact—"

"She was not alone," she said in a low, deliberate voice.

"Excuse me?" The rigidity returned, and his face contorted in a way she had never seen.

"She—"

"Enough of this, Eira!" He had swung about again, but she chased him around the long wooden table.

"Why are you trying to keep this a secret, Father? The Ignati was there that night! I saw the evidence with my own eyes. He sacrificed himself right alongside her. This is the perfect detail to prove to the council that the humans are not wicked!"

"You know nothing about the Ignati and his appearance that night!"

The force of his shout staggered her, and she grabbed the table for support.

"That . . . that . . ." This response was different, revealing not anger but a deep despair that only Eira knew he carried and that he seemed unable to keep from pouring out tonight.

She dug her nails into the wood, holding herself up.

"That man had ages to ask that of her. He had hundreds of years to stop Chaoic in his own realm and did nothing, cowering before the proof of his failures—his . . . his self-pity about the parchment he signed."

Her heart froze over at the sight of her father in such a state. This was not what she was expecting when she pressed the issue. This outburst was more emotional than it should have been from a warrior of such stature.

"He picked that night, after she finally . . ." He did not need to finish; one of the answers she sought was already clear to her. "Your mother's actions that night saved our people. That, and only that, will be what our people know."

The words stunted the swelling inside her. The cruel, arrogant tone she had only heard him adopt with the council made her shiver as she balled her hands.

"That is unfair."

"To your chamber!" It was over, the king's brief moment of vulnerability gone as he lifted his chin and turned his back.

She was trying so hard to keep the avalanche from tumbling out, but his final words broke the dam. "You are no better than those monsters!" She intended for it to hurt. It was meant to leave him with the same feeling she had as she drove her boots into the floor and strode out through the same door she had entered.

Once in the foyer, she shook her head. The conversation had supplied a few answers, but it also led to more questions that might not be easily satisfied.

"Eira." The hand on her arm stopped her cold. Cole's blond hair was combed now, and his eyes—deep blue, like the oceans she had seen in books—locked on her. "Please."

"Are you here to find out if your chair is ready?"

His expression was pitiful, and staying would only make this worse. The day's events had produced a frozen venom inside her that clamored to be unleashed.

"Goodnight, Cole." Without hesitation, she was up the steps, leaving the pleading face of her fiancé under the chandelier.

CHAPTER 10

"This place is amazing!" CJ's gawking—normally reserved for museums or digging in dirt—was in full force as they wandered the sizable room. "I mean, like, holy shit!"

The most magnificent experience of Chris's life to this point had been a trip to Disneyland when he and CJ were nine, a vacation donated to the group home. What they had discovered after stepping through the vines, however, was ten times more breathtaking, and his senses were overwhelmed as he questioned whether this new world was real.

The leap they'd entered took them into a relatively normal-looking shop, which Bernard had told them was used for items purchased in the human world—extremely rare goods. Their new environs had seemed simple when they first entered, but much like the room they stood in now, the shop felt somehow different from any place Chris had been. Every detail of every object was meticulously constructed. The chairs in the shop and the shelving, all of which looked to be made for people of Bernard's size, were perfect, a quality that was further accentuated when they stepped outside and into the city.

It was nothing Chris could have prepared for, nothing that a human book on futuristic societies could have predicted. In fact, as CJ eventually put it, it was more comparable to a nineteenth-century town than to the space-age cities created in movies.

Nonetheless, the faultless architecture left him feeling out of place and inadequate. Even the cobblestone sidewalk made for an uncomfortable stroll, as the streets showed not one tiny crack. To make it worse, the people who roamed these streets matched the buildings in which they worked and lived. Their physical perfection was obvious and yet somehow subtle to the naked eye.

Like Bernard, these lumi were all at least six feet tall and looked like professional athletes in the human world. The men, most just slightly taller than the women, seemed like they could all be brothers, with blond hair and muscles that would put any wannabe at the gym to shame.

"Damn." CJ's soft exclamation brought Chris back to the present; a tall, stunning servant was dropping off two impeccably sculpted glasses of water. CJ barely squeaked out a thank-you before her hasty exit. "Perfect," he exclaimed.

Chris could not help himself. "The glass or . . ." The uncharacteristic comment brought a snicker from his best friend, who threw out his arms.

"Both!" The two broke into chuckles, partly from the joke and partly because this whole thing felt crazy. "They all are just so perfect, man."

Every woman they'd seen here, no matter what their role seemed to be, had gleaming gold hair, long, perfectly toned legs, and proportions that would make a fashion photographer salivate. They also carried a mesmerizing grace.

"This is like a dream, Chris. These works of art!" CJ shook his head, sipping the water as he strolled over to the paintings hanging on the wall by the fire. "The architecture alone in this place is something I have never seen or studied, but the artwork, the paintings, and the sculptures . . ."

"A self-sufficient society," Chris marveled as he glanced through the room's lone window. The courtyard on the other side of the glass was of course perfectly manicured and housed a healthy set of trees that still held snow. "They farm their own food in the outside villages, raise their own cattle, and the wastewater collection system they have in place is absolutely amazing." It was his turn to express astonishment, his arms flailing as he thought about all he had seen and been told on his way up to the castle they now stood in. "They take only what they need from the land, in such a simple yet efficient way. This is nothing we could have ever imagined; it's perfect."

"Well, I wouldn't go that far, tree hugger." CJ played with the curtain on the window. "This is pure satin, and the feast I saw them wheeling in was overkill, for sure. Unless they're going to be feeding two hundred of those Legion soldiers Bernard told us about." It was a good point and not the only issue Chris had noted on his way in.

While everything gave off the impression of a truly utopian society, a few things still made him uncomfortable. The arrogance, for one, stood out right away—not just in the way their guide had spoken but also in the stares they'd received on the long dirt path to the astonishing castle.

The selection process was probably the aspect that had most taken Chris aback.

"Imagine being told at age eight what you're going to be doing for the rest of your life. I mean, I guess if you want to be good at something." He ran his hand along the iron table positioned between two long couches made of intricately crafted wood. The cushion he dropped onto was, unsurprisingly, the softest he had ever felt.

"Yeah, that shit is weird. And the stuff Bernard mentioned about all the arranged marriages." A shout from the other side of the door by the fireplace brought them back to their feet. "Who is that?" The alarm had returned to CJ's tone, and the two crept toward the noise.

"And you brought them here?"

Chris had little doubt who they were talking about; rustling and the angry screech of a chair suggested that this was not a cordial meeting.

"After everything that has happened? You bring humans into our walls?" The voice was close enough to a mumble that it drew them even closer to the wooden door, which was perfectly smooth to the touch. "We should kill them right now. They were probably sent here as spies, or worse!"

The friends glanced at each other nervously, and Chris began mapping out an exit strategy while they listened.

"We do not want their kind here! They are pitiful creatures, weak and pathetic." The insults continued to fly as Chris dug in against the door. A smash was followed by more screeching chairs.

They had been warned when they arrived that humans were not well regarded in these parts. The stories Bernard told had been very direct and, while not completely false in their treatment of the human personality or environmentally destructive actions, were wildly off when it came to humans allying with the king of darkness.

Their guide had been very adamant that they follow his lead, imparting definitive instructions to keep their heads down during the trip to this magnificent castle. Yet as the ranting became more unhinged and his body temperature rose, Chris could not help but grasp the doorknob.

"Chris." CJ was a pro at reading him, and his concerned grab at Chris's hand showed that he was ready to step in and stop whatever crazy idea Chris might have. "You heard Bernard."

"Their kind does not belong here! They should go back to where they came from!"

The words tore into Chris's ears as he tried to control the heat bubbling into his chest.

"Disgusting, worthless . . ."

The suppressed part of his mind screamed to let go and confront these people who spoke like they were too good for him and his best friend.

"I swear, Bernard, if I see them, I will—"

"Chris!"

CJ wasn't strong enough. The buildup inside sought release as he finally smashed into the door and yanked it open.

"Do what?! What the fuck would you do if you saw me?" The emotional scream turned the heads of at least ten men of Bernard's size gathered around a table.

"Shit, Chris." All of them rose to their full height inside the grand hall. Behind him, CJ whispered, "This might be the dumbest thing you have ever done."

Each of the gargantuan warriors brought their hands together, producing swirling canes like the one that had destroyed the robed monster and the wolflike demon just a few hours ago.

"Council members." Bernard's annoyed eye roll was strangely welcome, as he was the only one not wielding a weapon. "I give you the humans."

Eira mulled over her options for at least two hours as she sat in bed. A cold bath and a harsh, bristle-snapping session with her hair had only dropped her temperature lower as she struggled to rationalize the last few comments her father had so ignorantly spewed. Her ire came not just in response to the words or the fact that they were completely out of character for a man who normally had such self-control; no, their sheer force and the pain behind them was what had her fingertips frosting with each breath she took.

A meeting with the council was the last thing her father needed at the moment. Colden would only use her father's current weakness as a way to get what he so dearly wanted: a war that, after her discoveries in the temple, she knew was completely unfounded, given that the Ignati had joined forces with her mother.

Of course, it made sense that he would feel the way he did. The two great warriors had been specifically created to stop Chaoic and had spent thousands of years on that journey, both separately and together. The fact that her mother had chosen that night, the first celebration of Eira's birth, to face the Darkness head-on must have been almost impossible for her father to understand.

Nevertheless, her search had finally provided an important answer to why her mother, as weak as she was, had traveled to that location knowing that she might not come out. If Chaoic had indeed entered the frost and been regenerated, then only the two great warriors working together could have stopped him from obtaining the relics he sought in order to raise his complete army.

That thought brought her to her feet. The quietness of her chamber became too much, and she exploded through the door.

She almost expected Cole to be waiting by the spiral staircase. She had not forgotten the way she had left him, but the subject would have to be broached later.

Three Royal Guards stared wide eyed when she reached the marble floor at the bottom. Illuminated by the chandelier above, their blue irises shimmered with a touch of fear as she stomped toward them.

"Move." It was the only warning she was willing to give. Her pulsating forearms begged for someone to confront her.

"Princess. Um . . ." An opening of her palms produced a blizzard that mirrored the roiling forces inside her. She straightened in preparation to force her way in.

"I said—"

She did not need to finish. The three guards parted, and she took a deep breath, bracing herself to deliver a tongue-lashing to the people who deserved it most of all. She thrust through the door aggressively for show, announcing her arrival without words. The scene that greeted her, however, stopped her cold.

"You are the enemy!" Colden shouted, his spiratus at the ready. Then all eyes swung toward her. The strength of her father's glare intensified as he rose.

"Eira!" Bernard moved around the long table in the middle of the room.

"I appreciate your leaving without a word to me." She added a sarcastic smile to the rudeness of her interruption. "And I see now why the council has such difficulty making any decisions."

Two council members who had their weapons drawn instantly dismissed them and took a seat. Her glare, which she felt was as frigid as ever, shifted to Colden, who seemed less interested in her and more focused on something hovering in the shadows behind Bernard.

"Eira, you must leave at once!" She cringed at her father's demand, but the familiar judgmental stares made her more determined. "You have no idea—"

"I know exactly why I am here, Father! And after the attack at the temple today, and what I found, it is ridiculous for the council to even consider war with the humans."

"The humans have already started the war, Eira! Their weak minds have put them at the mercy of Chaoic!" Colden's hot anger was more manic today.

"Man, fuck you!" The crude insult was so sharp that she had no doubt that the speaker was the target of Colden's irritation.

"How dare you."

"Don't talk down to me, you piece of shit! Where I'm from, you open your mouth like that, and we have problems." The speaker's raw emotion was palpable, carrying a strength and unwavering passion she had never heard directed at a council member.

"Christopher, that is enough!" Bernard joined the shouting match, and his attempt to restrain the individual revealed their new guest's identity. She threw a hand over her mouth as the silhouette came into full view.

"What is that? Is that . . . ?"

Based off Colden's venom and this being's size and speech, she could only assume it was a human that now struggled against her advanced weapons trainer.

"I didn't ask to come here! He brought us here, and just so all you fuckers know, I never even knew my father!"

"Chris, stop," said a softer voice. Another human, this one with darker skin and slightly taller, stepped into the light. He looked worried, something the other one showed little regard for as he jerked away and adjusted a long-sleeve shirt with strange writing on it.

"Whatever, man, I just don't need . . ."

He stopped abruptly, his golden eyes grabbing hers and widening. She suddenly felt as if she were choking. The stories of these creatures, the pictures from her studies, and the myths she had been told growing up appeared to be completely wrong if this thing really was a human. He did not look barbaric at all, and his size, though unequal to the men around him, was not far different from that of a younger lumi.

His black hair, which had been described in her studies as similar to a ferlup's, was not matted but rather cut short with a small amount of facial hair of the same color growing in. His lanky body showed very little muscle, and he seemed underfed, which suggested the complete opposite of their gluttonous reputation.

"Is that a human?" she finally whispered.

"Eira, please," her father pleaded, as if worried for her safety. But it was clearly the two humans who should be worried, as they were undersized and outmanned.

"Why?" She had so many questions, so many thoughts flooding her brain, but this was all she could manage.

"Your Highness." Bernard stepped closer, and she was able to tear her gaze away from their visitors at last. "I am sorry I left without a word, but your father sent me to the human realm to get some answers." He turned to show the two humans. "On my trip through a leap your father opened, I discovered the human world was the same as we had left it." A scoff from Colden did not deter him. "But I also found some of Chaoic's creatures tracking a scent."

Eira found the first human strangely compelling. His posture, like his shouts earlier, remained aggressive as she felt herself pulled nearer. "When I found the source, I believe I found some of our answers."

It was as if they were being presented to each other. The human's quizzical expression indicated that he felt it too.

"Eira, I would like you to meet Christopher and his friend CJ, of Philadelphia." The pair laughed and exchanged a brief glance.

"Actually," the first human said, extending his hand as he directed a crooked smile at her, "it's just Chris. Chris Cho." She sized up his palms: no callouses or blood markings like had been described to her.

While it was rude to let him linger, she struggled with the forces tugging her in all different directions. But the feeling was very different from the anger or adrenaline she had felt earlier in this whirlwind of a day. Eventually, she could not stop herself; the curiosity and chance to touch a human was too much as she moved in.

"Good evening, Christopher. I am Eira, princess of Noel." A jolt at their touch shut her up and brought the churning winds inside her to an abrupt halt.

Everything that had happened with her father, everything at the temple and even before that, dissipated. A shudder ran up her spine, the force nearly bringing her to her knees. It was so overwhelming that she could not help but squeeze his hand tighter. The shaking ground and dimming lights, along with a few gasps from those around the room, were of little concern as warmth cascaded through her veins.

The human's grip increased as the new force inside her intensified into a rush of heat such as she had never thought possible. The energy did not seem to come from him, though, but from the chain of the necklace she wore. While normally a reason to panic, this warmth did not melt her insides but merely relaxed her, easing the stress in her muscles. Even the dull pain from her earlier injuries, which had almost healed, was erased in an instant as another shiver rolled up her back.

"Eira!" Her father's shout returned her to the room, which had been cast into darkness. The overhanging torches had somehow been extinguished, and the only light came from the moon.

The human named Christopher, now hardly visible but clearly breathing heavily, coughed, and a frosty puff escaped his mouth. Bernard stepped between them and deliberately yanked them apart as she blinked uncontrollably.

She felt the stares, but, similarly to when she was with Aspen, they meant nothing. Her interest was only in the individual before her. "Who are you?" The human's golden eyes stayed locked with hers as everyone else stirred into a frenzy.

CHAPTER 11

"Just keep your head down and follow me." Their guide had been on repeat, hardly giving them time to acknowledge his presence before he led them through the courtyard. Large trees swayed on either side of the dirt path as the two reluctantly followed.

CJ's inquisitive stare grew ever more annoying. "So," he finally said as they passed through an open gate flanked by two guards, "are we going to talk about what happened last night?"

A peek behind showed the courtyard gates closing. The guards' eyes did not leave the group as they headed into the city.

"Don't know what you mean." Chris ignored CJ's disbelieving stare. The dirt turned to cobblestone as they passed a finely crafted stone building emitting the unmistakable, delicious scent of bread.

Chris had no answers, even after thinking about the situation all night in the massive bed they had been assigned. His boiling anger as he confronted the group of men at the table had cooled immediately when he laid eyes on the stunning woman who introduced herself as the princess. Her long white hair, radiant under the torches, separated her from the other lumi in this strange place.

Chris could not get her astonishingly blue eyes out of his head. They had practically anchored him to the ground last night, and now her gaze was engraved on him, her soft white skin sparkling around him like a flurry on a winter's day.

"Chris!" CJ jerked him around before he barreled into a horse alongside the road. "Pay attention!"

The burly man who climbed to his feet nearby must have been its owner. A long, hard stare ended in a nod, and they returned the gesture.

"Look, I'm cool if you don't want to talk about what happened yesterday morning or afternoon. I'm even cool if you don't want to talk about your dad potentially being some human fire rod created to protect us. But the whole thing with the princess? The damn torches blew out when you two shook hands, dude!"

That was another thing that had kept Chris up all night. The shock at her touch had brought an icy calmness he had never experienced. It was not an uncomfortable chill. All the simmering tension had uncoiled with an ease that cooled his body, and he felt the remnants of that handshake even now, as if icy chunks still floated in his veins.

The scenery was especially charming today, and the vibrant flowers on the torchlights above gave off a friendly vibe. While a few horses trod up and down the stone streets, the hustle and bustle he associated with cities was nonexistent. And contrasting with the picturesque surroundings, the people seemed uneasy, the shoppers and pedestrians moving with a purpose. They reminded him of humans preparing for a hurricane.

"Where are we going?" He picked up speed to join their guide and escape CJ's questions.

"The king was nice enough to let you stay in the courtyard suite, even after your childish outburst." Chris was growing accustomed to judgmental digs from these people. "But he will not give you access to the castle or its library. If you wish to learn, you will need material, and this shop is the only one that can provide it to you."

Bernard threw open the door of a wide stone building without a knock.

"I think we found your new favorite place, CJ."

His best friend gasped. The store they stepped into had a very unique energy. Books lined each wall, and the scent of some unfamiliar herb nearly knocked him off his feet.

"Dude." CJ's eyes were wide as he slid toward one of the shelves.

"Do not touch anything!" Bernard said sharply.

Another outsized man emerged from a door in the back. "I see you made it." He appeared uncomfortable as he ran his hand through his whitening blond hair. "Are these—"

"Yes" was their guide's simple answer, but it held a twinge of pomposity that brought Chris closer.

"Does this one like to read?" The shop owner pointed dismissively at CJ, who was still analyzing the books.

"He has a damn name!" Another speedy retort emerged without thinking, and Bernard glared at him; surprisingly, though, the other man seemed to regret his original tone.

"My apologies, good sir," the big shop owner said, extending his hand gently. "My name is Whittaker. What is yours?"

He did not seem to mind Chris's hesitation.

"Chris," he eventually said, accepting the hand and clearing his throat. "And that's my friend, CJ. He does like to read, by the way."

"It is a pleasure to meet you, Chris. Again, I apologize for my dismissive attitude. I have not had the pleasure of human interaction in quite some time." He nailed the apology so well that Chris regretted lashing out. "I only ask that you please not use that language. My daughter is over there, and I wish to keep her from using those types of words in the future."

A glance at the counter running along the side of the shop revealed a young girl, who was curiously eyeing Chris.

"Oh, I'm so sorry! I never meant . . . It's been a long few days."

"I understand, Chris. Please, let me get your books and study material from the back." Chris's face was on fire from the original outburst. The embarrassment worsened when Bernard sighed heavily and joined CJ on the other side of the room.

The swish of paper drew Chris's attention back to the counter. The young girl hunched further down but couldn't hide her peek in his direction.

He had enjoyed working with the kids in the group home as he got older. Preparing them for school or playing games with them was a pleasant release from the stress of an orphan's world, a chance to get away from the stigma—to enjoy something and be himself.

"What's your name?" His approach straightened the little girl's shoulders, and he stopped a few feet away at her tense reaction.

"Aspen," she said softly, her head still down as she flipped another page.

"Does your dad own this shop?" A nod bobbed Aspen's blond hair. "I'm guessing your father likes to read from all these books. Do you as well?" Another nod brought her legs up onto the stool she was sitting on. Her hands wrapped around a cup of tea. "That tea smells good." Chris was struggling to get a feel for how old she was. Her features suggested that she might be around eleven or twelve.

"You should not have any. My dad says it is bad for humans. It will make you sick." She indicated a cluster of white flowers that Chris realized were the source of the smell.

"Well, thank you for the advice, Aspen."

The boost in her posture suggested that she was warming up to him. "Are you staying in the city?"

He could not help but grin at her sweet voice.

"Not actually in the city. I'm staying up in the castle."

The girl's eyes widened, and a broad smile revealed glistening white teeth. "You know the king? And Eira?"

The princess's name perked him up, and an idea jumped into his head.

"A little. Tell me something, Aspen. Where is the queen right now? I have met the king and the princess, but not the queen."

He immediately regretted the question as the little girl slouched low in her seat.

"My father says that the queen died a long time ago. She was our protector against the bad things on the other side of the frost. But we are not to worry." With a determined nod, the young girl then smiled vibrantly. "Eira will become our protector! She will fight off all the bad things."

Another droop in her posture had him inching closer in genuine concern. The girl's liveliness was a welcome distraction.

"What's wrong, Aspen?"

"Well, Eira is my friend," Aspen sniffled, an adjustment of her hands on the cup giving her time to compose herself. "And I wanted to be a warrior, just like her. But during my selection today, I . . . I was not selected for it."

Based on what he had learned regarding the selection ritual, this smart, well-spoken little girl was only eight years old, which was a little hard for him to process.

"I let her down." Her disappointment tore at him.

"Your books." Chris spun around at the sound of them hitting the desk. "You should probably go."

The shop owner's fatherly caution was crystal clear, and Chris honored it as he grabbed the materials and headed for the door.

"Thank you," he said, shifting around and trying to show that he had no intention of upsetting the little girl, who was once again straining over the counter. "You have done a great job raising your daughter." The words seemed to help some, as Whittaker nodded while glancing at her. "And, Aspen?" He could not help himself, although Bernard and CJ were motioning impatiently for him to follow. "You didn't let anyone down, and don't ever let anyone tell you what you can and cannot be."

She perked up with his goodbye, her smile exactly what he was hoping for as he stepped out into the warm sunshine.

"The son of the Ignati." Ivy rotated the gold utensil between her fingers as she gazed at the distant ceiling. "I heard he helped Bernard fight off five minima and three ferlup. Left them all dead in the human realm for Chaoic to find."

The chatter brought Eira back to their schoolgirl days in the library. Her best friend's rambling included gossip she had heard from other warriors at training that day.

The arrival of the two humans, one of whom might be the son of the Ignati, had set the castle abuzz. All of her staff members were chattering about them, and the trip into the city would draw even more attention.

It was not that she wasn't interested in what was being said. The stories of what humans had for breakfast and how they slept were of just as much interest to her. However, something about last night's run-in had kept her up all night as she tossed and turned in her bed.

"So." Ivy took a bite of chicken and leaned in. "Is it true that he tried to fight Lord Colden and the entire council?"

Another rumor that, while embellished, was not wholly untrue.

"That is nonsense, Ivy. You need to stop listening to the staff and trainees. They know nothing."

She still felt the warmth where Chris had touched her hand. Her blood flowed much faster today, as if it had been thawed to the perfect temperature.

"Agreed."

She tensed at her fiancé's approach.

"My father said the humans merely cowered when the council rose. Not surprising given how pathetic—"

"Your father would tell you lies again," she replied aggressively as Andri appeared by Cole's side. "But that should come as no surprise to anyone."

The two men stiffened when she stood—a reminder to Eira that she had not spoken with her fiancé after he had run to her father.

"I was just—"

"You were just what, Cole?" Again, even she was struggling to make sense of her hostility. "You were just repeating what he said? Is that what I am to expect when we serve on the council together? Can you not make your own decisions or think for yourself?"

Her blood coursed with new freedom at her caustic question.

The opening of the main doors interrupted them. The two figures who entered were full of joy as they laughed and slapped hands.

"And he was like—" The one who had introduced himself the night before stopped, and an awkward pause followed as all six stared at each other in silence.

"It's them," Andri squeaked softly, an uncommon deviation from his boisterous roars.

Chris and CJ hesitated. Then Chris finally shifted his golden eyes to hers.

"We, um . . ." Chris's voice was tentative, but the sound of it sped up her heart. "We were told to come here for lunch. It's been a pretty busy day, so we figured we'd better grab something to eat." With a shrug of his lean shoulders, he headed to the buffet, his friend staying close.

Cole and Andri lingered. Their bitter glares had Eira clenching her hands in disgust.

"You should probably go," she said to Cole, with a harshness that snapped her fiancé out of his trance. "You might want to be there when General Aquilo returns with the scouts you sent out alone." Another cruel jab at the warrior that only rekindled her feelings from the night before.

"Eira—"

"As your fiancée, I ask that you respect my wishes and leave." She marched to the long wooden table, frost lacing her palms as she eased into the seat and raised her chin high. She sensed his stare for a few more moments and welcomed the light breeze and click of his boots that announced his departure, followed by the main door slamming shut.

"Seems like a nice guy." Chris's plate, piled high with food, hit the table so hard that she jumped. "A shame he had to leave so quickly."

She was once more struck by how normal he looked, how similar to their own youth. Even the way he took his first bite was familiar. He was no ravening beast, tearing wildly at his food. Instead, he delicately cut a piece of meat with a knife. His friend, who joined shortly after, took a different approach before sitting, timidly glancing side to side before easing into a seat.

"Normally, you would need to ask to sit by the princess."

Ivy's whisper made Eira blush.

"Oh?" Chris's anger from the night before was gone, replaced by a sarcastic tone that fit him quite well.

"We are so sorry!" The darker-skinned one stood immediately, bowing his head as her cheeks grew colder. "We didn't mean to overstep. My name is CJ, and we were just hoping to eat something after our walk—"

"Please," Eira scoffed. "My friend here was merely reporting old traditions. You are welcome to sit wherever you want."

Chris patted his face with the cloth napkin and smiled.

"Well, maybe not last night?" By the way he said it, she assumed it was a joke. "This isn't poison or anything, right?" He examined the glass of wine he had picked up.

She was perplexed by how straightforward he was. Meals with guests typically resulted in silence or trivial chatter about politics.

"Why would you ask that?" Ivy asked. Eira was stuck on the golden eyes analyzing the glass.

"Well, I ran into this little girl at the bookshop today, and she warned me not to drink—"

"You met Aspen?" Eira gasped as she realized she had missed the little girl's selection ceremony that morning.

"Yeah." He seemed to no longer care about the potential for poison as he took a sip. "Super adorable. A little upset today because she wasn't chosen for a role she wanted, and of course you tell these poor kids what they can and can't be so early, but I think—"

"She did not make warrior?" The thought of how hard Aspen had worked filled Eira with disappointment on the girl's behalf.

"Well." Chris softened his tone a bit as he put on a crooked smile. "I told her not to worry. She shouldn't let anyone tell her what she can and can't be." He took another bite and peered around as if what he said were an apparent reality.

"But that is not true at all!" Ivy sounded astonished. "Once the council selects your line of study, you must commit to it for life. It is the way of our people, the way of the Essence."

Chris's friend stood abruptly, and Eira stiffened, preparing to leap in if the human dared to attack. But he only waved his hands frantically.

"I am so sorry! Chris tends to overstep regularly, and don't mind his sarcasm. As my professors back at school would say, he likes to deflect when he's uncomfortable with a situation."

It was a lot to unpack: not just the well-spoken contrition but also the information.

"Really, CJ?" The two men exchanged a glare of their own that made Eira snicker.

"You study?" Ivy's intrigue was palpable, the question bringing the attention of the men back to them.

"Yeah. I go to a university for school."

"He studies dirt and bones." This was another clear poke that had Eira lowering her head with a wider smile. The two possessed an unusual chemistry. While she would have loved to say she and Ivy had the same connection, these two seemed to read each other's minds, a tactic that the one named Chris was currently using to fluster the other one.

"I . . . I study anthropology. It's, like, the history of humans and the past, I guess you could say." He sat down in a hurry. A nervous grab of his cup betrayed a slight shake.

"Well, we have a library on the second floor; you should stop by and ask some of the pupils for a few suggestions while you are here." The tone was unusual for Ivy.

Chris glanced up. "That is very nice of you, Ivy, but CJ and I were warned about venturing outside this hall and the suite we were so graciously provided by the king."

The way Chris mentioned her father lowered Eira's temperature in a hurry.

"We'll just keep our heads down and stay out of everyone's way. Wouldn't want the puny humans messing anything up."

A quick punch to his shoulder led to another tense, nonverbal exchange between the humans.

"So, you believe that is how all of us feel?" She had been fighting the urge, but his taunting was too much to ignore.

"Listen"—he stood, plate in hand—"CJ and I know when we're not wanted. It's kind of, well, it's kind of our thing." Nothing in the way of a response came to Eira's mind. The absolute certainty with which he had spoken took her by surprise.

A staff member came running, and her attempt to take his plate brought on a chuckle.

"If you just show me where it goes, I can put it there myself. No need to come running in like that; I'm sure you have a busy day."

The woman remained upright, her eyes jumping to Eira, who patted her lips with the napkin and rose to her feet.

"Our staff takes great honor in serving. By not allowing them to do their job, you are—"

"No one takes honor in being someone's bitch, Princess." Her jaw dropped. "But I guess . . . I guess someone like you would have no idea about that."

The staff member looked just as dumbfounded as Ivy.

"You have no idea—"

He shot a finger into the air to cut her off. "Before you finish, I might not know much about what goes on here, but even in the human world, we have kings and princesses." CJ scampered off in retreat. "And you might very well be the perfect representation of them."

She was not about to let him leave like that, but her stomp forward did not move him an inch. "What is that supposed to mean?" Her cheeks were solid ice.

"It means you could never truly understand what your people need." The finality of his judgment punctuated his departure, which came as swiftly as his arrival.

Eira's hands were shaking by her side. "I cannot believe . . . !" The sentence was impossible to finish. The audacity was so unexpected that she could only march back to her seat with a scoff.

CHAPTER 12

The nighttime sky outside her window did nothing to quell the bitterness that had taken hold since Eira's afternoon encounter with the human. His disrespectful behavior had left her unable to concentrate during training that day. Bernard's constant criticism, which ordinarily would have her jumping in response, meant nothing as she thought about Chris's outlandish comments. The cloud of that immature exchange finally launched her out of bed with a disgusted flick of a small projection against the wall.

"The nerve." With a mumble, she flew out of the room. Her aggressive thrust against the door startled a young staff member bringing tea and dessert to her chamber.

"Princess Eira, I am so sorry!" A frantic cleanup was already underway. The young woman continued to apologize feverishly. "I did not mean to cause this. I will make sure to have some new tea made right away!"

It was as if the human had sent her to prove a point. The woman's nervous energy was so apparent that Eira could not help but bend down to assist.

"No, Princess! You do not need to help. This was my fault. I will have these rugs cleaned." The shudder in her staff member's voice made Eira shake her head violently in embarrassment.

"Please." The softness of the word took even Eira by surprise as they both paused. "I was in a hurry, and this is my fault. No need to fret." She wanted to say more, but it had dawned on her that she did not know this woman's name.

When Eira was young, the staff in the castle had rotated constantly. She only recalled the names of the nannies who watched her when her father was away. The older she got, the more independent she had become. Soon, she only needed help selecting an outfit or picking up in the dining hall when she finished her meal.

The young woman had already sheepishly returned to the mess. Eira, who felt obliged to remain with her, handed over a broken teacup from the floor before they both rose.

"What is your name?" The question appeared to take the staff member by surprise.

"My name? My name is Bianca." The curtsy was no doubt instinctual, the proper response when introducing oneself to a royal or lord.

"Bianca." Eira placed a gentle hand on her shoulder. "Again, I am so sorry. I will be heading out for a walk around the courtyard, so please, there is no need to bring me anything else tonight."

Bianca's nod and accompanying smile were forced but welcome.

"Thank you, Princess."

The clanking of guards making their rounds downstairs finally sent the young woman away and down the hall.

"Bianca," Eira whispered to herself before lightly descending the steps. "Interesting." She tiptoed to the end of the hallway, then under the chandelier and past the dining hall. Unlike when she was a child, there was no one to stop her from venturing out. The next open room was one Eira moved through on instinct. Her years cooped up in this castle had allowed her plenty of time to memorize its layout.

A glass door took her out into the middle training ground, which was encircled by the castle. The grass walkways and hedges sprawled at least two acres in length and were split into sections of dirt that housed obstacles for the daily training of students and soldiers.

This space had always provided a calm oasis for her to think, although she tried to ignore the menacing outline of the mountain to the north against the moon. Her bare feet glided across the freshly cut grass. The chill of the snow that still dotted the landscape helped clear her mind of recent, unpleasant interactions.

She had never once thought about her day-to-day relationships with the staff in the castle or the citizens outside the walls. Her main focus since she had received her selection had been on learning her craft and searching for something that none of her peers had the ability to find. Sure, the trips into the city had always been uncomfortable. Her inability to travel without an accompanying Royal Guard or Legion soldier had made it almost impossible to develop connections beyond Ivy and Cole. Whittaker and Aspen were the lone exceptions, but the thought of her mother's former head librarian and having missed Aspen's selection ceremony returned a tightness to her chest.

"Damnit!"

The shout sent her leaping behind a hedge, from which she spotted a silhouette training in the distance.

"This is stupid!"

The figure was alone, training with the wooden dummy designated for children who had just been selected to work on their offensive projections. Those lessons generally produced crazy flashes of wind, but this session was more subdued, as only a few huffs and puffs and the occasional flip of a page were audible. A snap of what sounded like a kick against the wood brought her closer as the shadow stepped back to flip another page of the book near its feet.

"Come on, Chris!"

The shout's target was the same as its source. The human flexed his hands and lowered the hardcover manuscript he had been studying.

He adopted a sloppy warrior stance, the stagger of his feet too wide and his arms not nearly close enough together. A deep breath was followed by a lazy thrust, and his subsequent movements were so unrefined that she snorted before she caught herself.

"Hello?" His steps in her direction were loud, with no effort at stealth. "Show yourself!" It was a feeble demand, considering the performance he had just put on.

"Sorry." She stood, and his golden eyes widened.

"Prin . . . Princess!" It was a surprising stumble after his earlier outburst. "I, um, I was reading some of the stuff in these books and wanted to see if I could . . ." He cleared his throat and retreated to the training pit.

"You are practicing?" It was not the tone she had planned to take when she stomped out of her chamber.

An embarrassed shrug was all he mustered in reply. He hastily closed the book and darted to the open gate leading under the castle's overhanging floors.

"It was a good start." She felt he needed encouragement after the way he had been berating himself.

The stuttering was gone, but the shake of his head reeked of defeat. "I appreciate your being nice, but I really was just messing around." He laughed sarcastically and threw his arms out. "You don't have to be nice to me. I don't deserve it, especially after this afternoon." The implicit apology was unprompted and sounded genuine. "CJ, he was right. I can be a little over the top. It's just, after the last few days, and everything your people have said to us—"

"You have every right to be upset." The words left her without thought, an automatic reaction to his defeated posture. "They have no right to say those things, and I cannot imagine how all of this new information has made you feel." She sighed. "And you were not off with your assessment. I have a lot to learn about my people."

He didn't move, but his smile popped out like a solitary flame, highlighted by the moonlight.

"Well, I had no right to say that. I don't know you, and I sure as hell don't know anything about you and your people. I hate being judged and I, well, I'm just really sorry about that. I'm a hypocrite." This gentle, rational side of him made her want to hear more.

The memory of their touch the night before flooded her body with heat, and her mouth refused to open as an inexplicable sensation rushed into her cold veins, something that made it difficult to swallow as he turned again toward the exit. She wanted him to stay, the feeling inside producing a kick that she did not want to go away.

"Would you prefer me to call you Chris?"

"Much more than 'human.'" He had returned to the sarcasm on which he so often relied. "But yes, Chris is fine. Do you prefer 'Princess'?"

A few lights flickered on in the surrounding windows, followed by more. Their conversation was clearly drawing interest from others in the castle.

"Eira," she replied softly.

He nodded and continued toward the gate as it swiveled open. His golden eyes briefly returned to her as he smiled once more. "Have a good night, Eira." The crook of his lips stayed visible until he disappeared into the shadows. An instant desire for him to return was so overwhelming that she had to exhale a cloud of vapor to breathe again.

"Pull yourself together." Shaking off her paralysis, she hurried back to the castle. The only lit window she noticed was at the far end, and she peeked up as she slipped inside.

Cole had likely seen who she had been talking to, and given his recent behavior, there was little chance he would not report to her father in the morning. However, she could not have cared less. The perfect temperature she had achieved in Chris's presence, now dwindling back to normal, had been so intoxicating that everything else faded away as she prayed for it to return.

"You should be careful about whom you speak with in this castle." The raspy voice tore Chris's eyes from the painting he had been analyzing. "And I see you followed my instructions to not wander, as well." The amused expression was the first Chris had seen from Bernard since arriving in this place, and he wondered if his sarcasm was rubbing off on the imposing warrior.

It had been a long two days. The reading, random trips around the castle, and hours of watching the so-called "training sessions" their guide had them audit had drained him to the point that he could hardly tell which way was up in this strange new world.

A chance to break away had presented itself after lunch when CJ not-so-subtly snuck off with Ivy, who had been smuggling him books to read each night. She seemed to have a genuine interest in his friend. And while her intellect was undeniable, it might have been her second-most impressive attribute after the power Chris had observed while she trained.

It was not as if they had intended to break the rules. Ivy had approached them yesterday at breakfast with a couple of books they had not been given in the city. A few questions during lunch led to a bigger delivery at the suite door that evening; the new reading material kept CJ awake all night.

Whether it was true or not, the information he had read aloud to

Chris was fascinating. That same history drew him into this gallery of art, the plant-laden door opening to reveal faces that filled in the blanks of the stories he had been told while he struggled to sleep.

"Sorry. I just . . ." He shrugged, the picture of the woman with green skin keeping him entranced. "Is this her? The one you all worship as the creator?" It was probably the wrong way to phrase that, but he was not religious.

"The Essence." Her name matched the aura she gave off. "She created everything we see today and some things we do not." The mysterious response was a clear attempt to steer him to the other painting, which Chris had tried to ignore since first entering the room.

"I look nothing like him." That was the first thought that came to mind as he beheld the grizzled warrior said to be his father. "He looks more like you than me." The assertion brought a slight chuckle from Bernard as he slowly paced behind Chris.

"From the legends, you may be more like him than you realize."

Chris's eyes were drawn to the jewels on the man's robe. The riches in the vault in New York started to make sense as he tried to picture himself in the elaborate clothes his father had worn. But it was impossible to envision anything past his contempt for this opulent look.

"How so?"

"He was said to be disdainful at times and extremely passionate with his decisions, one of the many qualities he must have picked up from being around humans regularly." It felt like an insult, and Chris could not help but think of the hypocrisy of the statement, given the behavior of everyone he had met in this place, including Bernard.

Even so, he could agree that he used sarcasm as a crutch, which took care of the disdainful part, and CJ would be the first to point out that the most irrational decisions Chris made were in the heat of the moment.

"He seems so . . ."

He trailed off, and Bernard's nudge indicated that he understood what Chris was trying to get out.

"Most lumi spend over thirteen years perfecting their craft, just to have it peak when they turn twenty-one." Chris jerked his head up at that. "But with you, no one can really tell you how long it will take, because no one has the power you do." A slight pause brought them over to another painting: of a beautiful woman with silky white hair. "Well, maybe one person does."

Chris adjusted his feet and replayed the conversation in the training yard.

"I know the princess is her daughter," he blurted out. "Can she help me figure this all out? See if it's true? The little girl down at the bookstore said Eira is the new protector. I read that her mother died twenty years ago. Can she—"

"Eira still seeks her powers as well," Bernard said as he moved over to the fire, which popped and sparked.

Chris was intrigued; the books mentioned nothing about her or her powers. "She can't project like the rest?"

"Eira's projections are much stronger than the spiratuses you have witnessed in the training pit. I assume, based on your studies of her mother, that you understand what they comprise."

He did understand. Her icy touch gave that away.

"But even after the recent passing of her twenty-first birthday, she still seeks her full potential."

A new curiosity chilled the inner bonfire that had refused to go away all day.

"When was her twenty-first birthday?" His strong connection to her gave him a slight idea of what it might be.

"I believe you call that day Christmas." Bernard's grin made him uneasy.

"Shit." It slipped out; the thought of her touch on his hand further twisted the pretzel of his mind.

Another crackle of the fire brought his attention to the other side of the gallery.

"Is this a painting of the war you told me about?" The canvas was different from the others and seemed to make the warrior by his side uncomfortable.

"Yes." The response was curt.

Chris could not help but ask, "My father helped stop it? With that, uh, parchment treaty in all the books?"

Bernard began pacing, his sigh indicating that he'd known it was only a matter of time before this all came out. "Our two peoples spent many years together. We survived the extinction and began to thrive."

He stopped beside Chris.

"However, our ability to project made us arrogant. Your free will made you thirsty for growth and knowledge. Your constant desire to expand, to grow—we could never understand that. That is what led us to this."

He pulled a cloth away from the painting next to them, revealing a massive, dark creature with a tangle of black hair that overwhelmed the length of the canvas. Chris was not afraid but instead drawn in by a curiosity he did not understand.

"Chaoic," Bernard murmured.

An eerie stillness filled the room. A pop from the fire shook them from their trance, and the warrior relaxed a bit as he motioned to the painting of the battlefield.

"During the war, the Darkness hid in the shadows. It engulfed the dead soldiers, both human and lumi, and began to build an army of its own, one made not of the living but of the dead."

A warm shiver raced up Chris's side as Bernard maneuvered them over to the first group of paintings.

"The two protectors could no longer simply battle the Darkness. Their peoples, who they hoped would find a solution themselves, refused to cooperate. Our ancestors were overwhelmed by hatred for each other, their differences too great to set aside." This story sounded a bit different than what was written in the books of this realm. "The two great warriors decided to take a stand. They came together and created a treaty, one that was given life with the powers of two relics—of fire and ice."

It sounded like a fairy tale, but he had read about the two relics just this morning, before breakfast.

"These relics were designed to separate our peoples. They provided a chance to start over and live in peace. The closing of the leaps and strengthening of the frost, of which you have heard so many speak, were accomplished by the ice relic. Its power was enough to keep anyone or anything out."

Chris considered that a bold statement, what with the various creatures breaking through.

"The fire relic, the one your father created, was used to wipe us from human memory. It was an extreme clause, to be sure, but one that your father believed was the only way to bring peace to both peoples."

For some reason, this all made sense. The books he pored through, everything he had witnessed over the last two days, and his initial trip to the bank made it feel real. However, the more he stared at the painting of his father, the more questions arose.

"My father was said to have died twenty years ago." Chris was back on the information about the princess's mother as he pieced together the timeline.

"You are much smarter than you like to show, Christopher." Chris let this insult slide as he awaited an explanation. "I cannot speak for why your father disappeared after the treaty, and I refuse to join in the chatter that many in this realm have repeated."

"They say he was weak. They say he went into hiding because of his failure to control the humans. Don't think I haven't heard and read about it already. They believe my father gave in to Chaoic. That he was too weak to defend—"

"History is merely told by the one penning it, Christopher." This blunt declaration carried an emotional heft he was not expecting. "Twenty-one years ago, the day you and Eira were born, it is said that Chaoic achieved a goal he had pursued since the Great War. It is said that after hundreds of years of feasting on the human realm, he achieved full embodiment."

The words were a strangling weight as Chris thought about the man he had never met.

"But your father was not the only one to blame for that." The slight shift in inflection returned Chris's focus. "The Iclyn knew of this growing danger. Like your father, she too did nothing about it."

"But why—"

"Because of powers much stronger than anything either of them had ever projected. Powers that did not bring death or destruction but regret and life." The towering warrior pointed to the two portraits, and then his finger came to rest on Chris's chest. "Twenty years ago, the two great protectors made their final stand together. But this time, they did not do it for a world of people. They did it for—"

"But why?" Chris had had enough of the dramatic irony and mysterious hints. His father's image taunted him as he thought of all the years in the group homes. "And what about my mother? Did she really die giving birth to me?"

"I am no historian of the Ignati, Christopher. To find your true powers, you must answer those questions yourself."

Chris threw his hands up in frustration. The boil intensified. "This is stupid! Why does it matter? If my father and this ice god killed Chaoic, why does it even matter if I find this power?"

Bernard seemed to anticipate the childish response, patting Chris's shoulder and leading him back to the uncovered painting of the monster.

"Chaoic cannot be killed, Christopher. Your father and the Iclyn merely destroyed his physical being and sent him back into the void. But their death created an opening he now seeks to exploit. Chaoic seeks to take over the world, to cast a shadow on everything. The great warriors were his lone obstacle to doing so for all these thousands of years."

The connected dots did not make Chris more comfortable with the situation.

"Before he can do this, he must regenerate and raise his army. But he believes he must do this quickly, before you and Eira gain your powers and restore the balance of our world."

"No pressure, right?" The magnitude of what Chris faced elevated his temperature once more as his cheeks heated. "This can't be real."

"You have always known, Christopher—always felt that something made you different." That hidden part of his brain churned as the words echoed in his ears. "It's what brought you to that train, what brought you with me through the leap, and what has allowed you to accept this place so quickly."

"Okay, so how—"

"The relics, Christopher. He seeks the power of the relics."

The painted eyes of the great protectors seemed to be judging Chris's response as he shifted and stood on his toes.

Two days ago, he would have thought this a sick joke or a hallucination he would snap out of when whatever drug he had been slipped wore off. But today, as he stood in this foreign realm, next to an enormous warrior who had not long ago killed two soulless creatures with a cane made of wind, he could only take a deep breath and accept it all.

"Okay." He clenched his hands into fists. "Where do I find my father's relic?"

CHAPTER 13

"And listen to this!" CJ rambled on, becoming little more than white noise as Chris eyed the wooden figure before him. The blank face and unseeing eyes matched those of the creature they had seen in the alley.

While the information CJ had gleaned was interesting and contained enough intrigue to keep them up all night, the encounter in the gallery focused Chris's mind on other, more personal objectives that began to weigh heavily on him.

Bernard had given him plenty to think about. The looming threat of this Chaoic creature, along with the stunning similarities he shared with the princess and his new need to find the relic, had him all tied up as he tried to slow his breathing and focus on the wooden figure.

"These relics are crazy, man!" Another outburst from his friend was no help as Chris inhaled and tried to make something come out of his hands. "If this is all true, the powers they possess are just incredible. The frost relic produced enough power to hide this entire region, which spans about a hundred miles up to that mountain range behind us. And the force of it keeps anything out of this realm by repelling it. At least for a while."

Chris opened his palms, something the other lumi did during training to produce the spiratuses they used as weapons.

"And the fire relic your dad used on most of our memories—just *poof!*" The twirl of CJ's hands ended any chance Chris had of concentrating. A slouch and a sarcastic shrug brought the two men face-to-face.

"Dude. Can't you see that I am trying to practice whatever it is I am supposed to be practicing?"

A raised eyebrow showed that CJ had little interest in shutting up. The purposeful flip of a page magnified that point, and Chris sighed. "Plus, you're wrong. The fire relic erased all of our memories, not just most."

"Well, I think the books are wrong about that." CJ's puzzling reply gave Chris pause, and he stared at his best friend, who grinned as he finally received the attention he seemed to be craving. "These lumi authors write from their own experiences. From just the first few chapters, I can tell most of them haven't been to the human realm in a very long time."

It was a wise observation, and based on Chris's conversation with Bernard, it was widely true.

"But think about it, Chris. According to the timeline, the treaty was signed after some of the first human civilizations existed. We have always marveled at how they created such grand structures and societies, but now it makes sense."

Chris had never pondered this before.

"The pyramids, Mesopotamia, the Roman sewage systems—these things are inexplicable wonders. Kind of like—"

"Where we are now."

CJ nodded in triumph. Chris's agreement seemed to satisfy him.

"After the treaty, these things still existed. They were part of a memory that humans could not explain, so we created—"

"You better be very careful with where you go next." Chris pointed to the sky, a reference to his friend's dive into religion in their younger years.

"I'm not saying it explains everything. And shit, I've barely even gotten to the Essence and who she was. But what about the leap we came through with Bernard?" This was another lesson Chris had let himself get sucked into. "These leaps are all over the human realm and link to the few that exist here. To use them, you press on the vines and let yourself be transported to the other side. It is said that the Essence herself taps into your mind and takes you to the closest leap to which it is connected. It's almost like a saying we humans use when we just let go and try something, eh?"

"You're going to say 'leap of faith' again, aren't you?" Chris rolled his eyes at CJ's chuckle.

"That term wasn't just created for the hell of it. Maybe we subconsciously still have some of these memories. And maybe the trading leaps that Bernard said he was a liaison for . . . Maybe not every lumi hates humans and wants to stay separated." That was a good point, but it would have to wait for another time, as the mention of their guide brought Chris's mind back to the impossible task he had been assigned.

According to his newly minted trainer, finding the fire relic would allow Chris to tap into whatever he had inherited from his father. It would require intense self-reflection of a kind he had never undertaken but on which he was due to be tested in the next hour or so, once Bernard returned.

He would not be the first to search for the relic itself. He had been told that many lumi warriors had tried to locate it over the years. However, the fact that none of them returned, combined with the emerging threat of this dark being, Chaoic, meant that his only chance of success and survival lay in his open palms.

He took a deep breath and attempted to block out the chirping birds by closing his eyes. A cool breeze eased his tension as he tried to parse the turbulence within. Perhaps he had trouble focusing because he was hungry; he had skipped lunch today due to the tight schedule Bernard designed to expedite his training. A longer reflection on the feeling, however, brought on a buildup of heat. The churning abruptly shifted to a boil that had nothing to do with his empty stomach.

His mind wandered down a path he had tried to tread many times over the last hour. *"Answers to the past will not soothe your mind, but when the time is right, your future you will find."*

The calming timbre of this voice from the past helped relax his breathing. He set his arms in the stance his trainer had shown; planting his feet and opening his palms was said to help loosen his muscles, which had begun to pulsate in the more instinctual crouch his mind had just fed him.

"Do not be afraid of it, Christopher. This is who you are. Let it—"

A swirling nudge from behind broke him from the trance, and he nearly choked on the puff of smoke that had been forced into his lungs as someone laughed. CJ scrambled back over to the books, and his tense, nervy expression prompted Chris to turn to see who was approaching.

"I thought maybe you had actually learned something!" The booming, arrogant voice of the man the princess had kicked out of the dining hall a few days prior was unmistakable. "But from the looks of it, you could barely recognize a small gust coming your way."

A snicker from the towering warrior by Cole's side carried the same pompous undertone. Their muscles flexed as they stepped onto the dirt.

"Tell me, human, do you really believe that you are the son of the Ignati?" Cole clucked dismissively, his condescending sneer making Chris's blood simmer.

"I don't want any problems, man."

De-escalation was the best bet for this situation. He and CJ were vastly outmatched.

"I actually hope you are, human. It would be nice to finally show the people how pathetic you and your kind are."

"Like I said, we don't want any—"

"Typical." The scoff reeked of something worse than the earlier arrogance. "I always knew the Ignati hid in fear. You are just the bastard son who will finally prove that point to our people."

That final remark hit a chord. The statement was not far removed from what he had so often heard while growing up, but with the newfound knowledge of his actual past and ancestry, it felt much more personal.

"Fuck off, man! We didn't ask to come here, and we never bothered—" A windy flash stopped CJ before he could finish, sending him flying back by the books he had just stomped away from.

"Hey!" Chris's response was instinctive. The warrior who had so far remained silent was the culprit, as he smirked and faced Chris. "What the fuck is your—"

A hard thump to his chest propelled him backward, his body in midair for an eternity before it finally thudded to the dirt. A ringing started in his ears upon impact; the laughs from the two lumi sounded like they were at the far end of a tunnel as Chris tried to shake off a likely concussion.

"Cole!" The sharp, feminine voice was hardly audible through the ringing. One figure darted past him, and he spotted another out of the corner of his eye. "What is your . . ." It was all just a mumble. The shouting grew louder as a cold, biting wind cut through the area.

He pushed his hands into the dirt, feeling the grains between his fingers as the boiling overtook the pain.

"They are pathetic, Eira! That one tried to strike Andri, and the way the small, insignificant one on the ground that you keep sticking up for speaks to me . . ." More insults from the petulant warrior pricked Chris's skin as he gathered the strength to climb to his feet.

"They should go back to where they belong."

The part of Chris's brain that he had always pushed away, the one that had always made him hesitate, screamed for him to let go.

"Weak . . . pathetic . . . worthless . . ."

Each new breath expanded muscles he didn't know he had as he dug into the sand, which started to smoke under his old sneakers. The hands that had so far failed him became scorching hot, begging to unleash what smoldered within him.

One more shout ended his fight against this newfound calling. An uncoiling of his fingers distributed a rush through every bone and fiber of his body. The motion seemed to release him from invisible chains. The ashy taste returned in force, but this time he did not push it away. A growing smell of sulfur pierced his nostrils with each inhale. The embers that started to pop in all directions did not deter him from his targets, who had become an obsessive focus that he could not—and would not—shake.

His readings and the brief lessons with Bernard came flooding out of that part of his brain. A cascade of what felt like lava coursed through him.

He could not hear a word nor make out the faces of anyone but the two lumi who had attacked them. His mind processed everything at warp speed as the spinning sensation wore off, and a comforting warmth eased through him.

"Are you ready?"

He spread his fingers.

"Your turn."

"Eira," Ivy whispered in the face of the growing fireball as embers hissed around them and the grounds filled with the distinct smell of sulfur.

It was a stark shift from what had been a pleasant day before the New Year Solstice. An early breakfast with the two humans had started it off, the meal ending in a few laughs after another exchange of smuggled books.

Eira had begun to enjoy their time together. Their meetings at meals provided a chance for her to not only get away from Bernard's increasingly difficult training but also to learn more about their human guests and the people they represented.

CJ was a scholar in the human realm, and his love of history made this trip that much more interesting for him. He was quite funny when he was not being overly polite, and his interest in Ivy had been evident from their first interaction. Eira had no doubt that the feeling was mutual, as Ivy had spent the trip to this very pit speaking about CJ's intellect. While not nearly the physical specimen Andri was, CJ had a certain appeal and pull that even Eira could feel; it was an energy she enjoyed being around and one that complemented his best friend's.

She was still struggling to get a firm read on Chris. His schedule was ramping up, like hers, as Bernard sought to teach him in a few months what lumi learned in thirteen years. Chris was full of sarcasm, but his genuine interest in keeping the world safe, along with a certain charisma of his own, left Eira wanting to linger over their empty plates.

Today, the humans had missed lunch. That was not surprising. Chris had been struggling to project at all, and she figured Bernard was working him overtime to make a breakthrough.

While Ivy had continued her own training, Eira took some time to collect herself. The past week's events had made her reconsider some of her earlier actions, and her mind wandered as she strolled through the courtyard. She had spent a relaxing and quiet few hours deep in thought, enjoying the abnormally temperate day. The fight at the temple, her missed trip to see Aspen's selection, and her run-ins with Chris all weighed on her as she took in the serene grounds. A surprise encounter with Bianca, the staff member she now knew by name, led to a conversation and even a few introductions to the caretakers out front.

Bianca's personality was infectious, and she seemed more comfortable with Eira the more they spoke. She even laughed once while explaining a mess in the kitchen that occurred during preparations for the solstice ceremonies. The accident, which according to Bianca happened because of a stray projection, had sent one unfortunate staff member to the floor—along with a freshly baked celebratory cake.

The encounter with her new friend was a lovely follow-up to the morning, and Eira rejoined Ivy with a smile as they began their search for the humans, who they assumed were still practicing.

The two friends' laughter as they walked through the hedges, however, had been interrupted. A blast of wind followed by a shout sent them running over to a standoff between the two humans and the women's respective fiancés.

"Chris." Another peep from CJ forced Eira closer to Ivy, who was helping him regain his feet after his fall.

"Get behind me," Eira commanded.

Chris's appearance seemed unfathomable to her. Smoldering where he stood, he looked taller as he straightened, his once scraggly shoulders bulging as he rolled them back. His palms were open, and newly formed biceps and throbbing forearms pushed against his shirt sleeves. As the heat around him increased, she could only stare. Something was building that she could not explain.

The inferno burning inches above Chris's hands rippled in the windy aftermath of the last push from her fiancé.

"Cole." She watched the burly lumi warrior steady himself. "Do not engage."

"I am not afraid of this human!"

She should have expected that idiotic response after his recent behavior.

"This is different, Cole."

The burning fireball grew with each passing second, and the sulfur smell thickened. A plume of smoke rose from the ground in front of Chris, who had not moved since standing.

"I will not be intimidated by him! This is a blatant act of war, and if this human wants a fight, so be it!"

Every fiber of her body told her to jump in and do something about the extremely formidable spiratus that had begun to circle in Cole's hands. There was no question where it was about to go and what damage it could do. But something told her to let it happen; somewhere deep in the recesses of her mind, a part she had never known existed shouted to her to let it go.

Another internal tug brought her a step closer. Chris's expanding aura was intoxicating, stopping her from uttering more pleas.

"Cole, don't!" Ivy made a final, feeble appeal. However, the thrust of Cole's hands showed he had no intention of listening as he flung his weapon toward Chris.

The initial blast of wind was recognizable; Eira had been on the receiving end many times during sparring sessions. Its power had made Cole one of the leading members of the Legion, and its strength had even thrown her on a few occasions.

The second, opposing shock wave, though, was instantaneous and earthshaking. The force of this eruption was like nothing she'd ever felt, and it brought her hands up into a defensive position as she projected a shield of her own to protect the two behind her.

The ringing in her ears increased as the new pulse produced enough heat to fill the castle for the winter. Her vision blurred, and she locked her feet into position to steady herself against the ground, which finally stilled. A thrust of her own provided clarity to the situation as she dispersed the dust swirling around the training pitch in another gust of wind.

The pit was now encircled by a ring of fire, inside of which her fiancé stood huffing, his armor scorched and tattered from an impact that had done significant damage. Andri lay sprawled outside the ring.

"Cole," she mumbled as the warrior began to spin his spiratus. "Cole, don't!"

The next thrust from his hands carried more power than she had seen him produce. Unexpectedly, his twirling cane missed the mark—another first. The jolt of heat that followed gave her little time to consider how it was possible. A flaming lasso similar in shape and size to the one she had used on the ferlup not long ago sprang out of nowhere and extinguished the weapon of wind as it boomerang back toward its wielder.

"Chris." She stumbled closer to him, no longer concerned with anything but the blazing body that was only getting brighter. He was clearly losing control of something he had no idea how to use. The embers sparking around him punctuated that point.

"Be careful!" Ivy cried.

But it was not fear that Eira felt as she took another step. An instinctual icing of her core had already ensued. The new part of her brain she had never spoken with explicitly directed her to head right over to the ball of fire and help with the situation Chris was facing.

"Stop!" She shot forward as Chris raised a hand and unleashed another attack, projecting her own shield in front of Cole. "Chris!" The impact was immense. Her feet buckled as she scrambled to find purchase on the dirt in the face of the advancing fire wall. "Please, listen to me!"

It was not so much a plea as an attempt to jar him from a mindset she had been caught in many times before, even after much more training.

"You *can* control it. Just focus on my voice!"

This was off script. No book or training from General Aquilo or Bernard could have prepared her for this scenario.

"I know you can do it!" The burning-hot, golden irises of the son of the Ignati locked on her. "Just focus on me, Chris!"

He was trying. She could tell, from the way his flame-filled eyes stayed on her, that he was trying with everything he had to stop what was happening. However, his lack of training and limited understanding of what he was projecting, along with the pain and anguish written on his face, meant that she had to do something else to end this.

"Sorry, Chris!" She snapped her left hand to the side, opening her palm as she grabbed an icy rope of her own.

A flick of her wrist sent it directly at his legs. His countermove took her by surprise as he caught the rope and pulled. The firewall intended for her fiancé vanished, and a new tug-of-war began that became increasingly difficult to contend with.

"How is this possible?" Never had one of her projections been answered so easily and dismissively. His face was expressionless, as if something else controlled his movements.

Another yank was meant to send him to his knees as she added a second hand, but the returning pull and strengthened grip showed he had no interest in doing so. The thought of lethal force began to cross her mind, and a growing whirlwind started to build as an icy blush hit her cheeks.

Her jumbled mind was humbled for a brief second; all her training went out the window as her ability to overpower any adversary failed her for the first time in her life. Chris's arms, bigger than when he'd first erupted, had steadied into a sloppy warrior stance that somehow made him look primed to strike at any second.

"*Eira.*"

The whisper startled her. The voice, calming and sweet, seemed to issue from that unknown recess of her brain.

"*Listen.*"

She struggled to lock in on it. Chris's explosion off his back leg allowed no time to discern where it had come from.

While his flailing movements gave the sense that he was merely testing and not looking to harm her, it was time for this to end. A tight pirouette sent him rushing past her with only a light touch. His warm skin added to that intoxicating tug from before as she landed and spun to face him. A quick thrust of her hand threw a ball of snow at his face; it was not meant to injure but to disorient and stop his pursuit. A cloud of smoke and his stumble upon impact showed she had accomplished her task. The final motion of her palms produced a gust of frost and ice so fast and accurate that even she was impressed.

"Chris!" His body landing on the ground quelled the blizzard that had built in her chest. In an instant, she was flying toward him as he coughed violently, puffing smoke in all directions. "Are you okay?"

People were shouting all around, but her mind could only process his face, which was back to its original tan with just a few remnants of black soot.

"What?" He seemed disoriented, the aftermath of her projections lingering longer than intended. "What happened?"

It was a good question, but they would have to discuss it later, as she had to catch him mid-collapse the moment he tried to rise.

CHAPTER 14

"It is a blatant act of war!" screamed the same man who had been so volatile when Chris and CJ first arrived.

"It was your son that started this! His actions against guests of this castle are unforgivable." Eira's voice was all he could concentrate on. Her toned arms waved with a force he had felt an hour ago on the training pitch.

His recollection of the fight was fuzzy. For a second, the part of his brain he'd always ignored had produced something unbelievable. From what CJ had told him, he had literally been on fire for some of it. He could not process that ridiculous notion, as he hadn't felt the slightest bit uncomfortable during the ordeal.

The voice in his head had walked him through each step as he tried to avoid another hard fall. He'd never intended to hurt anyone; his initial reaction arose from anger. As far as he could remember, the initial thrust was merely a response to the whirling weapon that had hit him, and the second action was supposed to be a warning to the belligerent lumi warrior.

The sight that greeted him when he regained consciousness,

however, suggested a different story—one that had Ivy's fiancé in a medical bed and Eira's holding bandages to his head while he glared at Chris from the far end of the table.

"You must understand who you represent, Princess! Your future on this council and your marriage to my son . . ." It was getting harder for him to listen, but Eira's stern expression reeled him in as she pressed hard on the wooden table.

The final interaction that delivered him to the ground was something he would never forget. Eira's voice had been so calm and collected yet her energy and aura so explosive and fierce that he could not help but want to experience it all again. Her pull on him was overwhelming; he struggled to hold himself back from her even now.

It was not just about her power nor the magnificent way she so easily bested him. The true reason—one that scared him—was that she seemed to genuinely understand what he was going through. Her encouragement and concern had been so real in that moment that he could not take his eyes off her as she stretched up on her toes.

"I know my role! It is you who does not, Colden."

"That is Lord Colden to you, Princess! And until you are married and sitting at this council . . ."

A peek at CJ showed that he too had little interest in this argument and seemed more interested in goggling at Chris.

"What?" Chris finally whispered.

"Are you serious right now? Chris, look at you!" The shrieked whisper drew the attention of the nearest council members. His best friend dropped his volume, becoming hardly audible. "Really look at yourself."

Chris did feel different than when he had sat here for breakfast; his knees hit the bottom of the table, and his body filled the seat. Whatever had happened had changed his physique. The more he ran his fingers over his newly crafted chest and abs, the more he realized how much of a change it had been.

The exploration of his new features lasted only a few seconds, though. Bernard's gaze from the other corner was enough to distract him, and the two exchanged silent nods. While not the primary person on Chris's mind, he was happy to see a familiar face after he awoke from his trance. Bernard's self-satisfaction—after all, he had been right—was crystal clear. The hulking trainer's smile lasted the entire walk back to the hall, in spite of the fact that they were both preparing for an inevitable berating.

More arguing was underway, the rising shouts bringing CJ in closer to be heard.

"You might want to try and find whatever you did outside earlier. I think we might need—"

"Do you have something to say, human?" Lord Colden cut CJ off. "You do understand that you are in front of this council now because you have violently broken the Treaty of the Parchment. Your actions have thus forced us to consider war against . . ."

The man's arrogance melted Chris's internal turmoil into a molten liquid. A new tug in his head told him to stand and confront this lord, who continued to hurl insults.

"He's lying about the treaty."

Chris jumped to his feet.

"I think our interpretations of the treaty are a little different, my man," Chris announced with biting sarcasm. His confidence in this new knowledge gave him clarity and made him comfortable speaking his mind.

"What would you know about the treaty, you pathetic—"

"Colden!" A shout from the far end of the hall halted the proceedings. The speaker's white hair ruffled slightly in a breeze as he approached. "Enough of these childish outbursts." Only Chris and Eira remained standing.

King Rori's power echoed in every footfall, anger and anguish plastered on his face when he finally halted near Chris.

"What do you have to say for yourself, human?"

The last word hung in the air as the hall went eerily silent.

"Chris." The king raised an eyebrow at his harsh tone. "My name is Chris, not human." No one dared move. Even the king's daughter, who had shown a distinct propensity to disagree, stayed still.

"I have offended you." The statement seemed to take everyone off guard. "I apologize, and I should rephrase. Christopher, please tell me what you have on your mind regarding the treaty."

Another unexpected turn: thanks to Chris's transformation, the two stood almost eye-to-eye. Chris glanced at Bernard, who gave him an encouraging nod. "Well, since it seems like I am the son of the Ignati"—when he opened his hands, a ripple passed through the group as they all leaned away—"I . . . I wish to speak on behalf of the humans."

It was probably the most pompous thing he had ever said, but he and CJ needed an out, and the voice in his head seemed to feel the treaty was their best bet. "We did not ask to come here. We did not ask for your insults, and we certainly did not ask for a fight."

Cole slouched in the darkness, his bandages catching the light of the torches above.

"Per the treaty, any human brought here by a lumi is said to be a guest who will not be harmed and will be treated like any lumi present."

"That is completely out of context! And the fact that you—"

"Colden, enough!"

Chris sneered as the man shrank into his seat.

"Continue."

Chris cleared his throat. Eira's eyes were wide, and he struggled to shake her gaze as he pushed forward.

"Even if you do not consider me a human due to my special

circumstances, my friend CJ certainly is. Your warrior, who unfortunately ended up in a medical bed, targeted him and committed an act against the treaty itself."

A few mumbles came from the other council members, and Eira returned to her seat.

"I see. And what do you wish to do with this information provided?" The question was condescending but also promised a bit of intrigue as the large man strolled toward his daughter, who refused to acknowledge him.

"Nothing." Everyone paused. "I want nothing to be done. We do not wish war on anyone, and I certainly do not wish harm to any innocent lives who would be caught in the middle." The message seemed to be received favorably by most, with only Lord Colden continuing to glare. "I only wish to go home." There was another shuffle within the group, and this time Eira jumped to her feet with obvious disapproval.

"Home? After everything that has happened?" The king's questions betrayed a tinge of annoyance at Eira's reaction.

"I wish to find the fire relic myself. If Chaoic truly seeks it, then I must find it first to prevent the killing of my people." Chris's words made little sense to him. The new, secret part of his brain churned them out as he tore his gaze away from the beautiful princess silently disagreeing with everything he said. "And maybe, by doing so, I can prove to you and your people that humans, though very different, are just as valuable as the lumi and just as worthy of peace."

A hollow laugh rang out from Lord Colden's seat, but the lack of a response from the king was much more telling.

"You cannot control it on your own, Chris," Eira said at last. He had to keep himself from shivering at her flawless voice.

"Maybe." It was as if they were the only two in the room. "But I know the feeling of not being wanted somewhere. CJ and I, we know it all too well."

His best friend stood with his mouth wide open, the conversation not going the way he must have imagined it would when Chris began.

"Well then." The king's voice stayed low as his boots clicked on marble. "It seems we have an agreement, per the Parchment."

"Father! You cannot let them go!"

The thought of Eira's wanting him to stay fueled a fire that Chris tried to keep banked.

"It is their wish, not mine." Relief cascaded through Chris's body as the king moved further away. "Bernard, I will have the trading leap opened again. Take them through, and let them go on their way. When you return, we will seal them off to prevent any other creatures—"

"Father!"

Chris could not stay and listen anymore. The realization that this could very well be the last time he heard her voice was too much.

"Chris." CJ was pulling on his arm, his look of worried confusion matching that of almost everyone else in the room.

"Let's go." Chris pushed out through the door. The compulsion to turn and face Eira brought on a nasty headache as he headed for their suite.

"How dare you let him leave, Bernard?" She was seething, the initial shock of what had happened in the hall giving way to an icy rage. "You saw what happened on the training pitch! There is no way he can control what is inside him on his own!"

The desperate point had her advanced weapons trainer shaking his head, but her shouts did not budge him.

"Eira, you have to understand that it was their choice."

"Their choice? My father nearly walked them to the leap himself!

The relief he showed the minute that Chris . . ." Eira inhaled deeply as a powerful cyclone whipped through her muscles.

"Eira, Christopher has made a choice—one that I do not agree with but must accept." She did not want to hear it. In disgust, she threw her hands up, propelling a gust of cold snow onto her bed. "You must control yourself. I know what happened earlier today has changed things for you. I know you are starting to feel things—"

"Do not act like you know what I am feeling!" The frigid interruption had Bernard straightening with an inhale of his own. "What did you tell him?"

It was becoming clear to her that this man's subtle hints and stories had been the driving force behind all they had gone through.

"Eira, I—"

"Do not lie to me!" Frost circled off her fingers and forced him to retreat. "I know you told me about the temple for a reason! I know it is not coincidence that you showed up with him right after!"

He scurried close, catching her off guard, and his look of concern shut her up as he peeked around the room.

"You, just like Christopher, are too smart for your own good sometimes." The odd retort added to his strange demeanor. "Yes, you are right about it, Eira. I knew your father had plans to send me to the human world to determine whether the council's theories were correct, and I was concerned that if I did not come back, you might never know what really happened."

His direct admission was out of character, and she struggled to understand where he was going with this as he turned away to check the door, again ensuring they were alone.

"However, when I got to the human realm, things changed. I caught the trail of two of Chaoic's creatures and found they were following Christopher and his friend wherever they went. The closer I got, the more powerful his pull was. After today, I am sure I do not have to elaborate in detail." If Bernard had already recognized it, then she was sure her father and Cole had as well. "Since he was never trained properly, his twenty-first birthday produced a magnet of energy that encircled him, one easy for a ferlup and minima to detect."

"His twenty-first birthday? When . . . ?"

A slight eyebrow raise confirmed the unexpected answer.

"You think your parents are all you have in common? Think about it, Eira! Like you, his powers are just surfacing." She gripped her necklace for support in the face of this revelation. "After I rescued the two in the human realm, I heard about the attack in the temple. I started to piece together what Chaoic and his forces might be planning."

"Which is what?" Her response brought them nose-to-nose, and his voice lowered to a whisper.

"I believe that he is looking for the fire relic, but not just as a step toward raising his army—at least not at the moment. When your mother and the Ignati sacrificed themselves that night twenty years ago, they left a void in this world, which I believe Chaoic is trying to take advantage of right now."

The clinking of glasses and sounds of muted conversation made them both shoot upright, but it was simply staff pushing a cart in the hall.

"It normally takes hundreds of years for Chaoic to collect enough souls to regenerate, but he knows that by that time, you and Christopher will have a chance to fully gain your powers. But if he can locate a relic and use its energy, he can give himself life again much more quickly. All signs point to him being stranded in the human realm, and in his current state, he would never be able to break through the frost to search for the lost ice relic. If I am right—"

"He will go after the fire relic—and Chris!" The swift realization was accompanied by the return of her rage as she stepped away from Bernard. "How could you let him leave, knowing that Chaoic will be pursuing him and knowing his inability to control his powers? You let my father close the last leap! There is no way to send—"

A soft knock jarred her, but Bernard headed directly for the door without hesitation. Ivy entered, and a nod between the two showed that this had been planned.

"What?"

Bernard held up his hand, a small smile growing as a cart rolled in, stocked with wrapped food and satchels that looked ready for a trip.

"Bianca!" Her new friend grinned as she hastily closed the door behind her.

"I have no more time to explain, as your father expects me downstairs." A few strides had Bernard grasping her hands. "I have taught you everything I can. Your next lessons—well, my dear, only you can find what is next." It felt like a goodbye. An expression of pride and worry spread across his face as he motioned to the other two. "Trust only those who you truly believe you can. These two already know what to do next, and I know that, deep down, so do you."

She was momentarily unsure. A glance at Bianca and the cart and at Ivy's warrior attire painted a clearer picture of what her friends had planned.

A slight headache set in as she tried to find some semblance of focus. "But how? My father had the last of the leaps closed, and even if we did find one, there is no way we could sneak out of this castle."

"I can take care of that," Bianca said, raising her hand. "I will have the staff keep the door closed. If anyone asks, I will tell them you have asked for privacy. It should give you enough time to get through."

Eira turned to her best friend, who smiled encouragingly.

"I must go, but, Eira . . ." Bernard dipped down to catch her gaze one more time. "He is what you have been searching for. Find him, find the fire relic, and maybe—maybe—you will find what you search for inside."

With a final wave, he left the room, leaving her and the other two alone.

The quiet after his departure gave Eira time to steady her mind. The frosty fog in her head dissipated as she scanned the room where she had grown up.

Her bed, where she had slept every night of her life, was elegantly made. The blanket was a perfect silky white that matched the walls, which were adorned with gifts—paintings of the surrounding landscape and portraits of herself as she grew. Precipitation clung to the wide window overlooking Noella, and the satin curtains were flung open, allowing the torchlights and the early-morning moon to illuminate the room.

No matter how beautiful this place was, no matter how faultless it looked, Eira felt burdened by the invisible chains that had always bound her to it. The new, deep recess of her brain interrupted her reverie with a muffled whisper that became clearer as she concentrated.

"Perfection on the outside can leave one blind, but when you find the strength on the inside, your future you will find."

She clutched her necklace, the voice waxing and waning as it repeated. The calm, nurturing tone, the clear picture it painted, left her nodding in agreement. Her abrupt turn to her two friends set them at attention as they awaited her order.

She smirked at them both. "So, what's next?"

Ivy motioned for them to huddle around the cart.

"We must take a trip to your favorite place, Eira." Her two visitors were already in motion. "We need to head to the gallery."

CHAPTER 15

The bustle of the coffee bar was at its limit when CJ sat across from him. The New Year's Eve festivities had already started, and screams and cheers rent the air inside and out. A sip of the dark roast hid another scan of the area. The sun sat high in the afternoon sky, reflecting off the buildings.

"You know, I always wanted to go down by the Birds' stadium."

An uneasy smile accompanied CJ's remark. While their trip back to Philadelphia had been effortless, their former guide had left them with an ominous warning about what might still be tracking them.

"You think we're good?" The nervousness in CJ's eyes matched his bouncing leg under the table.

Chris had been wondering the same thing as they sprinted from the sports complex where the leap had deposited them. The dark, cramped room of the abandoned factory near the football stadium, which they had indeed always spoken about visiting, was not where they had expected to end up.

Bernard had been considerate enough to wait until close to sunrise on the East Coast to send them through, and they quickly followed the rays to a nearby exit. While the sight of the field they'd often seen on television was a pleasant surprise, the thought of lurking creatures sent them running from the area as fast as they could. Their dash took them back into the familiar surroundings of buses, smog, and early-morning travelers who had no idea what might await them around every corner.

"Maybe." The word held no conviction. Chris was operating solely on caffeine and the rush of adrenaline at the thought of another giant wolf or faceless soldier melting from the shadows. "Might as well try." He stood abruptly and walked to the door. CJ, hesitating and peeking out the window first, soon joined him.

The two cautiously exited the café. The revelry did not match their attitude, but they tried to blend in with a group of city dwellers who were already well on their way to a blackout. Avoiding any alleys along the way, they soon turned onto a familiar street. Even then, they stuck to the sun-drenched sidewalk.

For Chris, it was not the fear of what he was about to do that had him tiptoeing toward their apartment. Since the fight on the training pitch, he had become in tune with the voice directing him, and while he had no idea how to control his projections, knowing that he could do *that* gave him some semblance of calm, even in the face of possible pursuit.

It was CJ who had him worried. There was still visible bruising on his cheek from the attack by Ivy's fiancé, and Chris had no doubt that something worse awaited him if they stumbled upon any monsters.

"When we get back, I'll pack up my things and get a hotel somewhere uptown."

CJ halted. "Chris."

An argument was the last thing Chris wanted. The revolving door to their apartment building offered a brief respite as they occupied their individual wedges.

"I'm not going to argue about this." A woman walked past CJ. Her pause and smile at Chris reminded him that he looked far different from when he had left. "I need to figure this shit out, and it could take time. Bernard said that those things can recognize my power now, and I can't take the chance that you—"

"I can handle myself."

It was a ridiculous statement. Sure, CJ and Chris had become embroiled in the typical schoolyard and playground fights that came with being orphans in the city when they were young. But this situation was altogether different. These were not bullies or rich kids poking fun at sneakers with holes in them; these creatures came from the depths of an evil that sought to take over the world—and they had shown what they could do to a human.

"You know this is different," Chris reminded him. He expected the annoyed glare he received in response. "We have no idea what or where this whole thing could lead me. I have no idea where to start, and if half the stuff Bernard said is true, well . . ."

They entered the elevator, joining the woman, who was still unabashedly staring.

"Which is why you need me," whispered CJ. The woman not-so-subtly tried to catch Chris's eye before he turned his back and pressed the button for their floor.

A few beeps took the group to the third floor. The woman's intensifying stare on his broad back made Chris uncomfortable as he tried to figure out if she was judging his outfit or trying to flirt. Having little time to recover after the fiery ordeal, he had kept the clothes Bernard had given him before they entered the great hall. A long-sleeve satin top matched gold-and-blue pants that hugged his newly muscular legs. The look and feel were nowhere close to his usual attire or liking.

The stitching was, of course, impeccable, and the flowing material offered a breathable fit that he could not deny was nice. But the golden lines, along with the sparkling cuff links for his shirt, gave him flashbacks to the tacky painting of his father.

"I know what you're trying to do." CJ brought him back into the conversation. A scamper out of the elevator finally left the gawking woman behind. "But I'm not going away, Chris. We have been doing this since we were little, and if you think that now, after all this, I am going to just let you—"

"You could die, CJ!" he finally burst out. "I have no idea what the hell I'm doing, and you saw what happened in that training pit! Shit, I have just as much a chance of hurting you as I do of successfully fighting off one of those things."

CJ's smirk showed that he wasn't going anywhere, no matter what Chris said.

"You think I'm going to miss the chance to see my best friend save the world? To see you face down some demon of darkness and his army? Wherever you go, I go."

It was settled, and even though everything inside Chris screamed that this was the wrong choice, knowing he had someone by his side for what was to come felt good.

He nudged CJ, and they laughed as they headed toward their apartment, returning as utterly different people.

One step inside, however, and Chris froze at a slight tug. Something was with them in the dark, and the familiar feeling that had started in Noella kicked in. A cooling rush through his veins heightened his senses, and he tilted his head.

CJ flicked on the lights, revealing two figures reclined on the musty old couch.

"So." Eira stood, her warrior ensemble almost comical against the dirty gloom of the apartment. "This is how humans live?"

"So, you just broke into our apartment?"

Even this rude greeting was enough to warm her cheeks. The mysterious pull electrified her body as he peered over at the window lock she had shattered.

Their escape had gone exactly to plan; with the help of Bianca and others on staff, along with a minor diversion by Bernard, the two arrived at the gallery without issue. Her remaining hesitation came from what she expected to find in the human realm. The stories painted a picture of savage creatures, of a world overwhelmed by gluttony and greed.

The cramped area they arrived in was not exactly nightmarish. It felt like a standard closet. Exiting the building brought them into the sunshine and unexpectedly coliseum-like environs. The arena, as Bernard had called it, was massive, with seating for thousands of humans to gather.

The lingering impressions of the stories she had heard and the knowledge that Chaoic was lurking sent them hustling to the precise location Bernard had provided Ivy before they left. However, along the way, they passed many humans, none of them fanged monsters. Most were smiling happily in celebration. There was a little gawking, but it was no worse than what she experienced in Noella.

She did briefly wonder if the celebration was related to the flaming ceremonies in Chaoic's honor. But upon further inspection, the festivities seemed to mirror the solstice parties that would be thrown in her own realm that night.

"It's impossible!" CJ finally managed, his eyes fixed squarely on Ivy, who had risen to stand beside Eira. "Bernard told us they were closing all the leaps."

"We found a master leap!" Ivy's playful undertone was unusual. "Remember that book I told you to read at breakfast? Well, there was actually one in the castle. The door to the gallery—it was one of them!"

A giggle accompanied Ivy's gleeful spin. Eira's glance at Chris showed he had also picked up on the flirtation.

"Incredible! I hardly got to read up on them, but that would mean the Essence herself made it. And if true, that would mean the leap is impossible to close. But how did you know where to find us?"

Eira inched across the worn flooring. Chris's warm gaze added to the growing swirl inside her stomach.

"Christopher of Philadelphia," she whispered, "Bernard gave us directions, the same ones you gave him before you left."

His eyes did not waver from her as she swallowed the cold air moving up her chest. His new appearance was striking, and although he filled out the lumi attire well, the new wardrobe gave the scene a feeling of unreality. Her desire to see him dressed in his original clothing confused her, given how ordinary those garments were.

Ivy and CJ continued their conversation as Chris finally opened his mouth to speak.

"Why are you here?" That was not what she was expecting, but she supposed it should not have surprised her.

"Why do you think?" If he was going to act like this, she had no problem burying the pull of connection that had helped bring her here in the first place. "Chaoic is weak. Our parents made sure of that." She pushed her chin up, the other two going quiet as she circled the table. "If he seeks to regenerate, then it will be the fire relic he tries to use."

"You think he'll go for the fire relic because humans are weak? Is that what you're getting at?" Chris's confrontational tone reminded her of when they'd first met.

"Of course not." The snappy response helped her keep her head high as her shoulders tensed. "But he cannot enter the frost or our realm through a leap in his current state. So, if he wishes to regain his powers before we gain ours—"

"So, this is about us?" The question was loaded.

"Look, Chris, it would be nice to have some help on this. Especially from the few people who know what the hell we're dealing with."

Eira appreciated CJ's interjection. It was what she had hoped to say herself, but their silly game kept her from doing so.

She glanced at Chris's hands to avoid his hot, golden eyes, which refused to let her go. She could not help but notice the biceps that flexed with his grip on the table. His crooked smile, which grew as she watched, took her by surprise. Once again, his connection with CJ was their saving grace.

"Well, it might help so I don't burn this entire place down. Not like anyone would really care if I did." With that welcome return of his sarcasm, he shuffled to a large, box-shaped object that opened to reveal an array of unfamiliar foods and drinks. "Thirsty?" He extended a bottle of something toward her. The top of it flew off as he twisted it with his fingers. "Since you'll unfortunately be missing your New Year's celebration, you might as well have a drink with us in honor of our own traditions."

He threw his head back to drain a similar bottle. A few gulps preceded a satisfied gasp as he leaned against a stone counter that appeared to support their water supply.

"Fake granite." He must have seen her inquisitive stare. "Nothing like the marble you have at home."

"You celebrate the changing of the calendars too? The chance for a new start?" They had spoken about some of their traditions over meals, but this was the first she had heard of this one.

"Oh yeah." A longer swig of the drink ended with him rising to his new full stature. "Humans go all out. But really we just use it as a reason to get drunk and party."

A laugh from CJ indicated that something funny had been said.

Chris finished his drink before Eira tried hers and ran his fingers through his black hair, seeming to draw out the gesture to let her gaze linger on him before he continued.

"We need to figure out how the hell to find this thing. Bernard might be good at fighting those demon creatures, but he sucks at giving instructions or even pointing us in the right direction."

She eased the liquid inside the bottle to her lips. The cold carbonation reeked of the hops used for making drinks in the outside villages.

"He has his own ways of speaking." The two residents laughed as she recoiled at the taste. The watery bitterness was too much for her, and she struggled to choke it down. "But he is not wrong about how you will locate it," she managed to say. "You must look inside yourself."

Chris rolled his shoulders and adopted a new seriousness.

"Is that how you intend to find the ice relic after this?"

She had been dreading this question since starting this journey. She gripped the necklace, her skin burning under the chain as the swirling from before balled up inside her.

"It is not my destiny to search for it."

They were the only words that came out—a repeat of what she had been told many times in the thirteen years since her selection when, after her selection as future queen, she had been instructed not to search for the relic herself.

Her father had always said the mandate was for her own good, but the gift of the necklace had renewed her hope that she might carry on her mother's legacy. The relic itself was a taboo subject in her realm, its form a well-kept secret. It had been described only as a spectacularly beautiful object. However, the reveal that the necklace was not the relic, along with the powerful emotional wall that her father maintained, hammered in the tenet that lumi were never to question their selection.

"How the hell is that possible?" Chris's crudeness returned, a drop of his arms ruffling his sleeves. "You're the daughter of the Iclyn. Your mother created the damn thing! And now that this dark creature is coming back, it would make sense for you to find it and keep it safe."

"That is not my selection!" Her shout set him back a step. A cold wind raced through the room and scattered the pieces of a food-stained box.

"Okay." His tone was apologetic, and she regretted the outburst.

"I'm sorry." She shook her head. "I have my spot as future queen. I have been selected to protect my people from the throne, like my father and . . . and my mother." She clutched the necklace again as she turned. The conversation and the sudden quiet churned her icy blood all the faster.

"I shouldn't have pressed. I'm sorry about that. It's just, at first, I thought maybe that thing on your neck was it, but after the stories we read and what I was told, I guess, well, I'm sure you have your reasons for everything, just as I have mine." Chris's gentle words helped, and her next breath released a frosty cloud that opened her lungs.

She managed to laugh. "This was a gift from my mother. She set it aside for me, for my father to give me on my twenty-first." The mention of her birthday had her spinning to face him once again. "I hear we have been blessed with the same day. Did your father give you anything for your twenty-first?"

CJ took the opportunity to jump in, slapping a box on the table.

"Sure as hell did! His father is super rich in this realm. He sent him a package with some cash and a note. It had some weird riddle we can't explain and a number for a bank."

"You got a note too?" she interjected. The tug inside her was growing.

"You got one? What did—"

"'Perfection on the outside can leave one blind, but when you find the strength on the inside, your future you will find. Love, Mother.'" The recitation was instinctual, her mouth opening before he had finished the question. "What did yours say?"

He slumped. A shake of his head told her all she needed to know—

another frustrating dead end. "It doesn't make sense." He threw his arms up, his muscles bulging.

"Maybe it's in the vault we visited?" CJ suggested, and the two recounted their trip to New York City.

"Did your father ever give you anything besides your birthday present?" Ivy asked Chris. The group now huddled around a fluffy, oversized chair that looked too soft to be comfortable.

"Nothing," Chris huffed, his irritation intensifying. "I never knew the guy! I lived in group homes when we were young and was only told stories that ended up being a lie. It's not like he even gave me . . ." He jerked toward CJ, bringing his hands to his friend's shoulders. "Holy shit, dude!" Chris turned to her, animation in his eyes. "I think I might know something that can help!"

CHAPTER 16

"So, you lived with a woman but were not wed to her?" The inevitable questions started as they entered the elevator of the apartment complex. Chris, who had until now been able to point out landmarks and interesting people to occupy Eira, was forced to provide an answer.

He had hoped that CJ would join him on this trip instead, but once he and Ivy went to the computer to perform additional research on his birthday package, there was no dragging him away. Chris's explanation regarding who Amber was and why his personal belongings were at her apartment obviously had not made sense to someone who still lived separately from her fiancé in the same giant castle.

"You sound like her dad." He smiled wryly at the thought of the Midwestern cowboy who had hated him so much. "He never liked the idea of us living together either." Her head tilt as the elevator started to tick off the floors to Amber's apartment showed that she still had a lot of catching up to do.

Chris hoped his ex-girlfriend had not thrown away the box as he had told her to do in his previous rage. When the metal door finally slid open, he could not help but think how different he was from the person who last rode in this elevator, not only in physical appearance but also in everything he had learned and processed along the way.

CJ, who had always been a little taller, had provided a pair of pants and a shirt that somewhat masked his new physique, which seemed to grow with each passing minute. While the long-sleeve university tee was snug, it felt more appropriate than the flashy Noellan outfit.

As they strode toward the apartment, his mind wandered. His ancestry and his frightening show of power had changed his outlook on himself and his world. For the first time in his life, Chris felt like he had a purpose—a purpose given to him by a man he had never met but who, over the last week, had finally begun to feel real.

"Is it common for fathers not to like you?" Eira's unexpected playful tone made him stumble as a new spark ignited.

"I don't know," he said, regaining his footing. "But it seems to be common lately." She dipped her head slightly, her clear blue eyes flickering as her white hair fluttered around her face.

He had not even thought to find her something new to wear before they left. The warrior attire she still sported was the only thing he had ever seen her in. For some reason, as they stood in the damp, stale-smelling hall, he could not help but wonder what she might look like in a pair of jeans and a T-shirt.

"So." He must have been too blatant with his stare because she broke away, her fingers flexing as they continued down the mangy red carpet. "Why did you leave her? If you two lived together, then you must have feelings for—"

"She left me. Well, she kicked me out." He was not about to get into this now, especially with an otherworldly princess he struggled to tear his gaze from. "She wanted to be an artist. She had ambitions to be much more, and I guess, well, I couldn't keep up."

The statement took him back to the last fight with Amber as well as their entire relationship.

"And you know what?" The clarity with which he was beginning to see was astounding. "Maybe she was right."

Once again, he grabbed at the doorknob by instinct. He cleared his throat and wiggled his shoulders to cover the mistake as he knocked softly against the scarred wood.

Eira remained a few steps back, out of sight, seemingly analyzing his last response and what it meant. He would have been lying if he said he was not doing the same.

"Well hello, Christopher." An older man with a Midwestern accent greeted him at the door. "And to what do we owe the pleasure—" Amber's father cut himself off, scanning Chris up and down unnervingly.

"Mister Hansen." A cloudiness returned to Chris's mind as he processed this new obstacle. "I . . . I just came for—"

"Chris?" Amber emerged from behind her father, looking the same as when he had last seen her. "What happened to you?"

He again had to remind himself that a great deal had changed. He rubbed his neck, his biceps bulging against CJ's shirt.

"Um, just going to the gym a little more. Hey, I was wondering if you still had that box I told you to get rid of?" One look at his old shirt, which she was wearing, answered that question, and she nodded with wide eyes.

"Yes! It's, um, it's . . ." Her nervous peep caught him off guard. The uncertainty brought her father forward with crossed arms.

"It's about time you cleaned up your mess from my daughter's apartment! What does this look like, a storage unit?"

The provocation normally would have slowed him down, but he had other, more pressing issues as he maneuvered around Amber and her father.

"Is it still in our—" It was Chris's turn to hesitate. The peek back at Amber showed that she had caught his slip. For a moment, he thought he detected remorse in her brown eyes. That half tilt of her head was something she did when recognizing that she had made a mistake.

"Yes." Her tone was soft.

The familiar grip on his insides differed from the tug he had felt over the last week. The warming sensation was much more subtle but still noticeable as he glanced at the pictures on the wall.

"Just get your things and go, Christopher!" Her father's shout ended the trance. He flexed his hands and headed for the bedroom.

The box had not been moved. He dug inside for only a second, the pocket watch catching a ray of sun through the nearby window. A quick flick unlocked the rusted metal. The fleeting, hopeful thought that maybe something had changed with the addition of his newfound powers ended as he studied the interior.

"Damnit." The icicle hands sat firmly on the twelve, and the place where the date was supposed to tick up still showed only ones. The inscriptions, the numbers, and Boston were also unchanged, faded as always.

"There has got to be something about this," he mumbled, rocking back on his heels.

"And the rest?" Amber's father was right outside the door, clearly looking for a fight, but Chris didn't acknowledge the question as he nudged past the angry man. "I always knew you to be rude, Christopher, but this! You know, I never liked you dating my daughter, and I never felt you were good enough."

"Dad, stop!" Amber's yell led to a momentary pause in the diatribe. Another glance showed she was struggling to look Chris's way.

"No, sweetie, I will not! This . . . this *boy* thinks that he can just show up after everything that has happened, grab one thing, and then just leave? Well, let me tell you something, Christopher, you were never good enough for my daughter, and you never will be! You cannot keep a job! You could never support her with her dreams, and to top it all off, you will never make anything of yourself in this world!"

This biting rant would have prompted Chris to fire back with some sarcastic comment about the man's divorce or his balding head in the past. Today, though, he had no time for that. The tug from outside the door was stronger than ever, and he could no longer stay in place as he simply nodded Amber's way.

"I know I wasn't perfect, and I'm sorry."

"Chris?" It was Eira's voice. The older man's eyes widened in disbelief at the new visitor. "I heard shouting and wanted to see if everything was all right." She spoke in a sweet whisper that increased the heat in his veins as she approached with an intentional strut.

"Yes." The simple word was all he could get out as she took his hand. His legs wobbled at her touch.

"Good." She kissed his cheek, cooling the flames flaring up in his body. A comforting winter breeze nearly picked him off his feet as she steered him toward the door.

Amber gaped after them. "Who?"

"We should be going, Chris. We have places to be and would not want to be late for any of them." Eira turned to Amber. "You have a beautiful home, by the way." She paused and motioned to the wall leading to the bedroom. "I love your paintings."

Without another word, Eira guided them out of the apartment, his jumbled thoughts the only thing keeping him from collapsing as they stepped inside the elevator. As the doors closed, he spotted Amber peering down the hall after them. Eira released his arm and shrugged with a coy smile. "They seem nice."

His heart thumped violently in his chest. "Why?"

She waited until the elevator opened on the ground floor, then pointed to the watch in his hand.

"Because you got what you came for, and we need not waste any more time." Though this was true, he wished there had been a little more behind her behavior.

"Right."

Her grasp on his forearm stopped him from moving out of the elevator, the smile growing as she leaned in with another whisper.

"And I could not listen anymore as that man lied to you." That was a much better answer, and he could not suppress a satisfied grin. "Now, let's go figure this out, together." The last word dispersed the rest of his tension. His feet gained extra pep as he ran in front of her, holding open the door as she gracefully curtsied and stepped through.

"So, this internet, you can find whatever you need on it?" Ivy hovered over CJ's shoulder. "And you can do the same with that little one. The . . . ?"

"Cell phone, yes." They both smiled—one of many they had shared that day. "I'm just trying to run down who might have sent Chris that package. It had no return address, and the post office won't give me anything." He clicked something he had called a mouse and moved the picture in front of them, but Eira quickly lost interest and paced to the wide-open window.

The chilly air was a comfort. Visiting the apartment where Chris had lived with a woman had revealed many things she found difficult to understand; the fact that they were not married, or even set to be, did not make much sense to her when taking into consideration the commitment cohabitation required. The odd swirling she had felt when she saw him lay eyes on the woman still had her reeling. The tug became powerful enough in that moment that she eventually could not help but push in and make an appearance.

Eira hardly knew this man, but the sound of that woman's father berating him had produced flashbacks to her own people's insults when the two humans first arrived. And something else had joined those shouts in her head—something that had nothing to do with her kin or even the task she had been sent here to accomplish.

The outside world was buzzing as she slid through the window. The lights around her illuminated the skyline as brightly as if it were the middle of the day.

Chris stood motionless, the city unfolding before him.

"I have a view of Noella like this back home," she said softly.

His head jerked around as she grabbed the railing of the ladders leading to the floors above and below. "That's probably much nicer than this dump." A tinge of sarcasm covered an opposing inflection.

"I think it is quite beautiful—charming, actually." Her intentional giggle brought a grin to his face, which meant she had accomplished her first objective in coming out. "The different structures and designs, I find them peaceful." She could not help but study the tall buildings around them as they fell silent.

None of the architecture matched, and a lumi builder would have fainted at the layout and spacing. But the flaws—the fact that it was built to house such inaccuracies and that the people living there accepted those flaws freely—made judging it impossible. Whoever put the time and effort into building something so enormous must have taken pride in it.

They remained in relative quiet for what felt like an hour. The only noise was the laughter inside, where Ivy and CJ seemed to be getting along just fine.

He finally broke the spell, pulling out the pocket watch and rolling it in his palm. "I guess when you grow up the way I did, you tend to focus on the bad." That genuine voice from the training pitch was back, pulling her in. "This thing . . ." He chuckled sadly as he flipped open the worn, gold-plated exterior. "I never knew my parents. I just, you know, growing up in group homes, you stop asking questions about your past and where you came from."

She had only learned bits and pieces of his family origin and recognized that he was now providing her a deeper look into how he had become the man he was today.

"I would make up stories in my head when I was young about who my parents were." He seemed to need her encouraging nod. "But this, I would have never." Another emotional laugh added to that strong pull, and she moved closer. "When I found out that my mom died giving birth to me, I—" His grief closed her throat. She had not given thought to his mother during all these talks of the Ignati and his future. "They said my dad abandoned me before he died. I thought he blamed me for what happened to her."

She had not come out to have this type of conversation, but given his firm grip on the pocket watch and his wavering tone, he had been holding this in for a while; she would help him expel it.

"It was not your fault, Chris," she said instinctively.

"I know." A smile and slight shake of his head said otherwise.

"I mean it, Chris. You had no control—"

"Answers to the past will not soothe your mind, but when the time is right, your future you will find." His interruption forced her to adjust.

"Excuse me?" She was the one shaking her head this time. He shrugged and turned to face her.

"It's what was written in my note." He craned his neck and rolled the watch across his palms. "I was being rude when you first showed up, and after you told me what your mom wrote to you—"

"Do you know what it means?" Excitement took hold, and her body found a happy medium between the freezing of her blood and the heat of his gaze.

"Not a damn clue!" His humorous shout startled them both into a laugh. A touch of her leg against his hand further balanced her internal temperature. "You?"

She could not tell if her cheeks were freezing or on fire. His eyes studied her face as a lukewarm shiver crawled up her side. He was genuinely asking, and she was enjoying every second of their conversation. For the first time in what felt like forever, she was chatting amiably with someone who truly understood what she was feeling—someone who wanted to listen to her and was not merely trying to gain a stronger political position.

"Not a damn clue either." Her playful words were unbecoming and yet right for the moment. He chuckled, shaking the platform where they sat.

A loud bang in the sky shot her over to him. The blackness above lit up in an explosion of colors that flashed and faded. "Fireworks," he whispered by her ear. Her grip on his shirt threatened to rip the cotton as her heart beat out of rhythm. "It's part of the celebration. Beautiful, aren't they?"

She hardly heard the question; her ears were ringing so loudly that minutes passed before she realized that more were firing off in the distance. The thud of her heart grew overwhelming. She tried to tell herself that it was her warrior response to a potential threat. Another few seconds locked with Chris, however, proved that to be a lie.

"Yes, yes it is." She gave up trying to figure out what this tug was. Her mind no longer focused on anything but the tan face of the man before her.

His breath held an intoxicating campfire aroma with a tint of birchy sweetness that ended any remaining fight. His palm against her thin, armor-plated top radiated heat, and her firm grip on his shirt intensified as her muscles coiled to bring them closer.

She had been in this position before, with her fiancé in his chamber or during trips to the outer villages. But all those times with Cole had felt different. And while his embrace whipped up a primal instinct to want more, it had never produced the energy Chris's presence did tonight.

The sheer strength and power in his touch and the increasing pressure on her side showed he was experiencing the same thing. Those calming golden eyes refused to let her go.

"Chris!" CJ's shout sent them scattering in opposite directions. An icy blush smeared her cheeks as his sparked bright red. "Sorry."

"What is it, CJ?" The annoyance of Chris's tone was replicated by Eira's motion to her own best friend, who had joined them.

"Well, I think we found something."

Eira found it difficult to catch her breath, although the exploding colors had already stopped.

"I think we found where the package was sent from."

Chris clutched his chest lightly, his breath coming in puffs. "Great. Where did it come from?" His tone reflected very little interest, despite the crucial nature of this information. He looked over to her, and the tug inside almost threw her directly back at him as she grabbed the metal railing for support.

"Boston."

Chris twisted back toward CJ in shock. The pocket watch in his hand shot open, and he analyzed the inside of the gold plate, though he already knew what it said.

"It said it was sent from Boston."

CHAPTER 17

"So, this Boston, is it close?" Ivy had been asking nonstop questions since they left the apartment. CJ, who had explained that the place they'd arrived a few minutes before was called a car dealership, seemed more than willing to answer whatever Ivy threw his way.

"Not too far," CJ answered with his typical politeness. "Finding a dealership that would take cash during a holiday made a late start to the day, but if we get lucky, we might make it by midnight." His eyes seemed to have trouble staying in place. The attire Chris had bought for the two visiting warriors did not help his situation.

Eira was still not overly comfortable in the long-sleeve wool top, which was pulled tight to her chest due to the weight of the satchel around her back. The lack of armor made for an odd choice for dress. She felt incredibly vulnerable. Even the pants, described as "denim," seemed unlikely to have value in the face of a minima or ferlup.

However, Chris had made a good point that the two visiting lumi would need to blend in; per the treaty, they should not have been here. Whatever the actual excuse, Eira had not missed the subtle glance from the son of the Ignati when she stepped out of the changing area earlier that morning.

"You have never been to this place called Boston?" asked Ivy breathily.

"No." The young man rubbed his neck. "But that pocket watch, well, Chris always said it was made in Boston—or, at least, had Boston written on the inside."

"And the numbers?" Eira broke into the playful conversation; the information was more important than a crush.

CJ turned to her. "We never knew what they meant, and Chris never cared. He thought it was just junk, but when we started to play around with everything last night, we found a connection."

A sudden roar from one of the machines they were trying to purchase made Eira jump, which she tried to play off by straightening on her heels.

"That giant castle!" Ivy followed her shout with a girlish titter.

"Mansion, but yeah, very close to a castle." CJ was clearly enjoying his time with Ivy, but while it was nice to see her best friend with someone who appreciated her hobbies, Eira had grown tired of the immaturity. "The numbers matched an address and area code located on a small island outside of Boston, but that is all I could find out."

A young child with a crown pranced by them. The smile on her ebony face was wide as she ran to an older woman who must have been her mother.

"I used some of the public directories, but it is said to have been built ages ago. Nothing else came up, but the last time any service was done, was, well, twenty-one years ago."

The little girl clinging to her mother's legs was no longer enough to distract Eira from the intrigue.

"Did you say twenty-one years ago?"

CJ nodded as the space they stood in began to fill up with humans.

It took Eira a few moments to settle down. While the time frame was not all that shocking, the fact that it had such a direct correlation to her birth made her uncomfortable. She adjusted the strap of her satchel and moved her hand to the necklace for support. The other two rambled about the upcoming trip as she familiarized herself with their surroundings.

She found it interesting that Chris had selected this type of transportation, as he often complained about the gases killing the Essence in the human realm. The machine they were buying seemed to be one of the main culprits. Nevertheless, the speed at which these devices allegedly operated was quite appealing, considering the potential threats hiding not far away.

The yellowish lights above cast a cheerless reflection off the fake-tile floor as she padded along in footwear the humans called sneakers. While this loose footwear was nowhere close to practical for the battles they were about to fight, the soft interior offered a cushiony comfort she was growing fonder of by the minute.

A hand on her shoulder jarred her from her thoughts. A cold rush accompanied the touch as a man with an untrimmed beard grinned lasciviously.

"You must be here to look at the Porsche." She cringed away from his slimy voice. The stench that had hit her when she entered this place was all over his tongue—the smell of that dark, heavy bean that humans liked to drink in the mornings. "You would look absolutely stunning in it."

The odd way he flexed out his mediocre chest did not do the fabric of his suit any justice. His eyes constantly flickered to her chest, and ice churned inside her as she prepared a swift reply to his crudeness.

"Mister." The little girl from before had joined them. Her sweet squeak steadied Eira, bringing back memories of Aspen. "Can I please have another cookie from the table over there? My mommy told me to ask you since I already had—"

"Quiet, kid!" That needless cruelty infuriated Eira. "Can't you see I'm busy? It's bad enough I have to wait for the banks to clear your mom's damn credit. Now I've got to babysit as well?"

"Sorry." The girl's puffed-out lip was too much to bear. Eira adjusted her shoulders as the icy blood in her veins surged.

"Kids, I'll tell ya." His arrogant laugh only dropped her temperature more. "But listen, sweetheart, if you want to take a ride in the one out back, I can have . . ."

She was done with this. The only thing keeping her from strangling the human in front of her was the treaty, which forbade such a thing. The bulging stomach and greasy black hair suggested that this man would hardly put up a fight if confronted; he didn't have such effort in him.

"It's got a lot of room, and I would love—"

She left the pompous man to talk to himself and closed in quickly on the little girl who had just been scolded. The false crown on her tiny head twinkled prettily in the lighting of the shop.

"Excuse me," Eira began awkwardly, having never spoken with a child of this realm. "Was this the treat you were looking to have?" The little girl twirled around, her expression matching those of the children in Noella as Eira pointed to a plate of desserts.

"Yes!" the little girl squealed with pleading eyes that revealed an innocence entirely at odds with lumi stories of a human realm filled with thieves and vandals.

"Here you go." The baked treat felt hard and stale when Eira grabbed it from the table and handed it over, but the immediate joy on the girl's face inspired her to ignore the flaws.

"Thank you!"

Eira smiled wider when the first bite sent crumbs in every direction. The young girl remained in place, munching away with a grin.

"Are you a fairy princess?" Eira asked. A poke at the crown confirmed that it was crafted from a flimsy material.

"I wish! But Mommy says that fairy princesses aren't real."

"Well." She peeked around, knowing that what she was about to do was incredibly foolish. The man from before had already moved on to another target, and everyone else seemed absorbed in their conversations. "From what I was told by a *very* important human"—as if on cue, Chris came into sight as he chatted with a salesman—"you can be whatever you want in this realm." She had not come to break any amendments of the treaty, but her failures with Aspen inspired her to do something special for this little girl, who seemed to need it.

As she slowly opened her palm, a sparkle came to the child's eyes. The small swirl of snow building from her veins made the little girl gasp in amazement.

"Don't give up on your dreams." An inner tug prompted her to close her hand immediately. She stood upright at the feeling of being watched, though she remained focused on her new friend.

"Are you . . . ?" The whisper was so faint that Eira had to lean down again to hear.

"A secret, just like that treat." The little girl clapped joyfully, the baked dessert no longer of interest as she fixated on Eira's palm. "You should be getting back to your mother. But remember, use your free will to be whoever you want to be."

Chris's mantra sounded stilted coming out of her mouth, but the girl didn't seem to notice or mind. She finally skipped off, her spin and final wave soothing Eira's slight angst related to breaking the rules of the treaty.

"You could get in trouble for that," said a steady, calm voice behind her.

"I am still surprised you even know what is in that treaty."

Chris, who was holding a set of keys in his hand, only shrugged and smiled when she turned to face him.

"You got a Mercedes?!" CJ raced up to them. "I'm driving! You have to let me drive."

"No way," Chris scoffed with a wink. One more glance her way sent the comforting warmth flooding through her veins again. "I paid for it. I'm driving."

The chatter around them became a mumble as Eira fell in step with him. Her cheeks welcomed the cool breeze that awaited them when they finally stepped outside.

"So, it is common for human males to blatantly inspect a human female for primal fun?"

Eira had been stuck on this subject during the meal in the small diner. The clock on the wall, which seemed to be running in slow motion, became the main source of Chris's attention as he contemplated how to make up for lost time. It had been a long few hours of driving. The New Year's traffic and the constant questions as they passed landmarks and cities generated a headache that he was now trying to fight off.

"Well, yes. I mean no, but yes." CJ's attempt to help out their species met with little success. Eira's run-in with the sleazy car salesman held all her focus as she tried to wrap her mind around why he would be so forward.

Chris was tempted to supply the real reason. The snug fit of the long-sleeve tee and jeans had caused even his mind to wander when she exited the fitting room. His original thoughts about what she might look like in such attire were nowhere close to capturing the mesmerizing figure across from him. The car salesman, probably acting on the same toxic masculinity that had drawn him to the job in the first place, had no doubt been taken by her appearance, which had drawn quite a few other eyes in the dealership as well.

"I think what CJ is trying to say is that humans tend to judge people based on what they look like. Of course, we are not all perfect, like your people." It came out wrong; the women frowned, and he regretted intervening.

"You believe us to be perfect?" Eira's question was dangerously playful, and he feared what was to follow. "What makes us so perfect?"

He had backed himself into a corner. CJ attempted a valiant rescue.

"Well, Chris is always trying to save the world. So, I think he means that the way you operate, with your self-sustaining lifestyle and agriculture, is just so perfect." Their guests did not look convinced. "He always hates how our people pollute and use politics to keep most of our people down."

"I see." Eira leaned over her plate with a judgmental grimace. The eggs were still steaming, but she shuddered after she took a bite.

"What? Not perfect eggs?" Chris could play the game too, and the lowering of her eyes preceded another forced swallow as she tried not to let him gain the upper hand.

"They are just fine." She cleared her throat, unable to hide her dissatisfaction with the taste. "And you're wrong about our being perfect. We have our problems, some of which are very similar to yours."

This was obvious from his trip to Noella, but he was surprised she could admit it out loud.

"But it does intrigue me." A more lighthearted tone kicked in. "Are you saying you do not have the same values as the men around you? Do you not enjoy the physical features of a woman?"

The cracked plastic of the seat popped as Chris shifted uneasily. His insides cooled under the force of Eira's stare.

"I . . . I, um . . ."

She had won. The careful flip of her white hair made it impossible not to study her in more detail. The placement of her hands under her chin also came across as a purposeful tease, and he had to clear his throat. "You tell me. Do you not do the same thing? I mean, look at your fiancé." A slight edge infiltrated his voice, to his instant regret as she tensed her shoulders.

"We trust the Essence to set us up with the right mate," Ivy jumped in, rescuing her friend. "She selects for us a perfect complement, one who will better our people." She trailed off as she looked at CJ, and Chris could only assume that her pained inhale was because she had just remembered what that truth meant for her.

The awkward silence lasted for a few minutes. The only sound was of clinking plates and a fryer bubbling on the other side of the wall. When the check arrived, Chris hastily grabbed it and followed the waitress to the register.

"Do you know of any motels nearby?" He still could not tear his eyes from Eira, who had not said a word since his petulant comment.

"There's one a few miles down, but I wouldn't stay there. I heard they had bedbugs not long ago." The helpful answer had him smiling as he fumbled with the bills before handing them to the younger woman. "But if you head up Ninety-Five a little more, you'll run into a few nicer chains."

The bags under her eyes gave the impression that she had been working for quite a while. A peek at the stained apron and untamed ponytail of black hair drove that point home.

"Long day?" He had not come here for small talk, but the sagging of her shoulders and defeated return of his change begged for a modicum of human decency.

"Double shift," she said. Her skirting of the question was a familiar defense mechanism he had used many times.

"I'm sorry. I didn't mean to pry. Thank you for the information on the motel; appreciate that." A connection to her pain had him digging for extra bills. She looked taken aback as he handed over three hundreds.

"What's this for?"

"Tip," he said softly. Given his new resources, he felt it was only right to share with someone who needed it more.

"But why?"

"I know you probably don't want handouts or my sympathy. But I also know you'll put that money to better use than I will."

A slight grin finally emerged as she folded the bills and jammed them into her apron.

"Thank you." She nodded before wiping her cheek. "Thank you so much."

He started back to the booth while the other three stood.

"Typical Chris." His friend's inquisitive gaze told him that the group had overheard the conversation. "Always trying to save the world." CJ's wholesome quip made Chris chuckle.

"Was it her physical appearance?"

Eira had him chuckling louder; her genuine interest, however, kindled the spark in his stomach as she peered at the waitress, who was disappearing into the kitchen as they headed for the door. "Do you enjoy the look of her working—"

The lights flickered, halting them in place. The shiver up Chris's spine was so hot that he almost cried out in pain. The diner went completely quiet; not even the hum of the heating system was audible as an eerie stillness set in.

"Do you feel that?" Eira inched closer to the long counter, which held only salt and pepper shakers and a few napkin dispensers.

A scream from the kitchen struck him like lightning. Cognitive thinking shut off, and Chris became squarely focused on the terror emanating from the swinging door behind the counter, his field of vision narrowing into a tunnel of outer darkness.

An ear-piercing shriek was followed by the sight of a familiar black gown. The faceless creature glided toward them from the darkened end of the diner where they had just eaten. As Chris regained his center of gravity and began to piece his surroundings together, he searched for the guiding voice in his head. A mix of instinct and unfamiliar basic training maneuvers prompted each step, but a heavy fog fought for control of his body even as his skin started to boil.

Undeterred by a yell, he jumped around the stools at the bar and through the swinging doors. The speed of his jarring entrance nearly snapped the flimsy wood off its hinges.

"Christopher." He had heard that low moan before. Flashbacks of the bar in Philadelphia and the alley in New York added to the swirling fireball in his stomach begging to be unleashed. *"Christopher."*

He could not block it out. The whisper grew louder as he passed a wooden prep station and two old stoves gone cold.

"Christopher." A few more seconds saw him through the kitchen and into a smaller back room. Shelves on either side were filled with bread and condiments for hungry customers.

"Christopher." It was louder. A tug from the fiery inferno inside him finally halted his body in the face of the external magnetism drawing him forth.

A blank, ghastly face suddenly filled his field of vision. Cloudy white eyes were all he saw before the room went pitch black, the shadows seeming to press in on him like a trash compactor.

"You could not save her." The jolt to his insides returned with the slithering new voice. The tone had changed. His body overheated in an instant, and he doubled over in pain. *"Her soul is mine now."* The sound drifted closer. His eardrums were on the verge of exploding as the intense pressure reached an unbearable level. *"You have failed her, and now you will be—"*

An arctic blast from behind him ended the moaning. The room brightened ever so slightly as he dropped to his knees.

Another shriek forced his hands to his ears. The compression felt likely to crush his skull, and a headache pounded through him. Every breath was more strained. He gasped for what oxygen he could find as the ashy taste returned in force, a thick smoke choking him with each wheeze.

"Take control, Chris!"

The mysterious inner voice supplanted the screeching moan that had been controlling him.

"Take control!"

One more wave of ice lent him the relief to control his breathing. A chill crept around him, marshaling his focus.

"Chris!" He lifted his head enough to see Eira returning from the loading area. The tips of her fingers were frozen over as she dropped by his side. "Chris! Are you okay? What were you doing?"

He had not realized how far he had traveled. The frozen specks coating the walls showed that he had missed a battle while in his comatose state.

"I . . ." The shuffling of feet brought more awareness as he struggled to unclog his mind. A cloud of ash hung about his head, and his gaze finally came to rest on the area where the minima had initially greeted him. "She's . . ." A body lay motionless on the floor. The evil whisper now made sense. "She's gone!"

He could not prevent the tears. The fear and pain strangling his every muscle felt like they came from a direct feed from the waitress's body, whose eyes still seemed to be begging for him to help.

CHAPTER 18

Eira stood on her toes and pushed her ear against the hotel room's steel-framed door but heard nothing on the other side. She had hoped to pick up an indication that Chris had recovered somewhat. While Ivy and CJ had decided to stay down at the area serving wines and carbonated hops drinks, Chris wasted little time paying for the rooms before leaving.

The group of minima had appeared without warning. The stealth and strength of their arrival was likely due to their ability to feed in relative peace. Since the passing of the Ignati, they'd been free to roam this realm, unlike in the lumi realm with the Legion tracking them.

A brief moment of surprise had given the first minima the upper hand. A snap of Ivy's spiratus rocked the windows, her prompt action allowing Eira to regain composure, but the attack came too late. The minima caught Eira just enough to force a stagger. Fortunately, the gash from its long nail began healing immediately, thanks to her icy blood.

Although the original attack caused the foursome to scatter briefly, that was the lone strike Eira would permit the minima to land. An instant follow-up thrust of her hands sent the initial creature back to where it had come from, the resulting flash of black smoke a chilling indication that they were not alone in this space or realm.

Early in her training, Bernard had told stories of Chaoic recycling his soldiers and, when he was strong enough, collecting their souls upon their defeat. Ivy's swift strike at another minima reinforced those claims as it likewise erupted into smoke.

A third minima was the last to meet its fate in the main dining area. Its thrashing nails ripped toward CJ, who had dived under their table for safety after the initial shrieks. Another quick thrust by Ivy disoriented the creature, and her whirling cane smashed its black skull, making it stumble with a resounding scream that threatened to shatter the windows.

Eira wasted no time finishing off the monster. A snap of her wrist produced the ice whip she so enjoyed using, and one powerful pull turned the rope around its neck into a noose. The subsequent silence and plume of black soot ended the fight in that arena. However, a new worry sent them all on a frantic search for Chris when the lights came back on.

"Chris?" Her knock reverberated in the empty hallway. The graying rug below her was stained from years of traffic. "Are you okay?"

While the first three minima had behaved typically, the fourth had used the female server as bait, drawing Chris in with her suffering as it feasted on her soul for power. Chris had somehow escaped into the back room, avoiding the other three minima but coming into direct contact with the last one, which stood without striking.

In place of physical aggression, a mental attack had him struggling to breathe when she burst through the kitchen. A lightning-quick thrust of her hand prevented the minima from accomplishing its goal. Its feeble attempt to escape was halted by a rush of ice from her nails that pinned it to the wall by its black robe. Her instincts had fully taken over at that point; one emphatic point with her finger launched an icicle at the struggling creature's jugular. It went quiet upon impact. The lights flickered a little brighter once the final soulless creature burst into the abyss and disappeared.

"Chris?" The only noise she heard as she gently nudged open the unlocked door was one she had rarely heard in Noella. She struggled to comprehend the sniffling and eased into the room.

"Chris?" His weeping faded in and out. Her chest tightened as she drew near the bed. The lone light by the desk illuminated him where he sat with his head in his hands. Her hesitation was unfortunately the only reaction she could offer.

No lumi warrior would ever show such vulnerability, especially at a time like this, when every decision had to be carefully processed. To most in her realm, this behavior would be considered weakness, and it would only prove the council's point that Chris was incapable of completing his task.

"I can't do this," he mumbled between sobs, shifting violently on the bed. "I can't!"

Her feet stumbled where the tug inside took her, and she dropped to his side without thinking, her arms enclosing his broadened shoulders. He shivered under her touch.

"Chris." She had not been trained to handle this. Her tongue froze as she contemplated what words might help him.

"I'm not who you think I am, Eira. I can't be this person." He was fighting her, but her arms refused to give in to his strength. "I'm not strong enough. I can't be him!"

The despair in his eyes when they looked at each other was so heavy that Eira could not help but hold him tighter.

"Chris, you can—"

"Don't even try, Eira!" He broke from her grasp, bolting up and clasping his hands together. "I have no idea what I'm doing. Just a week ago, I was just another guy. Sure, I was a failure, an underachiever, but that was who I was! This . . . this is not who I am."

The returning smell of sulfur propelled her off the bed, a not-so-subtle warning that he was again losing control of the force inside him.

"You *can* control it, Chris." She tried her best to stay calm in light of the smoldering above his open palms.

"I felt it, Eira. I could feel her fear, the terror before she died." Regret played across his features. "She was innocent, and I couldn't save her. She was just working a double shift, for fuck's sake!"

Now it made sense. The image of the dead servant came back to her as he started to pace sporadically.

"The only reason she's dead is because of me, just like that poor homeless man. Because that thing was looking for me! It used her to get to me." She was a bit shocked that Chris had picked up on its plan—a good observation for someone just learning the ways of the minima. "How can I save this whole world if I can't save one person?" The thrust of his arms nearly produced a projection, but she stopped it by grabbing his hands.

The heat was tremendous. Her blood began to simmer, but she refused to let go for fear of what might happen if she did.

"Chris." She struggled not to tremble. His begging eyes made her forget about the pain as she searched deep for an answer. "I know." The burning began to die out. "I know how you feel." The sentence caught her off guard. Clarity returned to his golden irises as he leaned over inquisitively. "I understand being scared of your future, of not feeling worthy of their sacrifice." She thought of the picture of her mother in the gallery, the power in the Iclyn's fingers prominent as she rested perfectly poised on the canvas. "Sometimes I wonder—"

"You're wrong." His interruption brought them closer. The sulfur smell was gone, replaced by the birchy sweetness of last night. "You are worth everything. You are just like her in every way. You are powerful, intuitive, and beauti—"

She had to pull away. The grip on her insides took her mind to a place she had so far valiantly fought off.

"I'm sorry." His sincere apology merely added to the blizzard whipping through her body. "I didn't mean to make you uncomfortable." This was a turn of the tables, given the position he had been in a few seconds ago, but it cooled her temperature to a comfortable level. "I just see myself and how I have no idea what I'm doing. And then you, what you did on the training pitch that day, I felt it! You were so precise."

"You *can* control it, Chris." The avalanche cascading through her muscles took her right back by his side. "I too felt it that day, and I know you can control it." Maybe it was wishful thinking or the immense pull this young man had on her, but she believed every word she spoke.

He was not the perfect choice for this task, but neither was she. Her flaws were just as significant, even if they were better hidden. It was not only her fleeting attempts to find her true power that made her ashamed, although the thirteen years of working with the best lumi trainers had still not produced half of what her mother could do. It was also her disconnect from her own people, the ones she was tasked with protecting and the ones who—until this man had so bluntly noted her failure—she had been ignoring for the sake of her self-pity.

"What if I fail?"

She almost smiled. She had asked herself this same question many times while growing up, and even now.

"What if I can't figure out where this fire relic is? What if I can never control—"

"You *can*, Chris." Her finger rolled over the back of his hand, holding it open as she gently rubbed against veins that burned hot.

"How do you know that?" His eyes locked onto her, the gusts coming to a stop as his palm turned over and pressed down on hers.

"Because you are different."

The answer was so obvious that she could not believe she had missed the real reason she could not stay away from him, why she wanted nothing more than to pull him close.

He was not a warrior. He was the furthest thing from it, and yet, as all of this craziness unfurled before him, he never flinched. After all the insults, he took on this task, even volunteering to perform it alone. She knew it was not the search for his father's power that motivated him; his inability to control it was so telling that she wondered how Bernard did not see it in the first place. What motivated him, and what drove this growing tug inside her, was his selflessness and willingness to sacrifice everything in an instant, no matter the odds.

"You care, Chris." The interlocking of their fingers brought her body to rest against his. "You care about them all. The waitress, your friends, your peop—"

His lips met hers, ending the battle she had been fighting. A rush of fire and ice decimated the blockages she had built up.

No training or stories could have prepared her for this; no night with Cole in his chamber remotely compared to the ecstasy racing through her. Chaoic, the relics, and her search for her hidden powers all seemed trivial compared to what was happening in this room. The touch of his hands on her lower back elicited an unfamiliar moan as she shivered from a comforting chill.

"Eira." Just her name in his mouth was too much. Her fingers dug into his firm shoulders as he dropped them to the bed.

"It's okay, Chris." The confirmation was for both of them. Her final thought, as he ran a hot fingertip over her bare skin, was not of a relic or a vile creature but of this young man's kind smile. "I want to be here, with you, tonight." The firmness of his hand grew with her whisper. His hot palm cooled against her thigh as her body tingled with the caress of his lips against her neck.

Surely this was not how her selection was supposed to play out.

Her entire life, the lessons she had been taught, and her training were all meant to stop her from an impulsive and emotional decision like the one she was about to make. However, as Chris's warm thumb slid up her ribcage, she could not have cared less about any of it. Because right now, in this realm, all she wanted was the man lying on top of her. The fiery blaze in his eyes was the final push toward an agreement that was just between them—one that required no forged relic or signed parchment and one that, no matter how hard they had tried to avoid it, they had been moving toward from the minute they met in the great hall.

Chris directed the Mercedes into the right lane. His eyes refused to leave the windshield despite the weight of the direct gaze from the woman beside him.

"Shouldn't be long now." His poor attempt to keep from cracking drew a broad smile from Eira in the passenger seat, which was clear in his periphery.

The roller coaster that somehow ended with them in bed together had left him more confused than when he had been dragged out of the diner. He had been so focused on the waitress that he had not realized the full scale of the ambush. The icy splatters and the overturned and snapped chairs illustrated the ferocity of the battle that had occurred while he was in his trance.

Even the short ride to the hotel was blurry, his mind trying to shake the image of the woman—who had only wanted to make an honest living—lying stricken and motionless on the floor. A hot shower and hard liquor from the minibar did not remove the stale taste from his tongue. An hour or so alone only made it worse, until Eira entered with a soft knock. The sobbing that had refused to subside took him back into that part of his brain that had abandoned him in the diner, and he had seemed on the verge of another meltdown.

On this occasion, though, Eira's touch, along with the softness of her voice, helped him find a semblance of command. The fire subsided as she voiced her own fears and struggles. At first, he'd thought she was trying to prevent another explosive encounter, but the force of her admissions convinced him they meant much more.

"Traffic wasn't bad; we actually made good time."

Another smirk greeted him as he finally locked eyes with the woman who had changed his world.

The sunlight breaking through the wintry northeastern clouds sparkled off her pearl-white skin. The gentle brush she gave her matching hair brought her gleaming fingertips into view, sending a shiver up his spine as he remembered how they had sent his skin into a frenzy the night before.

It was not just the physical release that had been different. While that primal pull had kept them busy for quite some time, the other, more profound connection was what had him struggling to take his eyes off her as the traffic around them began to move forward.

"This place looks so elegant!" Ivy snapped him from the daydream. The thought of Eira's touch on his bare chest left every hair on his arm raised as he straightened his hands on the wheel.

"Boston is one of the older cities near us. It might remind you a bit of where you're from."

CJ's response had Chris peering into the mirror. The two in the back exchanged one of their frequent glances, which seemed especially weighted with meaning today. Chris had not caught up with his best friend before they left. However, based on the soft, suggestive tones in the back seat, something had also happened between them.

"Look at that!" High-rise buildings surrounded the Mercedes as they took a turn onto one of the main streets. The midday traffic brought them to a stop at a red light. "All these people!"

Eira joined in on the gawking.

"Some of these buildings are used for workspaces, offices where people trade goods and information." CJ was becoming a pro at explaining the human world to them. "That over there is a church. The different worship groups we spoke about last night—that's where some of them have their services."

A turn down another street had Chris adjusting the cell phone in his hand. The GPS directed them to their destination as he tried to remain steady and focus on the road ahead.

"Eira, look at that waterfall in the open! It reminds me so much of the one near the courtyard. The one we set up for your wed—" Ivy's sudden silence was a wake-up call. Eira's eyes, which just seconds ago had been filled with so much joy, widened as a harsh realization set in.

Disquiet overtook the group. Chris had never been good at dealing with such situations, and the twinge in his stomach jumped out of his mouth before he could stop it.

"Yeah, about that. When is the date?" He hated the sarcasm he always reverted to, but this reminder hit him like a kick to the gut.

"Spring." Eira's whisper was scarcely audible as she shifted and peered out the window.

A knot of heat formed within him. His attention jumped to the woman in the back, who had ended the fairy tale they were all living in.

"And how about yours, Ivy?" The plea in her face forced an ashy swallow. Regret took Chris back to the phone in his lap.

"Late summer." Another whisper, one that revealed the growing disappointment among them. "My selection was, I mean, during my selection with Andri, it was deemed we would be married in the summer or fall."

He was not about to peek in the mirror again. The lack of movement from CJ told him all he needed to know.

"Well, I'm sure they will be very beautiful." It was childish to have pushed it this far. His exhale and spin of the wheel rolled them around a bend as they exited the city's busy downtown.

The rest of the ride was not accompanied by conversation. The skyline slowly disappeared as they made their way to the harbor district. A weight had been added to Chris's knots from earlier as time ticked away. His thoughts refused to eliminate the picture of Eira with the bulky lumi warrior who had attacked him a few days before.

"I think this is as far as we can go in the car." He bobbled the Mercedes into park. A dock housing boats of all kinds broke through the fog as the smell of raw fish took over.

"Wow!" CJ spoke for all of them as Chris threw himself out of the vehicle. A cloudy smoke in his head kept him from truly engaging with the stench.

"We should move." Chris tried not to sound dismissive. Eira and Ivy's polite attempt to ignore the reeking fumes kept him in check. "The only way to get to the island is by boat. The ferries are closed this time of year, so we might have to throw some cash around to get a ride."

A brisk walk took him away from the car in a hurry, but the sound of brand-new sneakers chasing after him meant he was not getting away easily.

"Chris!" The image of Eira in his arms was overrun by that of the large, blond warrior she was engaged to. "Chris, please! I would like to talk about—"

"No need." The sarcasm returned as he spun with a smile. "We have work to do. It's why you came here, right?"

Her shoulders sagged.

"Please, Chris. Now is not the time to make emotional—"

"Emotional?!" He cut her off; the other two, who had kept their distance, stopped at his shout. The rising smoke in his chest nearly choked him. An exhale and clench of his hands released some of it as he caught himself. "There is nothing emotional about this, Eira," he said, his voice dropping to a deep, stern tone. "You came back to help me find the relic. Now we have a chance to find it." A glimpse at Ivy and CJ found them lowering their heads to avoid his gaze. "So? Are we going to do this or not?"

The directness made his point. Eira hesitated only briefly before stomping forward.

"Yes," she responded with strangled defiance. "We should not waste any more time." She flashed by in a huff as she headed toward the dock and boats below.

CHAPTER 19

"You should have stayed down in the hub. It's wicked cold out here!" The boat captain's thick Boston accent wafted over the rhythmic splashing of the icy bay waters.

"Why does he sound so weird?" Eira asked softly as the weathered, muscular man chatted with CJ and Ivy by the boat railing where they had all gathered for their journey.

"It's an accent. They all have it up here."

The captain had been the only person down by the harbor not yet out during this winter season, and he was more than willing to take the cash Chris provided for the trip. The last hour on the boat had given the group time to recover. Sure, the thought of Eira with her fiancé remained. Given the night they had shared, he had little doubt that things would change, but reality brought him back to his mission and the pocket watch rolling in his fingers.

Jamming the watch back into his pocket, Chris joined the small talk. "You been out to this island before?"

"No suh!" The captain tilted his head before adjusting his camouflage beanie. "Normally just hikahs going to this place, and never in the wintah." Another curious glance from Eira was surely due to the accent. "But I know the place you're lookin' fah. It has a private dock. I'll bring it in close."

"If you've never been out here before, how do you know about the dock?" Chris asked. He studied their captain. A tattoo peeking up from his collar suggested that he had been military at some point.

The man's laugh was deep and reverberant as the boat slowed. "I've heard talk. The place yah lookin' fah been shut up fah twenty years and gets no visitahs." An old, rickety wooden dock appeared in the distance. The late-afternoon haze gave way to a snowy-white patch of grass at the far end of the platform. "Until you, of course."

His smile was profound, his words carrying an undertone so allusive that Chris could not help but pry.

"Do you know—"

"You said you want me back by sunup?" The interruption seemed deliberate. "That still yah plan?"

Chris had every intention of asking more questions.

"It's time."

The interruption of the crystal-clear voice in his head synced perfectly with the appearance of the old mansion.

"It's time to go."

A mossy green tint had taken over the white siding. Thick vines and verdant leaves draped over all three stories of windows. The sprawling backyard held an old stone firepit and a few decrepit lawn chairs overturned and covered with snow.

"Charming." CJ's snide remark took the boat captain over to the side with a snicker. The rope he cast out wrapped around a warped wooden post.

"Like I said, been shut up fah years." The man's cracked hands were hard at work. A slight bump and creak announced that it was time to disembark.

"Half now, half when you—" A wave cut Chris off, the money he extended disappearing as the captain peered up at the mansion.

"I figure yah good for it." Chris had little time to analyze this oblique remark as the rest of the group shuffled by and onto the uneven planks.

With a final glance at the man, he followed his friends off the boat. The wood bowed under his feet, and he hastily made his way onto solid land. The captain wasted no time pulling away as a wintry gust kicked up over the island, the engine's roar growing and then disappearing into the fog.

"So this is where your father lived?" While Eira looked comfortable and unbothered by the chill, the rest of the group shivered and gripped the sweatshirts they had purchased at a rest stop that afternoon.

Chris didn't know how to answer. The tug from his insides enticed him to march right up the snow-covered yard and in through the two steel-hinged doors that probably hadn't budged in twenty years. However, the thought of what might await him and the tranquil scenery around them kept his feet stuck in the mud patch he had discovered the hard way after stepping off the dock.

"It's quiet," Ivy commented as Chris scanned the area.

The island itself was not extensive. Their approach on the boat had provided a good look at the layout. Normally, this area was reserved for tourists, hikers, bikers, and beachgoers making their way to this cozy spot during the warm springs and hot summers. Today told a completely different story. The buildings in the distance, set aside for lifeguards and rangers, were empty, the beaches they passed were barren, and the snowy trails barely visible in the haze showed no signs of riders or walkers.

The few trees that had sprouted up around this one-acre property stood unmoved by the light wind. No animal presence—or any life at all beyond the thick undergrowth—seemed to exist nearby.

"Well." The pull was too much. Chris's curiosity and the slight anxiety at standing defenseless in the open drove him across the lawn.

A peek at the balcony overlooking the bay showed more mossy covering. Its two sliding doors were shuttered with blinds. As Chris approached the brick patio, his muscles coiled, and his thoughts drifted to a week ago, before everything changed. Storming out of that coffee shop, he could never have imagined being in a place like this just a short time later. He was standing outside a crumbling old mansion that might have been his father's—a man long forgotten but said to have been created from fire itself to protect humanity. The weight of this legacy held him in place.

"Are you okay?" Eira's touch sent his thoughts spiraling back to the night before, gently cooling his body just as it started to overheat.

"It's time, Chris."

The voice had returned. Its familiarity added to the softening of his shoulders as he held Eira's gaze.

"I am." He forced remnants of the building smoke out through his nostrils, his steps lightening as he confirmed the two words with a nod. He had no idea what he was doing. But no matter what came next or what fate he was to meet, he knew he was where he was supposed to be.

"I'm ready." His whisper elicited a return nod from Eira and validated what that inner urge was telling him. "Let's do this."

When Chris opened the doors to the gigantic house, they did not see what Eira was expecting.

They had been told that it had been abandoned for the last twenty years, a time frame that matched the altercation between the Ignati, her mother, and Chaoic that had ended the Battle of the Frost. The untamed yard reinforced the tale of abandonment. The vine growth reminded her of the temple where she and Ivy had been ambushed. She wondered what kept the more temperate plants alive in this region's cold and blustery conditions. Their color was not nearly as intense as in the Temple of the Essence, but they were clearly thriving.

She had expected to find the interior in a similar condition when they walked through the front doors. However, what greeted them led her to believe that they had indeed found the place they were seeking. It gleamed as if untouched.

While not a castle or manor like those the council leaders occupied back in Noella, this structure appeared to have a similar layout and style. A high ceiling was the first feature to grab her attention, its massive chandelier comparable in size to the one back home. Four giant pillars stretched the structure's height, unexpectedly illuminated by glowing bulbs. A spectacular, open view unfolded under the lights, with multiple doors, some open, lining both sides of the hall.

CJ had explained electricity, and while Chris had been very vocal about the poisonous greenhouse gases generated by its production, Eira saw how efficient this energy could be; the spiral staircases on either side of the main entryway sparkled with it.

The marble steps were pristine. A few flowers sprouted on a wooden table not far away, their vivid colors contrasting strikingly with the white walls and tangled greenery so prominent outside.

"It's . . ." CJ stammered as they crept in, padding across the floor. "It's so clean." His swipe of a mantle revealed none of the moisture or dust that would indicate twenty years of neglect. "How did it—"

"The Essence," Ivy whispered as she pointed to the top balcony, where green vines and flowers flourished from some epicenter they could not see. "She must somehow—" She cut herself off at Chris's movement on the staircase. His eyes were locked on something as he gently eased up the steps.

"Chris?" Eira followed, obeying a slight tug of her own.

The second story of the mansion boasted more doors, all of which were closed. None interested the man in front of her, though, who jogged to the next group of steps.

"Chris, where are you . . ." She didn't catch the rest of CJ's question. She had to stay close to the man who had brought them here.

Chris's gasp spurred her on as he abruptly stopped on the next level. The overgrown forest scene awaiting them denoted an extreme change from the spotless floors below. She again thought back to her visit to the temple. This healthier, more radiant setting was easier on the eyes than was the devastation their parents had left in the wake of their final battle.

"In here." Chris seemed to be working on instinct. His feet crunched on the grassy floor as he headed straight for a set of double doors that stood slightly open.

A surprising hesitation hit her as the others hastened through. It was not just the worry of a hidden ferlup or minima that inspired this pause. For the first time, she was uncertain if she wanted to know the answers Chris sought.

Maybe she dreaded the truth. Her brief trip to the human realm had shown that most of the stories and legends were false. The descriptions of the fire warrior as a coward and ally to the creature they sought to destroy grew more fictional with each discovery. And the humans he had been forged to protect were practically identical to the lumi.

Maybe the truth she feared was about something else, something she had never thoroughly considered but now, using a new part of her mind, began to question as she clutched her necklace.

"Eira?" Ivy popped out of the door, her eyes wide. "You need to see this."

The confusion settled. A forced nod took Eira over the last of the grass and vines and into a roomy study.

"Wow!" She had never seen anything like it. The walls of books were so expansive that even Whittaker would have gawked. It was more extensive than the castle library, and she had no doubt that the pupils back home would go crazy for a chance to roam this enormous room. The sheer number of volumes and the weaponry decorating the walls were overwhelming after the starkness of the rest of the house.

"This is amazing!" CJ had already started combing through different sections. Glancing at Chris, Eira drifted closer to a desk at the far end, near a closed balcony window. "These . . . these are first editions! And I don't even know what some of these languages are!" CJ had skipped to another shelf close to a rack of steel swords. Ivy tucked in behind him, and they started to pull books from the shelves.

For Eira, everything had reduced to a mumble. Her internal struggle returned as Chris eyed something on the desk. He fiddled with a few papers, eventually sliding around the desk to a picture frame. His hand shook as he picked it up and stared blankly into space.

"Chris?" The alarm in her voice must have been noticeable; the other two paused their jubilant chatter as Eira inched closer. "Is everything alright?"

The jut of his lower lip made her more nervous.

"I . . ." A clenching of his fingers had her readying her own. What had happened on the training pitch remained fresh in her mind, and she prepared to subdue him if he lost control. But there were no projections nor burning sulfur this time as he slammed the frame onto the wooden desk.

"What?" She moved around him and picked up the frame. "Chris." She knew immediately who this was. The woman's delicate, long black hair, perfect tan, and slight smile matched the features of the man who stood a few feet away from Eira. Her red lips were slightly pursed, and her elegance radiated from the image. She posed with a graceful turn to the side, her floral dress flowing down to the grass at her feet. The modest attire perfectly accentuated her beauty, which stood out above all else.

"It's my mother," Chris whispered. He turned away, took a deep breath, and paced to a bookshelf on the other side of the balcony doors.

"Shit." CJ appeared, his eyes revealing a mix of concern and shock. "She's beautiful, man." The words carried none of the slimy undertones she had noticed from the man at the car dealership. "You okay, Chris?"

It seemed like the two needed this time together, like this moment could only be shared by true friends who had known each other for almost a lifetime.

"Eira." Ivy motioned her over. The wall before her supported a colossal map covered with pictures and tacks.

"What is this?" Eira tried to make sense of the markings. The photos accompanying the different areas were clear enough to show human bodies sprawled across the ground. "They look like attacks. Attacks by . . ." She leaned in and shuddered at the realization.

"It looks like ferlup and minima attacks!" Ivy gasped. The gashes marring the bodies matched those on Eira's arm. "Was he tracking them?"

Eira spun away and pressed her palm to her forehead. An icy rush brought on a few beads of moisture that trickled briefly before freezing on her cheeks. She flicked away the beads. A headache built as she pieced the mystery together. "That would mean . . . ?"

"He wasn't a coward." Chris's voice behind her made her jump. "He didn't run; he was tracking him." She felt the satisfaction in his tone was warranted.

"For a long time, too." CJ rifled through the papers on the desk. "Some of these go back hundreds of years. He kept records and looked to be following the growing strength of the attacks." The information added to her headache. A logjam inside started to freeze her throat over. "There are notes scribbled all over, but I can hardly make out the writing. Some of this is English, but some—"

"Eira!" Ivy's cry plunged the room back into silence as she pointed toward the bottom of the wall, where one image was clearer than all the rest.

"The Temple of the Essence!" Eira slapped her hand to her mouth, an unintended icy projection stinging her lips.

"He must have known." Chris traced the other areas, carefully examining each photo. "He did this all, tracked them all, on his own." His final statement forced a frigid, hard swallow as the cause of Eira's anxiety and the blizzard in her chest and lungs finally started to surface.

All the stories she had been told when she was young, all the legends of her mother and the great battles she had fought, culminated in this instant of utter betrayal. As she looked on in horror at what had taken place while the Iclyn had hidden inside the frost, any doubts were washed away; everything she had been told was a lie.

Each photo communicated a heart-wrenching fate. The images spanned an entire wall of this huge house, and each one showed innocent lives needlessly lost. Perhaps, in her realm, they would be described as "only" humans. After what she had witnessed of these people, that common lumi phrase stung her worse than any projection. She had been raised in a fairy tale, worried about a few random attacks. Meanwhile, on the other side, the Ignati had been fighting an endless battle—alone. The fire warrior had been abandoned to deal with this himself, forced to watch the people he cared about suffer at the hands of a monster roaming free and growing in strength.

"But why?" The hero she had worshiped and sought to emulate crumbled in her estimation. She could not pull herself away from the horrific images, and Ivy's welcome hand against her back was all that kept her upright.

"Why would she—"

"Chris!" CJ gestured at something he had found. "I found—"

The bookshelf to her right swung open with a click and churning noise, and she jumped back in surprise. A small, unlit bulb hung in a passageway leading to a hidden place below.

CHAPTER 20

Eira's pounding headache momentarily froze as they tiptoed toward the opening.

Chris was the closest, and he yanked on the old string attached to the bulb, illuminating the passageway. "I guess this is for me." The objects and clues in his father's house pointed squarely to this secret opening, but he hesitated. Eira knew he needed her support.

"I'm right behind you."

He nodded gratefully, and with a deep breath, they descended into the damp unknown, leaving CJ and Ivy to watch over the library.

Eira kept her hand on the cool, uneven stone alongside the staircase. They quickly reached the bottom, and Chris hit a small switch on the wall. With a buzz of electricity, the door at the end of the passageway became visible, and they hunched under the low ceiling as they maneuvered toward the rusted steel door.

Chris hesitated again.

For some reason, she felt this was as far as she was supposed to go. What lay on the other side was meant for him alone. "Chris, I think—"

A crash above sent them both spinning back the way they'd come.

Her stomach dropped.

"We need—"

She cut him off, her arm flying in front of his chest. "No, Chris. You *have* to go in there."

His desperate stare showed that he'd returned to the memory of their night together—and the tragedy that preceded it. "I can't let anything happen to them. They followed me here."

She wanted to wrap him in her arms. His desire to help his friends even now, when everything he had been searching for looked to be at his fingertips, reinforced how different he was.

"I'll go." He slumped at her words. "This is where you belong right now."

This simple truth softened him, and he reached for her hand.

"Eira." His touch brought comforting warmth. The rumble beneath her feet did not deter her from responding to his gaze, which again pulled her forward—until another bang wrenched them away from each other. A familiar, terrible shriek sounded above, echoing and multiplying by the second.

"Go. But be careful," Chris murmured.

As he turned toward the door, she willed her feet back to the steps. Her best friend was probably alone in the fight, but she lingered, peeking over her shoulder one last time. This seemed like a final goodbye. And while she hardly knew this man, the pain accompanying this feeling was worse than any injury she had suffered.

"Go, Eira." The urgency of his voice finally pushed her up the steps.

The shrieks were punctuated by the thuds of falling books. She spread her fingers wide as she strove to eliminate the doubts of her past and focus on the powers she needed now more than ever.

"CJ, get down!" Ivy's shout brought that icy rush to the surface. Eira's blood froze over as she focused everything swirling inside to her palms. "CJ, get—"

Eira kicked open the door. At her arrival, the three minima trying to encircle her friends turned to her. They shrieked, ear-piercingly, in unison.

"Eira, look out!" screamed Ivy. Eira barely dodged the ferlup's slash as the creature flashed by her. Her instinctual grab clamped around a handful of fur, and the massive wolf yelped in response to the projection that she had been growing when she entered the library. A swift thrust of her knee sent the creature into the air. The next push from her other palm hurled it against an emptied shelf.

She had no time to judge the damage she had done. The closest minima joined the fray, lunging with breathtaking speed. But her attacker never came close. An avalanche of a projection threw the monster across the room. The defensive joust gave Ivy and CJ a chance to scramble to Eira's position near the door.

Another ferlup not far away struggled to its feet. Ivy's spiratus must have smashed it to the floor.

"Look!" CJ pointed at the entrance where two more ferlup stood, their long, dripping fangs snapping as they called out to their brethren. "Shit!" A flailing minima took their pause as an opportunity to approach, but Ivy sent a partially formed spiratus into its chest. The action staggered the soulless soldier for a moment, which allowed Eira time to respond with an icicle through its head.

"We're surrounded!" CJ's scream confirmed what Eira was thinking. The four ferlup fanned out as three new minima joined the original two.

Eira recalculated. "Ivy, you need to get CJ to the chamber with Chris." There was no other option; the creatures seemed oblivious to the dim passageway. "I'll draw them off, and you—" The wounded ferlup leaped, the force shattering Eira's hastily erected ice shield, and they tumbled to the floor.

The fall gave the rest of the attackers momentum. Ivy struggled to get her bearings as a handful of enemies closed in.

"No!" A flick of Eira's wrist launched another projectile at the closest minima. The strike hit home but did not deter the ferlup behind it, which prepared to attack. "Ivy!"

Eira screamed at the sudden, searing pain in her leg as the ferlup that had broken her shield clawed into her calf, causing her muscles to seize. On instinct, Eira extended a weapon of her own. The icy sword pierced right through her assailant, which let out a small whimper before toppling.

"CJ!" At Ivy's shout, the pain vanished for a moment. Her best friend crawled over to the young man, who lay moaning on the floor.

"Ivy! There are more coming!" Eira projected a blast of frigid particles. Its power and deadly precision provided her an opening to hobble over to her companions.

"What happened?" Eira had missed the encounter. A ferlup sprawled nearby with a sword through its chest.

"He . . ." The terror in Ivy's eyes was palpable. The barks and shrieks all around them grew louder as their attackers regrouped. "He saved me." The gash on CJ's neck spilled red blood, a sign that his actions had not come without a cost. Eira had read enough books to know that the poison was already spreading through his system. A human hardly stood a chance.

"How did he—"

A cough interrupted her as he came to. Ivy gripped him tight and helped him sit up as their attackers prepared another strike.

"What are we going to do?"

Eira's chest tightened at the plea. She gazed down at Ivy and the man who had somehow saved her with a human weapon.

"Stay behind me." This feeble command was all she could manage. "Whatever happens, just stay behind me."

She straightened her back and faced the group of minima and ferlup, their clamor strengthening the headache she had been fighting since their arrival on this island.

"I know you're with me." She had a hard time committing to the statement. Her recent discoveries floated to the surface, but she tried to block them out. "Guide me." The half-hearted attempt flickered a projection in her palm as claws scraped on marble. "Come on!" A howl from the biggest ferlup sent the group forward. Her body coiled as she tried to call on what strength she had left. "Guide—"

A massive gust took her to her knees. The sound of a whistling wind overtook the room.

A ferlup's loud cry at being bent in half by a spiratus broke through the sounds of the whirlwind. The swirling cane quickly returned to the imposing warrior who had just emerged from the vines of the double doors.

In response to another blustery snap, she projected a shield of frost to protect the two behind her. A few seconds of intense effort allowed her to lock it into place.

"Bernard?"

He winked, and the creatures pivoted away from her and took aim at him.

The steel was cold when he finally touched the door. Rust particles crumbled under his fingertips. He had been standing there for a few minutes now, Eira's abrupt departure and the rumblings upstairs not helping him commit to the task he knew had to be done.

The image of his mother added to the anchor holding him in place. The caring nature of her gaze, the elegance of her pose, and her radiant beauty were everything he had expected.

"It's time, Christopher."

The voice came clearer than ever as he slowly turned the doorknob.

A stale, musty odor greeted him as he entered the dark room. There were no books or shelves. When he flicked on the light, he saw only a desk in the corner of the spacious and otherwise empty area. A few papers were scattered on the desk, but the main attraction, which drew his eyes like a magnet, was an exquisitely decorated goblet. Its golden exterior featured the most tastefully cut gems he had ever seen; they shimmered, even in the half-light of the room. The loneliness of the object stood out in the barren space, with no water or wine to accompany it.

A red flicker from one of the jewels pulled him closer. The tug in his chest was so intense now that he felt it might burst through if he did not follow its urges.

"*Touch it.*"

Again, the voice was crystal clear, and the command sent him into action.

Scorching heat blazed around his hand. He gawked as a fiery ball erupted from the goblet, which had grown brighter at his touch. His every fiber heated up with this new development. His fingers clenched reflexively around the goblet, as if they knew what to do without direction.

The ball began to expand, the pulsing syncopating with that of his muscles. A figure formed in the fire as the temperature of the clammy room reached boiling point in an instant. The pressure on his palms disappeared into a blinding flash, accompanied by a thunderous bang that clapped against the stone walls.

He struggled to comprehend what was happening. The glowing figure gradually took the shape of a man above the goblet.

"*Christopher.*" The man's mouth did not move, but the voice was the one from inside his head. He extended his massive hand. "*It is really you.*"

The sight would have sent Chris sprinting in the opposite direction a week ago. Swirling flames surrounded a massive warrior figure levitating over a golden, gem-covered goblet. However, after everything else he had seen, this moment felt inevitable.

"Dad." A hot tear formed as he directed this word at someone for the first time, the moisture steaming off his skin. The voice in his head, the one that had been coaching him and that he had been blocking out for so long, finally had a face.

"*I am sorry it took so long, son.*" Chris wobbled as the last word forced a hard swallow of smoke. "*But now, the time—*"

"But when the time is right, your future you will find." The pocket watch was already in his other hand. His eyes darted between it and the fiery figure, which only shook its head.

"*If only it were that easy, Christopher.*" The hesitancy caught Chris off guard. "*This relic is not your future.*"

"I don't understand." His hands tightened around the objects they held, his eyes moving back and forth between the two. "I found it; I found the fire relic! The address, Boston. It was inside the pocket watch. The same from where the package was sent. I followed your directions. I fulfilled my destiny!" He now knew what it felt like to plead for parental acceptance.

"*This is not your destiny, Christopher.*" Chris's slouch of rejection strengthened the burning smile that looked back at him. "*This is merely a mistake. One of many I made during my existence.*"

Chris tried to make sense of it. The picture from the desk brought back the thought of his mother's death and the role he had played in it.

"*You cannot carry the weight of the world on your own, Christopher.*" The touch from the flaming finger was gentle, almost cooling, as it lifted his chin. "*And you cannot blame yourself for the decisions of others.*"

He had forgotten that this warrior had been in his head all this time.

"But I—"

"*She was one of my biggest mistakes. But also*"—a new smile formed on the figure's face, a smile he recognized—*"my most precious gift."*

The words hung in the air.

"I have so many . . . What am I supposed to—"

"Answers to your past will not soothe your mind, son." The flames flickered as the figure moved.

"I'm sick of all these damn riddles!" The simmering he had fought to control finally reached a rolling boil. "If you were in my head for so long, why did you wait until now? Why didn't you give me time to train? Why did you . . . why did you make me live as an orphan?" He flexed his fingers, nearly dropping the pocket watch.

"Because, Christopher," the figure said in a calm, nurturing tone that diffused some of his tension, *"you are different."*

"I—"

"You are not like me, Christopher. And I hope you never will be." The figure crossed its arms. *"I was created to protect the humans. But my faults led to more failures than successes."*

The lumis' stories roared to mind, and Chris wondered if some of them might be right.

"But they called you a coward. They said—"

"I was, my son." The answer was direct. *"You see, I was merely created to protect them. I was never one of them. But your mother . . ."* The laugh returned joy to his voice. *"She was everything and more."*

Chris had every intention of asking about her, but the stare from the gigantic figure seemed to pan across the room, so he clamped his mouth shut.

"I never knew my purpose, Christopher. All the wars. All the fighting. All the . . . all the pain and agony that I felt and watched." The waitress's face popped into Chris's head, and a quick shake only partially removed it. *"The minute I saw you, though, I knew."* The burning figure grew brighter. *"Tonight is just the beginning for you, my son."* The figure moved higher, toward the ceiling. *"Tonight, you make your own destiny."*

Chris sensed where this was headed: the increasing temperature and slow rise were setting up an exit.

"Wait! I don't understand! What am I supposed to do? How am I supposed to control all of this?"

He realized he had let go of the goblet only when he looked down at his palm. His eyes went wide at the fireball projecting above his skin.

"You are the best of both of us, Christopher. The star that burns the brightest and brings hope. Your strength is not just in your hands but also inside you." The flames around his father swirled faster. *"Use that strength. Find your own path, and when the time is right, you will have your answers."* A blaze overtook the figure who spoke with his father's voice. The heat was so powerful that Chris had to end his projection and step back. *"I love you, Christopher. You are my one true success."*

A final flash blinded him as a jolt beneath his feet nearly took him to the dirt. His vision blurred, and he blinked uncontrollably, trying to focus on the lone light still burning in the room.

"What?" He glanced at his fingers. The goblet was no longer on the desk; instead, it was nestled in his palm, which no longer held a fireball. In his other palm, the pocket watch began to freeze over before he hastily shoved it back into his sweatshirt.

A line of sweat cooked on his forehead. His temperature, while cooler now, was still nowhere near what any human would consider normal.

"Jesus Chr—" The foundation of the mansion shook. A chorus of shrieks and howls sent him rushing back through the doorway. After a final glimpse back at the table, he gathered himself and pushed the steel door shut.

"Eira!" The shout made his heart skip. The urgency from the yell overtook any thought of his encounter with the burning silhouette and sent him sprinting toward the steps.

CHAPTER 21

The wind died, and Eira's advanced weapons trainer rushed toward the trio.

"Get back!"

She followed his demand out of habit. "How is he?"

Two black clouds hung where Bernard had laid their attackers low, signs that the creature they sought to defeat was close.

"Where are they going?" Eira asked as the remaining assailants slunk out the door Bernard had just entered. The last ferlup's yellow eyes disappeared around the corner.

"Most likely regrouping." A groan from CJ signaled the need for action. "We need to hurry. The poison is spreading through his blood."

The gash on CJ's neck was still bleeding. A sudden revelation brought Eira close, her palm open.

"What are you . . ." Ivy trailed off as a projection eased out of Eira's hand and sealed over the wound. Layer by layer, she carefully built a frosty covering over the gash as she surrendered to an impulse she could not explain.

"Shit!" CJ's squeak was loud and agonized, but any movement

was a positive sign. "Goddamn, that's cold!" Ivy restrained him from grabbing at the newly covered wound.

Pulling back her hand, Eira stared up at the serene circle of snow hovering in the air around them. It seemed created not to destroy but to heal, and it gingerly circled, awaiting further instruction.

"Impressive." Bernard smirked by her side. His eyes wandered the room as Eira took a deep breath and closed her fingers.

She had no idea how or why she had just done that.

"Where is Christopher?" Her trainer appeared no longer concerned with the injured CJ and had started toward the desk. "There will be more of those creatures. We must get him to safety."

"He went down there." Ivy pointed to the passageway. Bernard perked up as he approached the opening.

An unnerving silence took over. The smile stretching across the warrior's face carried an almost manic quality she had never seen. She rose and approached him with a question fed to her from the back of her mind.

"Bernard." He seemed distracted. "How did you know where to find us?"

A tug from her insides told her that something was amiss with this situation.

"The master leap by the gallery." The answer again felt distant; his attention was clearly not on her.

"But how—"

"Ignati steel." Bernard cut her off. He analyzed a knife he had retrieved from where it had fallen from the wall. "No wonder the creature's body remains."

He nodded at the dead ferlup CJ had slain, and Eira slid closer, watching him run his finger along the small blade.

"They say these weapons allowed the humans to penetrate our projections during the war." She was halted by the familiar force inside.

The warrior shook his head with an arrogant laugh as Ivy helped CJ to his feet. "The Ignati developed this steel to strike against Chaoic's armies, to accomplish exactly what you just did."

CJ was breathing heavily, his curled upper lip showing that he had picked up on what Eira was sensing.

"You son of a—"

"Be careful, human." Bernard's snide interruption was accompanied by the reappearance of two ferlup, their nails clicking on the marble. "My friends here have taken notice of what you did to their brethren."

Eira's throat snapped shut. The look in the eyes of the warrior who had guided her all these years confirmed her fears. He prowled back toward them, pressing the blade's tip into the pad of his finger and drawing blood as his sneer grew.

"Traitor," Eira forced out, the tug replaced by a rush of icy wind.

"Me?" He seemed shocked by the accusation. His head tilted back as he erupted into the most condescending laugh she had ever heard, which was saying something. "*I* am the traitor?"

The group of minima glided back in, and the knife settled by Bernard's hip as he rubbed a black liquid on his cut.

"Your family are the true traitors. You have forced our hands!" His statement dulled the gusts in her chest. "But I do not have to tell you that, do I, my dear?" She clenched her hands into fists. "You can now see all the lies they have told, the façade we have hidden behind!"

There was some truth there.

He positioned himself between the vile creatures, ignoring their snapping and shrieks. "You really believe in your selection? To sit on the throne and waste all that power inside you?" Rolling her shoulders did little to ease her tension. "You? The daughter of the savior?" With another laugh, he stepped forward. "Do not tell me you inherited your father's ignorance."

She could not stop the thrust of her hand.

"How interesting," Bernard said, batting away the massive projection. "Maybe it is not just your father who has rubbed off on you."

An icy blush hit her cheeks. The thought of Chris alone in the passageway fought for attention in her mind.

"Why?" Ivy finally yelled from her side, the noise enough to bring Eira back to the confrontation at hand.

"Three years." Bernard seemed comfortable enough to turn his back on them, and given the way he had just fended off her outburst, she understood why. "For three years, I tried to break down the barrier your father put up—to help you find your true destiny!"

A tremble bloomed in Eira's wounded leg. Her strength was almost exhausted.

"But you never could quite find it inside you. You never had the strength to find the relic your mother created!" CJ and Ivy were frozen in place; the disclosure of this man's treachery and everything it meant carried a paralyzing weight. "And then we felt it! The rising power of someone else. The scent of someone who might actually have the strength to fulfill his destiny."

She darted her eyes to the open passageway.

"You could never quite break the chains of your past. Your father shielded you from the power you were meant to wield." She grabbed at her necklace, which had grown warm against her skin. "But you were still good for something. The night I saw you two touch—the look he gave you and the weakness all humans have!"

"No," she stuttered. Her role became clear as she clutched the gem in her palm.

"No human man could resist the beauty of a lumi woman, especially if she is the only one who can understand what he faces." That hit her harder than any of the day's other attacks. The next throb from her bleeding calf nearly brought her to the ground. "And unlike in your training, you managed to succeed this time!"

Again, she could not stop it. An overwhelming force swirled into her chest, and she flung it at the cackling traitor who had so misused her.

He had no trouble with this projection, either, flicking the iceball into one of the minima, which exploded in a puff of black smoke. "So human of you, Eira." The cold remark was joined by an equally chilly breeze that began to circle them.

"What are you . . . ?" Ivy muttered, slumped under CJ's weight.

"No need to continue, my dear. For you, this will be quick. I have no more need for you or that annoying, loud-mouthed human you have been forced to drag around." The howl of a nearby ferlup indicated an imminent attack. "It's a shame. I always liked you, Ivy, and felt you had a bright future. But my master needs your friends more than I like you."

A pump of his fist produced the mighty whirling cane once again, and he fired it at Eira's friends, who ducked for cover.

"No!" Eira's feeble shield cracked in half under the spiratus's force, sending them once again to the ground in a heap.

"Pathetic," he said, though his words were almost drowned out by a whistling and humming in her ears. "What? You intend to fight me, human?"

She could only somewhat focus on CJ, who was using a bookshelf to pull himself to his feet. The sword he had used earlier was in his hand as he struggled to maintain his balance, and the fear he should have felt seemed nonexistent; his lowered brow conveyed only fury.

"Fuck you." The young man's curse was just loud enough to hear. Another chuckle followed.

"Fine then." Eira's headache pounded hard enough to bounce her eyes out of her head. "Die, like the rest of your kind!"

A blast of wind sent Eira back to the ground. The bounce off the marble floor did not help her blurred vision, and the ringing in her ears grew deafening. She grabbed for something sturdy enough to support her and pulled herself half-upright against the desk.

"Ivy," she gasped as her eyes found her friends.

Ivy crouched on one knee, her spiratus spinning at a speed Eira had never witnessed as it shielded Ivy and CJ against the terrible force of Bernard's weapon.

"Fool!" Bernard's furious glare marked Ivy for the next attack.

"Look out!" Eira shouted as a minima snuck up behind them. CJ turned too late to lift his sword.

What strength she had left brought Eira's finger up. The icicle projectile was sloppy, but it connected, striking the minima in the shoulder and sending it spiraling into the opposite bookshelf. She had no control of her next movement. Her hands opened as she unleashed a projection of snow and ice that barely held shape but somehow cut the next two gliding assailants in half.

"Eira!" Ivy's scream signaled that Bernard had shifted his attention back to Eira. Her shield this time took the brunt of the spiratus better than the last.

She stumbled into the desk as Ivy tossed aside an approaching ferlup. Eira's next thought was to finish what her best friend had started, and a flick of her wrist produced a sword that sparkled under the lighting above. However, a stab of pain changed her plans. The knife Bernard had been holding was no longer in his hand but instead jammed into her side.

"You see." A long, scaly black arm retracted back to his body. Another jab took the wind from her chest as frost puffed from her mouth. "I have tricks too!"

She could no longer swallow. The rush of energy she had miraculously discovered dissipated as thawing blood trickled from her wound.

Chris was out of breath when he reached the top of the stairs. Two ferlup twisted toward him and howled, but his eyes were fastened to the young woman bent over by the desk.

"No! Eira!"

Jaws snapped inches from his face as one of the creatures sought to prevent his advance. Meanwhile, Eira sank to the ground. The large man who had first approached him in the subway turned to face him, revealing a dagger and a diseased black arm.

"You!"

Bernard's wicked grin erupted Chris's insides into a blazing tornado. The man yanked on the weapon, and Eira cried out in pain as she crumpled.

"Give it to me, human!" The goblet in Chris's hand was scorching hot. "Come on, Christopher. If you want this to stop, then hand over the relic!" A scan of the room showed Ivy and CJ cornered by another group of attackers. The situation deteriorated with each passing second.

He had no time to figure out what had happened. The treacherous man who had sought to train him now held the upper hand.

"Chris." Eira's pained tremble had him opening his left palm as one of the ferlup approached, eyeing the sparkling gems in his hand. "Don't . . ." The click of the monster's claws ended what restraint he might have shown.

He grabbed its throat, stunning the creature. Its yellow eyes widened as lava coursed through Chris's veins and out of his palm. The ferlup never had a chance to squirm. Its neck snapped effortlessly, and a puff of black smoke rose as the ferlup's companion retreated. But Chris would not let it escape so easily.

"Come here!" The flames produced another lasso, and the demon wolf screeched as Chris ripped it to the ground.

"Impressive." Bernard was still smiling as Chris ended the life of the flailing creature in his grasp. A look at Eira showed her struggling to her feet. "But you forget." A flick from the massive warrior took her back down. Her agonized scream drew a whimpered plea from Ivy. "Now give me what I came for!"

Chris couldn't focus on the request. The eyes of the woman he had spent last night holding were full of incredible suffering.

Bernard taunted, "Christopher, if you want this to end—"

"Enough!" Chris's voice was deeper, stronger, and angrier than he had ever heard it. The pinpricks across his body began to smoke with the beginnings of an inferno.

"Then give me what I came for." The two men were locked in a stare. The swirling blackness in the warrior's eyes was new, showing that his threat was no bluff.

"Chris." Eira shook her head, the strength clearly leaving her.

"Take it!" His mind had been made up long before. No tug or hidden portion of his brain spoke for him as he extended the sparkling relic toward Bernard.

"No!" Ivy implored as the minima towered over her.

"I have to."

Bernard's smile grew as he pointed the knife at Chris.

"No games, or I send this directly through her icy heart." The minima seemed to take this as a cue, their movement toward the entrance allowing Ivy and CJ to rejoin Eira.

"Wise." Bernard's voice had become as piercing as the squeals of the minima. The long nails of another demon wolf wrapped around the goblet as Chris let go. "Very wise." A wet, bitter breeze picked up in the room, and Bernard's eyes fixated on the gems soon nestled in his grasp.

Not a word was spoken as the ferlup crept away. The cup burned bright once again, and the air felt heavier with each tick of the clock. A tingle hit Chris's spine as he looked toward the library door, which gaped open.

"This is it!" The big warrior headed to the far end of the

bookshelves, and Chris took the opportunity to maneuver to the group by the desk. Neither the minima nor ferlup seemed to care about him now. The sparkling goblet kept them entranced as it projected a swirling black cloud.

"It is time for him to take his form!" Bernard lifted the goblet above his head, his shout echoing off the high ceiling, but Chris's focus had shifted to the floor, where his friends all lay.

"Eira," he whispered. The hand Ivy held against her side overflowed with a bluish liquid.

"What have you done?" She stared at him, her eyes wide.

"I had to." Eira's breathing became more inconsistent with each inhale. "You can't stay." A mysterious instinct rocked his body as he focused squarely on the beautiful princess. His hand opened without prompting, and he rubbed his fingers together before hovering them above Eira's gaping wound.

All the anger and balled-up aggression was gone, and a calm flame flickered in his palm. Warmth flowed through his stomach like a summer breeze. He let it enter his veins and then his fingers.

"Chris!" CJ's gasp was mere background noise; everything else in the room became meaningless as he concentrated on the gaping wound covered in thawed blood.

The initial touch made Eira lurch in pain. His other hand grabbed her tight as she dove headfirst into his chest.

"It's okay." He had no idea why, but he knew exactly what he was doing. "Just give it a few more seconds." The hand on her wound began to cool, indicating that it was time to pull away.

"Chris." She shuddered, and as he embraced her, the strength he had felt the night before was hardly recognizable.

"It's going to be okay."

Ivy peered through the gash in Eira's sweatshirt. The wound was charred, her skin smoking slightly from his touch.

A howl split the air, drawing their attention back to Bernard and the relic, which had become fully engulfed in darkness. The minima that had initially cornered the group were circling above the goblet, just as Chris's father had in the basement. They watched as a ferlup followed suit, its feet jerked into the air by the cyclone.

"He's coming!" Ivy pointed at the door, and Chris squinted as the lights flickered above. At a massive flash, he flattened to the floor for cover, his grasp on Eira unwavering even as the frigid air around them became explosively hot.

"Holy shit," CJ blurted out, his hand wrapped around a neck wound.

Further words failed CJ because they did not do justice to the image before them. Bernard, or the creature that had once been Bernard, had grown even taller. His fingers unfurled to razor-blade tips that reflected the little light left in the room. His once perfect, whitening blond hair had shifted to a jet black that matched the robe taking shape around him, flowing to the ground around his feet.

"Interesting." The deep, slithering voice from the diner set the stage for a foul smile full of fangs.

"What happened?" shrieked Ivy. The answer was the least of their worries, however, as the newly formed monster, standing at least ten feet tall, examined itself.

"Ivy," Chris said quietly. Eira was weakening in Chris's grasp, but the disappearance of the other creatures presented an opening to reach the door. "You have to get down to the dock! You have to get back home so Eira can get help."

"The entrance!" CJ pointed toward the double door. "The shithead said he used it to get here from the gallery. It must be a leap to the castle!"

A piece of the puzzle fell into place, but Chris had no time to ponder it as the dampening swirl of wind continued to strengthen.

"You will need cover." A massive surge of power that seemed to draw from every dark crevice of the house began to grow as Chris pulled Eira up with him. "Go now." He gently handed her over to Ivy. A new flame appeared, flickering in the wind.

Chaoic's yellow, beady eyes were locked on him. The demon's wide smile stretched leathery skin that had once been perfectly toned and pale. The ponderous rolling of its broad shoulders showed that it had retained the trainer's impeccable physique. Every muscle was growing firmer and larger, and the creature looked to be preparing to strike as it sent Chris a grotesque wink.

"Chris." Eira's whisper twisted him around to face her.

"You have to go." He could not let her finish. The thought of what she might say and what it might prevent him from doing was too much. "It's your destiny. You know what he will do next." The heat intensified in his palms as he inhaled. "Find the ice relic. Be who you want to be, Eira." She shivered and grabbed at her cauterized wound. "I believe in you!" His turn was emphatic as he again faced the creature. "Now go!"

The shout set his hands ablaze, every muscle tensing as his temperature reached a level that would melt sand.

"You have failed, Christopher." The monster stepped forward, shaking the house. "You have given me my vessel. And all for that thing that has shown more weakness than—" A fireball struck the massive figure, but a brief stumble was all that came of the impact. "So passionate." The word made Chris grit his teeth. His skin sparked, and flames sprouted around him.

"Go now!" He could tell the group was still frozen in place behind him. The creature knocked his next projection away.

The pattering of feet drew Chaoic's attention. An extension of his hand unraveled the sharp knives of his fingers and aimed them at the three heading for the door.

"No!" Chris produced a burning whip to wrap around the five daggers. The monster's scream nearly shattered Chris's eardrums.

The silhouettes scampered to the vines. A baleful glance from the demon prepared Chris for the next projection, a black gust that he blocked with flames. The pressure of the impact was such that the marble cracked beneath his feet. A humid heat smashed him in the face as the projections fought for supremacy.

"You cannot stop this, Christopher!" A mounting mass of steam made the creature difficult to see. "I have my form. And when I am done with you, I will have my arm—"

Chaoic's voice erupted in an agonized scream. The steam dissipated instantly as the strength pulling at Chris's lasso disappeared.

"Go!" It was CJ's turn to echo Chris's words. A sharp shield rested on the floor near him, and the disembodied, daggered hand flopped beside it like a fish on land. Ivy pressed on the vines, shaking her head as she gripped Eira tightly to her chest. "Ivy, go now!"

Ivy and CJ wore the same helpless expression. Circling black clouds expedited their silent farewell, and Chaoic's screams turned into roars as the room darkened.

"You pathetic human!" Chaoic's remaining arm shot a black torrent at CJ, too quickly for him to touch the shield at his feet.

The wall of fire Chris projected clenched every muscle in his body upon contact with the cloud. The force of what he was up against dropped him to his knees as he tried to hold on with every ounce of energy he had left. "I can't—" The warming of his stomach produced one final flow of lava. A swirling fireball exploded up and out of his hands as he screamed at the top of his lungs.

The collision that followed was unlike anything he had heard or felt before. His feet left the ground in slow motion, and he floated as if in a dream.

With an abrupt smash against a hard surface, he snapped out of the smoky fog he had been lost in. He rolled to his side and heard only ringing. The smell of charcoal and decaying flesh was so pungent that he gagged as his senses reset.

He strained to get his bearings. A voice at the end of a tunnel called him fully back to consciousness as he lost the strength coursing through his veins.

"Chris!" It grew clearer; the voice was familiar, but his eyes refused to focus. "Chris, are you okay?" CJ's soot-covered face was a welcome sight. The outline of his best friend holding a blackened shield helped him breathe a little easier.

The scene was a crispy mess. Smoke wafted from every surface. A turn to the double doors showed that the entire frame was gone. The colorful vines had been burned to char by the explosion.

He sensed no other figures in the room with them. The emptiness was a rapid shift from what had so recently been the site of a massive battle.

"Did they . . . ?" The mumble brought his friend down beside him. A moist breeze drifted aimlessly through an open balcony window.

"They did, Chris." They steadied their backs against a shelf. "They made it. They're gone." The finality of the statement drained the rest of Chris's strength.

CHAPTER 22

Noella sparkled beneath a bright winter sun. As Eira peered out at the city that now felt so foreign, Ivy's daggering stare intensified.

Gloom had encompassed the region as the news of Chaoic's regeneration spread. Noella's quietness today had become common since her return through the leap a month before.

Though the streets were still, gossip was rampant. The citizens' chatter was undoubtedly intensified by a leak in the council. Most variations, wildly off, portrayed her as responsible for Chaoic's success.

"I know you will not agree with this." Ivy finally broke the silence with the truth Eira had been trying to hide behind a cheery smile.

"Ivy, please." Eira winced as she stepped forward. Her wound was still not fully healed, even after a long regimen of bed rest. "This is your decision."

"And you are not making the same decision. Your eyes tell me that." Eira struggled to respond as she shifted back to the open window.

The crisp air had been helping her breathe until Ivy arrived, but Eira's circumstances overwhelmed the lightheartedness that should have accompanied a day of wedding arrangements for her best friend.

At first, she'd had little time to think about Cole and her own wedding in the coming spring. Her sudden entrance through the gallery door had sent the castle into a frenzy as the explosion on the other end spiraled the two to the floor. The puncture wound had stopped bleeding thanks to Chris's intervention, but the healing process from the Ignati-steel wound was taking longer than from any previous injury.

A cooling breeze wafted in as Ivy whispered, "What they did for us—"

"Please." Eira did not want to hear this again. "I can't."

Recent reports from the human realm suggested that the two who had saved them were unfortunately deceased.

Initially, she had held out hope for Chris and CJ's survival. As the days passed, her hopes faded. A small rescue party headed by General Aquilo finally put an end to her prayers when they returned with news that the house had been destroyed and the two men pronounced dead by the humans.

That night had been the toughest on her. She was haunted by the thought of the man she had grown so fond of dying because of her failures and inability to recognize Bernard's duplicity. Chris's final touch made it linger. The scar from the heat he had used to seal her skin brought his face back to her when she closed her eyes every night, making the healing process that much more difficult. The days alone, as she refused any visitors but Bianca and Ivy, rolled together while she lay in her bed and fended off the tears.

Her father had tried his best to get in, even using Whittaker and Aspen as decoys when they stopped by to check on her. That had backfired. Her anger with the former librarian for all his lies about her people, especially her mother, along with her pent-up guilt over Aspen's selection, sent her into a blizzard that had her father running out soon after the other two had left.

"This is about you, Ivy." She was surprised she could maintain this calm tone. She wandered over to the nightstand and picked up the blue gemstone necklace. "This is about your marriage to Andri. By the end of summer, I will be standing right by you." This was not a lie. Her devotion to Ivy was unwavering, even with the decision Eira herself could not make.

The return nod seemed to signal defeat. They stood silently under the weight of their burden while another cold breeze circled the perfectly arranged room.

"Okay then." Ivy's forced smile helped them push forward with the day's plans. "Bianca is setting up everything in the hall. Her team will have everything laid out for us to go over, and my parents will be meeting with your father."

The air of normalcy disappeared again with the mention of the man Eira had been avoiding. She jammed the necklace emotionally into her nightstand and slammed the drawer shut.

"Good." Eira had no interest in hiding her animosity. "If Bianca says it is ready, well, then I trust we can head down without interruption." Her new friend had become a watchful eye throughout the castle. "We will need time to—"

A voice broke in cautiously from outside the door. "At some point, you will have to speak with him. He worries about you and asks how you are doing every day."

Cole's unannounced entry went against her wishes, as she had made clear when he first tried to check on her during her recovery.

"I, um, I will see you both downstairs." At Ivy's scamper through the door, Eira realized that the two must have staged this meeting.

"I wish for you to leave." Eira's demand cut his first word off dismissively as she raised her chin. "If you wish to discuss arrangements for the wedding, that can be done down in the hall. I have made it clear that I will respect all of Ivy's wishes and will stand with you."

"Eira. I . . . I wish . . ." He rubbed his neck, the cracks and dried blood on his calloused fingers reminding her of what her failures had forced him to do.

The breaches had become more frequent with Chaoic's regeneration, with each instance producing more creatures, monsters with power never before seen in their realm. The Legion was venturing further out toward the frost—her father's new strategy to stem the enemy advance and avert attacks on the outer villages in the east and south.

"I only came to tell you that if you wish to not stand by me, I have told Andri that we should be separated." His eyes and posture told her that while he hated every word he had just uttered, they were true. "You have been through enough over the last few months, and I have done nothing to support you through it. I have lost your trust, and for that, I do not deserve to stand by you."

She struggled to keep the frozen swirl in her stomach today. The dejection on his newly grizzled face sparked her sympathy, given what he had no doubt witnessed over the last few months himself. She analyzed his new lines and creases. The battles with Chaoic's creatures had taken a toll.

"Cole," she sighed.

"Please." He moved toward her, grabbing her hands and squeezing them tight. "I only want to see you smile again, Eira. To see that smile I dream about every night and that keeps me alive."

A rush of ice froze her cheeks, and she instinctively shied away, but his grip refused to yield.

"Just tell me what you want me to do." The desperation returned. "If it is to leave, then I will leave. I will no longer bother you with my presence, and I will leave you to whatever you wish to do. But know that I will never stop thinking about you. Know that every day I am in battle, every night I go to sleep, I will—"

"Cole." She put her finger to his lips. He leaned in, his blond bangs falling to the side of his face as he clasped her hands like this might be the last time he ever held them. "I do not wish for us to be separated." She fought off the tug in her chest and focused on the man in front of her, who was lighting up like the chandelier downstairs. "I just . . . need time. Time to heal and time to figure out—"

"Maybe this will help." He produced a book. The unexpected gift's worn binding cracked and nearly crumbled as he placed it in her grasp. "I know a few scholars at the library. I offered to give them lessons on the side if they did some research for me."

This gift was out of character, and she stared at the words on the cover. The title lifted her to her toes. She had been obsessing over the topic since her return from the human realm.

"How?"

"I spoke with Ivy. I figured that you might need help getting started on your search." Eira clutched him harder. They were practically nose to nose as he continued, "The scholars said these books are the earliest they could find on the ice relic. However, they will dig deeper and put in a word with Whittaker. Confidentially, of course."

For the first time since she had returned, her insides began to unknot. The touch of this man and his thoughtful gift set her sluggish heart pumping at a rate it had not achieved for weeks. She assumed this arousal was pent-up adrenaline, her body's primal desire to find release after stewing alone with her troubles and failures for so long. "Thank you."

Before she could touch her lips to his, he stopped her. The smile on his face was genuine as he turned and opened the nightstand.

"You should not be caught with that." He gently slid the book into the drawer and removed the blue gemstone. As he placed it on her neck, the chain's heat brought back the thumping of the scar on her side. He whispered, "But if you would like to join me, I believe we have some planning to help with."

He extended his muscular arm to her. She hesitated, her mind flying in different directions as the tug grew more assertive with the chain touching her neck.

"I . . ." Her stutter made him sag a bit. The reaction was probably not what he was expecting after her attempt at a kiss.

She was sick of the chaos. She was sick of fighting herself and sick of living in a dream world that no longer existed. "I guess we do." She slipped her arm through Cole's, and he perked back up. "We should not keep them."

A muggy spring breeze surrounded Chris on the balcony overlooking the old city below. The Tangier skyline did little to distract him from the events of the last five months.

Every face he met, each conversation he had, and the night he had spent with the amazing lumi princess lingered with him when the sun set. The nightmares when he closed his eyes were not of the demon he had fought but of the losses his actions had triggered.

A group of tourists not far in the distance pulled him back to the present. Their laughter provided a stark contrast to the howling screams he had faced less than an hour ago in that same alley when he had struck down two prowling minima.

"Crazy that they have no idea what they just missed down there," CJ scoffed as he set down some type of fish soup. "But I guess ignorance is bliss, as they say." He wasted no time diving into dinner. Their travels over the last month had left them with little time to enjoy the kind of hearty meal now sitting in front of them. "Here." CJ barely looked up from his food as he slid a pair of newspapers across a map they had been analyzing. The headlines stuck out to Chris as he joined his friend. "Looks like this time they hit San Francisco and Tokyo."

The murders splashed across the front pages had been deemed an escalation of gang violence. However, Chris's trained eyes left him with little doubt as to the true culprits.

"They're getting worse." CJ patted his lips with a napkin. The scar on his neck was still visible, even after months of healing. "Right now, the papers can't seem to put it together, but the stronger he gets, the better the chance he—"

"I know." Chris did not want to get into this again. The heat in his stomach had only begun to dissipate after they'd returned to the hotel room.

A day spent hunting the two Grim Reapers had proven successful when the creatures tried to strike a group of street vendors heading home after work. CJ's decoy, along with Chris's ever-growing powers, had made the fight a short one. The potential prey never knew what awaited them, as CJ had diverted the group in a safer direction.

Unfortunately, the last few months had produced their share of failures. A trip to Buenos Aires, in particular, had occurred a day too late, as a pair of hungry ferlup had already found an unsuspecting team of backpackers to feast on before Chris and CJ arrived.

"Well, we're not in the clear either." Another slip of paper halted Chris's last slurp of the fresh, fishy soup. "From what it looks like, the hotel we stayed at before Boston got another call from the police checking about our stay. I don't have all the details on the call, but I think it has something to do with the dead waitress from the diner. Her body was never removed by that minima."

Chris tried to block out the memory of the murdered server's face.

"I can throw more cash around down here, but our contacts are drying up. If we head to Europe, we might pick up a few more details if I splash a few million—"

CJ paused as Chris lifted a tired hand. The thought of more travel was too overwhelming right now.

All those months ago, they had spent the first hour after the battle sitting in silence, unmoving. The aftermath saw Chris exhausted and defeated by the injuries and Eira's forced exit. However, as sirens drew near, the two quickly decided on a course of action, burning the house and everything in it to protect the stories the location could tell about a realm that was not ready for them.

The abundance of money at their disposal made it easy to disappear. His father's account, which seemed to be untraceable and under law enforcement's radar, helped them cover their tracks. A few million to a shady character outside the Boston morgue tied up the remaining loose ends, and they were pronounced dead in the fire that had engulfed the house they were said to have been vacationing in.

It was rather easy after that. Untracked flights were simple to secure with an endless amount of money, and their luck got better when they finally left the country and made their way to South America to regroup and heal. A few stops in different countries caused no disturbances, and they began to piece together the information they had brought with them from the Ignati's house.

It was at that point that Chris had decided to seek Chaoic again. The increase in attacks forced his hand; the human realm seemed to be sinking further into darkness.

"Any, um, any sign of anyone, or if they—"

"None." CJ's answer was the same as last time. "No indication that any lumi were present at this locked leap, either. Chaoic's creatures are clearly hanging out close to each leap on your father's map, but the lumi seem to have shut them."

Spinning on his heel, Chris headed back out to the balcony. "Maybe they're searching their realm for the ice relic. Maybe they've already found it." The hopeful thought did not inspire a reassuring nod from CJ. "I mean, I told her to find it. I gave mine to Bernard because—"

"Chris." The hand on his shoulder told him that CJ needed no explanation.

Seconds became minutes as the two stared out at the peace and quiet. The stars seemed to sparkle more brightly in the North African night. The building heat of the impending summer helped to ease what had become chronic tension in Chris's shoulders.

"You know, we aren't that far from Cairo." CJ's comment made them both smile. "At this point, my professor and the team are probably all set up and digging. Maybe we can surprise them and rise from the dead, like the mummies." CJ had become very good at providing comic relief since their world had turned upside down.

"Europe," Chris suddenly said, jumping back to the topic CJ had broached. "I think our next stop should be to the leaps in Europe."

He visualized another cramped trip in the shadows. The lurking creatures were only one of many possible reasons to hesitate, but their individual reveries gave way to a joint nod.

"Okay then." CJ headed for the door without prompting. He patted his pocket, showing that he still had the card that would produce whatever cash was needed for the next trip. "I'll cover up and head to a few of the banks in the area. If I take out a couple hundred thousand, with the half million we have stored—"

"Here." Chris tossed CJ one of the cold beers he had ordered, which nearly hit the ground before his friend snagged it. "That can all be done tomorrow. Tonight, let's try and relax."

A smirk stretched across CJ's face before he plopped down on an old couch by the television, which was currently showing a soccer game.

"You know, this sport really isn't that bad if you just . . ."

CJ rambled as Chris grabbed a drink himself. He took one more peek at the moon, which was now high in the black Moroccan sky.

"Beautiful," he murmured, retrieving the watch from his pocket.

His pain subsided as he gripped the gold plating. The cool surface dried his sweaty palms, and he closed his eyes, thinking back to the smile of the woman he refused to forget. Eira's face was the one thing that still brought him peace, a snapshot of a brief but monumental time in a life now changed forever.

"It's just . . . perfect." That faultless smile was a memory he would not repress. He yearned to see it again, and no matter how much time had passed, he would seek it with each step he took on this journey.

www.ingramcontent.com/pod-product-compliance
Lightning Source LLC
LaVergne TN
LVHW041659070526
838199LV00045B/1115